BRUSH WITH DEATH

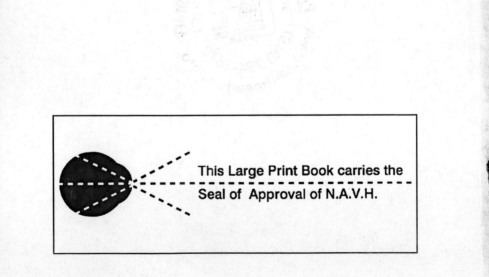

A GRAY WHALE INN MYSTERY

BRUSH WITH DEATH

KAREN MACINERNEY

WHEELER PUBLISHING
A part of Gale, Cengage Learning

GALE
CENGAGE Learning®

Detroit • New York • San Francisco • New Haven, Conn • Waterville, Maine • London

GALE
CENGAGE Learning

LIBRARY OF CONGRESS CATALOGING-IN-PUBLICATION DATA

MacInerney, Karen, 1970–
    Brush with death : a Gray Whale Inn mystery / by Karen MacInerney. —
Large print edition.
        pages ; cm. — (Wheeler Publishing large print cozy mystery)
        ISBN 978-1-4104-6114-8 (softcover) — ISBN 1-4104-6114-9 (softcover)
    1. Hotelkeepers—Maine—Fiction. 2. Bed and breakfast accommodations—
Maine—Fiction. 3. Murder—Fiction. 4. Cranberry Isles (Me.: Islands)—
Fiction. 5. Large type books. I. Title.
PS3613.A27254B78 2013b
813'.6—dc23   2013016773

Published in 2013 by arrangement with Midnight Ink, an imprint of Llewellyn Publications, Woodbury, MN 55125-2989 USA

Printed in the United States of America
1 2 3 4 5   17 16 15 14 13

Dedicated to my creative, beautiful,
and talented daughter Abby —
who happens to be a darned good
storyteller in her own right.
I love you, sweetheart!

ONE

I'd heard it said that "life imitates art more than art imitates life," and as I stirred a bowl of chocolate cookie batter and looked out the window at the frozen, glistening world, I found myself wondering if it was true. My life was certainly more artful than it had been three years ago, when I'd quit my job and thrown my life savings into a small inn on a Maine island. I had plenty of non-artistic years to my credit, that was for sure. In fact, if I were still at my old job, I would be just finishing up a sandwich and returning to my seat in front of a computer monitor, with the padded beige partitions of the Texas Parks and Wildlife Department office for a view.

Instead, I was tucked into my cozy kitchen on Cranberry Island, Maine, with my ginger cat, Biscuit, napping on the wood stove and a scene from Currier and Ives framed by my frosted window. Life as an innkeeper wasn't all coffeecakes and walks on the beach — some months, it was tough scraping up money to pay the mortgage, and I spent a lot of time washing sheets and tidying rooms — but I was deeply satisfied with the transformation I had made in my life. And between the busy tourist season and the refinance I had completed just a few months ago, the fact that I had no bookings the second week of December was a welcome respite rather than a cause for panic.

Art was certainly on my mind, though. Ever since my niece had been selected to display her work in a gallery show on the mainland, there had been talk of little else at the inn. Between my fiancé, John, who was a talented sculptor in his own right; Fernand LaChaise, Gwen's mentor (and a recent fixture in my living room); and Gwen herself, with her obsession regarding the upcoming show, there had been talk of little else. As ashamed as I was to admit it, I was almost relieved when John had to leave the island to do continuing education to keep his deputy sheriff badge.

Which didn't bode well for our impending nuptials, said a little voice inside my head, but I pushed it aside.

In my niece's case, anyway, art definitely was imitating life, since the subject of her paintings was the gorgeous landscape of Cranberry Island. She preferred to work in watercolor, and her paintings had an ethereal, magical quality that was entrancing. I was thrilled she had been offered the show, but not at all surprised. As wonderful as the opportunity was, though, my normally happy-go-lucky niece had been a nervous wreck since the announcement — and the gallery owner's request for a different style of art. It was a good thing we didn't have too many guests this time of year. Twice she had run the coffeepot without adding water, and she'd put my new red sweater in with a load of white sheets, making everything pink. If this was what an artistic temperament looked like, I decided, I was glad my creative talents didn't extend beyond baking.

I gave the batter one last turn and then began spooning it out onto a cookie sheet. The radio was on, giving the weather forecast; highs in the twenties, lows in the teens. A big change from balmy winter days in Austin, but I didn't mind. Summers were divine; although summer was my busiest season, I still found time to enjoy the warm days, with wild raspberries and blueberries I could pick on my walks and transform into pies and muffins, the slap of the waves against the rocks by the dock, and the sweet scent of pine in the air. Unlike Texas autumns, where the leaves don't fall off until they turn brown and die in February, fall in Maine brought a rush of crimson and gold, with smoke-tinged air and apples heavy on the branches. Winters, though long, had their high points as well. It was peaceful and cozy at the inn, despite my perennially cold toes, and I had learned to love the absolute hush of a new-fallen snow, the crackle of a fire in the fireplace, and the icicles that hung like jewels on the eaves of the house. All of it was better than the six-month broiler blast of Texas summers.

Now, I tore my eyes from the snow-dusted pine trees out the window and tasted the batter. It was rich and buttery, with a deep chocolate flavor from the cocoa I had added. Today, I was trying a new recipe — Candy Cane Chocolate Sandwich Cookies — that I planned to take to the Winter Knitters' meeting at my friend Claudette's house. I wasn't a knitter — not by a long shot — but when Claudette issued the invitation to join one of the island's oldest groups, I was so honored to be invited that I couldn't say no. And of course I'd offered to bring refreshments. But it did make treat-baking a challenge; one disastrous session involving fudge and white yarn had taught me that knitting and sticky fingers are a bad combination.

I had just popped the trays into the oven when I heard Gwen's footsteps on the stairs. My niece had been with me almost since the inn began, helping me out with the cleaning and serving (but generally not the cooking) while she studied art with Fernand. Although she and her mother, a high-powered attorney in California, were often at odds, my relationship with my niece had grown roots since she arrived at the inn. Bridget, my sister, was still making noise about Gwen returning to UCLA to finish a business degree, but I was glad my niece had chosen to pursue her twin loves — art, and a kind-hearted young lobsterman, Adam Thrackton — instead. As much as I wanted her to be happy, though, I had to admit to a selfish motive; I would miss her terribly if she left.

"Hey," she said, her greeting unusually subdued. She was all bundled up in a gray wool sweater and a burgundy scarf that would have brought out the roses in her cheeks — had she had any. Her face was wan, and her usually bright eyes were dull. Ever since Herb Munger, the retired vacuum company mogul who had recently opened an art gallery on Mount Desert Island, had invited her to display her work, she had focussed on little else. Privately, I had reservations about Munger. He had insisted that Gwen change her style, moving from her delicate watercolors to large, bold oil paintings. As far as I could tell, though, his background in art was limited to drinking wine at the occasional opening and networking with potential future clients. I had only met him twice, but his preference for plaid and polyester golf pants added credence to my suspicions regarding his aesthetic sensibilities. Gwen, however, was determined to please him, and had been killing herself trying to do so. Even Adam had taken a back seat to her preparations for the show.

"Did you sleep okay?" I asked, pouring a cup of coffee into a travel mug and wrapping up a pumpkin spice scone for her to take along to the studio. She hadn't been sleeping well, but I wanted to make sure she was at least eating; she was naturally skinny, but lately, she'd been closing in on gaunt. Although Gwen was usually impeccably turned out, lately, she seemed to be taking a page from my book and embracing the low-maintenance approach to grooming. This morning, her long, curly hair was pulled back in a yellow scrunchy, and there were dark circles under her mascara-free eyes.

"Not too bad," she said, reaching down to rub Biscuit's head. The round cat purred appreciatively.

"Off to finish another painting?" I asked as I unwrapped two sticks of butter and plopped them into the mixing bowl for the filling that would go between the chocolate cookies. It was a basic buttercream frosting, but with peppermint extract instead of vanilla and some crushed candy canes mixed in for color and crunch. I turned the mixer on low and opened the canister of powdered sugar, then turned my engagement ring on my finger. It was an antique that had belonged to John's grandmother, and John had given it to me when we visited his mother over Thanksgiving, but something about it was irritating my skin. I rubbed at my finger as I reached for the peppermint extract.

"I hope I can finish another one," Gwen said, giving Biscuit a last pat and eyeing the snow-frosted scene outside the window. "Although with the new snowfall, I might sketch out one or two more."

"No hurry," I said as I reached for the confectioner's sugar. "According to the

13

radio, we're going to get a few more inches tonight." Although many islanders groused about big snowfalls, I was secretly excited; I loved curling up in front of the fire with a mug of hot cocoa while snowflakes drifted down outside.

Gwen wasn't as enthusiastic. "I hope it doesn't mess up Fernand's party."

"I'm sure it will be fine," I said, measuring out two cups of sugar. "Charlene told me he already picked up the food order." Charlene, the local postmistress and island store owner, was the island's gossip and news clearinghouse — and my best friend.

"Zelda Chu will be there," Gwen said, giving me a pointed look.

"I figured," I said, stifling a sigh as I added the sugar to the butter and turned on the mixer. Over the last month, two New York artists had suddenly decided Cranberry Island was the place to be. Fernand's party was in honor of one of them: Nina Torrone, a young artist whose work had caught fire and was selling for over half a million per painting. She had evidently decided to rent one of the island's mansions for the winter, as a retreat from the hustle and bustle of the city, and she was scheduled to arrive today. Zelda Chu, on the other hand, was less celebrated but more business-minded;

she was attempting to put together a summer artists' retreat to rival Fernand's, and had asked me to partner with her by hosting her retreat participants. Gwen was vehemently opposed to the idea, as she feared it would infringe on her mentor's business. I hadn't decided how to handle it yet.

"Did Fernand invite her, or did she just announce she would be attending?" I asked. Zelda Chu was not one to take no for an answer.

"Fernand invited her. It would be rude not to." Gwen narrowed her eyes at me. "You're not going to support her, are you?"

"The business would be helpful," I said. "But I understand your feelings." As much as I appreciated her thoughts regarding Zelda Chu, and as much as I liked Fernand, I wasn't sure I was in a position to turn down a potentially lucrative partnership. "Nothing is decided yet. John and I will talk about it."

"Fernand would never forgive you," she said, making me feel a pang of guilt. She looked out the window with a moody sigh. "Is there really more snow forecast? What if Nina Torrone can't make it to the island because of the weather?"

"I'm sure it will be fine," I said.

Thankfully, the phone rang. I turned the mixer off and answered the phone, cradling the receiver with my shoulder. "Gray Whale Inn, can I help you?"

"What are we baking today?"

It was Charlene, of course. "Candy Cane Chocolate Sandwich Cookies. I'll save you a few."

"Oooh," said my food-loving friend, whose well-padded curves had been the object of many local bachelors' unrequited love for years.

"I'll drop them off on my way to the Winter Knitters," I said, rifling through the pantry in search of peppermint extract.

"Have you learned how to purl yet?"

I groaned. "Not yet, but I figure as long as I keep bringing treats, they won't kick me out." I glanced at my niece, who was looking at me expectantly. "By the way, Gwen wants to know if there's any word on Nina Torrone."

"The artist who's moving into the Katzes' old house?"

"That's the one." I thought of the house, which presided over a point that jutted out just east of the pier. The previous owners had passed away and/or gone to jail a few years ago, and the house had been vacant — until now. Although there was predictable grumbling about wealthy outsiders, I knew many of the islanders were looking forward to having a luminary in residence — particularly Fernand, who was hosting the welcome party at his studio to introduce her to the islanders.

"Not to worry. She got in last night," Charlene said. "Along with her agent. A puffed-up guy named Mortimer Gladstone, according to George McLeod." George was the captain of the *Sea Queen,* the mail boat that ferried passengers, mail, and all sorts of things, from chickens to refrigerators to building supplies, back and forth from the mainland.

"She's here," I reassured Gwen as I measured out a teaspoon and a half of peppermint extract and poured it into the creamy frosting, along with a dash of red food coloring. "And Fernand has everything he needs for the party, right?"

"Even the two cases of champagne he ordered. Came over on the morning mail boat."

"He's got all the food and two cases of bubbly," I told Gwen. "You can stop worrying now."

"Good," said Gwen, looking relieved. She had shrugged on her coat and was reaching for the doorknob; I held up a hand and pointed to the wrapped scone and the travel mug. She mouthed the words "thank you" as she tucked the scone into a pocket and grabbed the mug. Then she slipped through the door, letting a burst of cold air into the warm kitchen. Biscuit curled up tighter on the radiator, and I shivered.

"And how is your zombie niece?" Charlene asked.

I sighed. "Dead on her feet, as usual."

"It's not fair; I always gain weight when I'm stressed, and she keeps dropping it."

"I know." I had long envied Gwen's ability to eat like a draft horse and retain her slender figure, but lately, even her size 2 jeans had been hanging on her. "I'm worried about her; I keep plying her with scones, soups, and sandwiches, but I'm not sure she's eating them. She's worried about Zelda Chu — and about getting things ready for the show." As I talked, I retrieved one of the boxes of candy canes I'd bought on my last grocery run and plucked four of them out. I had bought three boxes: one for baking, and the other two for the tree John had promised he'd cut for us when he got back. Charlene sucked in her breath and lowered her voice. "Don't tell her I said so, but I was out at the gallery yesterday to deliver some of Fernand's order, and I got a look at what she's working on."

"And?" I asked.

"I hate to say it, but those new paintings of hers? They're nowhere near as good as what she normally does."

"Well, she is working in a different medium. But that's what the Munger wanted," I reminded her.

"Munger also buys pink plaid pants," Charlene pointed out. "And wears Hawaiian shirts with naked women on them."

"I know, but he says the bigger, more abstract paintings are selling better." I unwrapped the candy canes and put them into a zippered plastic bag as I spoke. I'd use a mallet to crush them, then instead of mixing them into the frosting, rolling the finished cookies in them. "You may question his taste, but you can't fault his sales experience."

"Well, I hope he's right," Charlene said. "But the new stuff is nothing I'd want in my living room." I heard a rustling of papers. "Oh, before I forget, there's an official-looking letter for you that's been sitting in your mailbox for a couple of days."

"Who's it from?" I asked.

I heard the sound of papers rustling in the background. "It's from Cornerstone Mortgage Company. The envelope is pink, and it

19

says 'FINAL NOTICE'."

"That's my old mortgage company," I said, feeling my stomach lurch. "I refinanced a couple of months ago. I knew there were a couple of snafus, but the attorney told me he was working it out."

"Doesn't look like he did a particularly good job," Charlene said. "Did you ever get a payoff notice from them?"

"I assume so — the attorney was handling all of that."

"Well, I'd call to make sure," she said. "And I think you should get down here and pick this up ASAP."

I usually found Charlene's penchant for stating the obvious endearing, but this was not one of those times. "I'll pick the envelope up when I drop off the cookies," I said.

"If you can get them here while they're still warm, I'll be your best friend."

"You already are my best friend. But I'll bring them warm anyway." In fact, I'd bring them as soon as I could load them into the basket. I knew I wouldn't be able to stop worrying until I got my hands on that letter.

We hung up a moment later. As I closed the bag of candy canes and reached for a mallet, my eyes were drawn to the painting-like scene outside my window. The snow-dusted pines looked the same, but the buoyant feeling of contentment I'd felt less than an hour ago had collapsed faster than a soufflé in a breeze.

Two

The Cranberry Island Store was decked out with Christmas lights twinkling in the windows and a fragrant Balsam wreath on the front door when I pulled up outside in my van an hour later, parking between a battered green pickup truck and a white sedan with only three doors; the fourth had been replaced with black plastic and duct tape. Despite the ominous letter waiting for me, I grinned as I put the van into park. If the vehicle inspectors ever opened an office on Cranberry Island, 75 percent of the cars would fail.

I stepped out into the cold air and hurried up onto the porch. The rosebushes — or what was left of them after Muffin and Pudge, the island's resident goats, had had their way with them — were dusted with snow, and as usual, the mullioned windows were covered with local notices. Jingle bells rang as I pushed the door open, a basket of cookies in my arms and a giant knot in my stomach.

Eleazer White, the local boatwright and husband of Claudette, the Winter Knitters' organizer, was ensconced on one of the big floral couches in the front of the store, sipping a big mug of what looked like hot chocolate. Despite my sense of impending doom, I found myself smiling; Claudette tried to keep Eli on a strict no-sugar diet, but I was guessing neither the hot chocolate nor the mound of whipped cream on top of it were sweetened with Splenda.

"Hi there, Eli!"

"Good morning, Miss Natalie," he said with a semi-toothless grin. "How's the new skiff treating you?"

Although it had been three years since he'd given me the *Little Marian,* the dinghy I used to get back and forth from the mainland in fair weather, he still inquired after her every time. I loved the fact that he viewed the boats he'd worked on almost as children. Anxious as I was to rip open the letter Charlene had called to tell me about, I decided to stop for a moment. I hadn't seen Eli in several weeks, and he was one of my favorite people.

"Just fine, although she could probably use a fresh coat of paint."

"Bring her by, and we'll take care of it before spring." His eyes strayed to the basket in my hands. "What goodies do you have today?"

"Candy Cane Chocolate Sandwich Cookies," I said, turning back the cloth napkin I'd covered them with and offering him one.

"You won't tell Claudette?" he asked, eyes twinkling.

"I won't breathe a word," I said as he took a cookie from the basket and dunked it into his hot chocolate. His eyes closed in sugar-fueled bliss as he chewed the first bite. "Do you like it?" I asked. "It's a new recipe."

"It's a keeper," he said, then took another bite.

"I'll tell Claudette to save a few for the grandkids," I said. Claudette's son, whom she had given up for adoption forty-five years earlier and recently reconnected with, had moved to the island with his wife and two children only a few months ago. "How is it having family in town?"

Some of the twinkle faded for a moment, but he responded with a smile. "The children are grand. I'm teaching Zoey and Ethan how to fish, and Claudette's got them finger-knitting already."

"Are they liking the new teacher at the school?" Sara Bennett, a fresh-faced young teacher with lots of big ideas, had just started in the fall, moving to the island from Bangor. Her partner, Terri, was a lobsterman who still worked with her father out of Southwest Harbor. Although a few on the island, including our selectwoman, Ingrid Sorenson, had had their feathers ruffled when they learned Sara was gay, I had heard nothing but good things about her teaching. Several parents had pulled their children from school during the prior teacher's five-year reign, but Charlene told me at least four families had reenrolled since Sara had come to the island — good news for the little school's chances of survival.

"They love it, except when there's homework." He glanced around, then lowered his voice and leaned forward. "Just between you and me, though, their mum isn't taking to the island too well. Some days she's bright-eyed and bushy-tailed, but most days she stays in bed and won't eat, or even look at her young'uns. If it weren't for Claudie, Ethan and Zoey wouldn't make it to school until lunchtime."

"That sounds tough for everyone," I said. "Could it be depression? Some people are susceptible to it when the seasons change . . ."

"I don't know," he said. "But I do worry."

25

"Natalie! Bring those cookies over here before Eli finishes them off!"

Charlene's voice reminded me of the letter that was hanging over my head like a proverbial axe. I offered the basket to Eli, and he snagged two more. "I'll check in with Claudette this afternoon," I promised as I flipped the napkin back into place.

"I'd much appreciate it," Eli said. "I want to help, but I don't know how."

I wasn't sure I knew how to help, either, but at least I could provide a listening ear. As he balanced a short stack of the cream-filled cookies, I hurried toward the back of the store.

Charlene was holding court behind the counter, where two lobstermen, Ernie and Rob, were sharing a "mug-up." Ernie looked as cheerful as ever; he was always a jovial man, full of jokes and stories. Rob, on the other hand, was quiet and reserved. He looked haggard today, as if he hadn't slept in some time. Rather like Gwen, in fact. I wondered what was troubling him.

"Come bring those cookies to the back," Charlene said, motioning me behind the counter. She wore a fuzzy purple cashmere sweater that set off her ample curves, and her manicured fingernails were painted a coordinating shade of lilac. She smoothed a strand of caramel-colored hair from her eyes as she opened the door to the back room. Like most of the island's lobstermen, Ernie watched Charlene's every move. Rob, on the other hand, seemed too distracted by whatever his troubles were to notice my friend as she sashayed past. I said a brief hello to both men and followed her through the door to the back room.

"Here it is," she said, thrusting the envelope at me as soon as I'd closed the door behind me.

"Take these," I said, handing her the basket as I tore open the envelope. The words FORECLOSURE NOTICE were printed in bold across the top of the page. I felt faint.

"What's wrong?" Charlene said.

"They're threatening to foreclose on the inn," I said.

"What do you mean, they're going to foreclose on the inn?" Charlene asked, a furrow forming between her plucked brows. "You just refinanced three months ago!"

"The letter's from the old mortgage company," I said, still in a fog. How could this be possible? "It says I haven't paid in three months. But I *have* paid — on the new note. I don't understand."

"You have a new mortgage, right?"

"Exactly. I've made all the payments since the changeover. I even paid extra."

"And you haven't gotten any previous notices?"

"There was a notice a month ago, but the attorney told me they just hadn't recorded the payoff yet, and that he was handling it."

"I'm sure it's a clerical error, Natalie. A few phone calls should get things squared away," Charlene said, although she didn't sound convinced. "You're not the only one, though. Someone else got an envelope just like that recently; I can't remember who, though. I didn't think about it at the time."

"I can't believe this," I said. The words on the page seemed to swim as I stared at them.

"They say I owe $15,000 immediately," I said, my voice husky. Where was I going to come up with $15,000? And what had happened to the payments I'd been making since September? The words on the page were like physical blows. Thirty days to pay. After that, I'd owe the balance of the mortgage, or the inn would be auctioned off. The business I'd worked so hard to build, my life savings, my home — even, I realized, John's carriage house — all of it would belong to somebody else. I'd be broke, homeless, and out of a job.

"Natalie," Charlene said, putting her

hands on my shoulders. She smelled like lilacs, and despite the dire news on the paper in my hands, I found myself thinking how impressive it was that she'd even managed to color coordinate her perfume. "If you're in a pinch, I'm sure John can help out."

"Fifteen thousand dollars is a lot of money," I said. Even though we were going to be married soon, I wasn't sure I was comfortable asking for help that way. "But I shouldn't need help. I've been making payments. I've got the bank statements to prove it."

"I'm sure everything will be fine, then," Charlene said, a forced chipperness in her voice. "It's probably a miscommunication between the new company and the old one. Didn't Murray's buddy Lloyd Forester handle the closing?" Murray Selfridge was one of the island's wealthiest residents — and also the one most intent on turning the island into the next Kennebunkport. Murray and I had crossed sabers more than once in the past over our differences in vision for the little island we called home.

"Yes, but I didn't hire him because he's Murray's friend," I said. "He's got a good reputation despite that."

"Do you want to borrow a phone and call

29

the attorney here?" Charlene glanced at the door to the store. "I'll close the door and go up front; no one will hear you."

"Yes," I said. "Yes," I repeated, more firmly. "I won't be able to think straight until I get this cleared up."

"Go right ahead," she said. "I'll make you a cup of coffee. Heck, I'll make you an Irish coffee. You look like you need it."

All the Irish coffee in the world wasn't going to get rid of the foreclosure notice, but I smiled at my friend, who I knew was trying to help. "Thanks."

Her carefully made-up eyes softened. "I'm here if you need me."

She gave me a quick hug and bustled out to the front, leaving me standing alone among the boxes of canned goods and a bag of unsorted mail, the receiver of the store's ancient Bakelite phone in my hand.

Charlene was waiting for me when I emerged from the back room a few minutes later, feeling as if I'd just been mugged.

"Oh, Natalie," she murmured.

"It's fine," I said, too heartily.

The two fishermen paid Charlene, stretched, and walked to the door, leaving a faint but pungent scent of herring in their wake. Ernie cast me a speculative look, but

30

I smiled bravely, even though it felt more like a rictus than a smile. When they were gone, I sank down onto a stool.

"What happened?" Charlene asked.

"The old mortgage company never got the payoff. I gave them all the information about the new loan, but they have no record of it."

Charlene's lilac-lined eyes widened. "You're kidding me. What did the attorney say?"

"He didn't," I said bitterly. "His reception-ist said he's out in Colorado on a ski trip. Won't be back until next week."

"He has a cell phone, doesn't he?"

"Apparently they're in an area that doesn't receive service."

Charlene snorted. She had just drawn a breath to tell me something when the front door jingled. We both turned to watch two people walk in whom I had never seen before.

One was a stick-thin young woman in a trench coat, with dark glasses and a black fur pillbox hat that wouldn't have looked out of place on Jackie Kennedy. Next to her, one arm placed possessively over her shoul-ders, was a balding, portly man in a black boiled wool coat and a brightly patterned

31

silk scarf. He looked old enough to be her father.

"It's our local luminaries," Charlene murmured before greeting them with a cheery hello.

The man steered the young woman up to the counter. "I'm Mortimer Gladstone, and this is the artist Nina Torrone. We just moved to the island. The house with the turret, near the dock."

I had to suppress a chuckle; he spoke as if Charlene hadn't known for weeks. They would soon get a crash course in island communication. Cell phones might not work on the island, but news traveled at lightning speed even without the benefit of technology.

"Pleased to meet you. I'm Charlene Kean, and this is my friend Natalie Barnes, our local innkeeper."

"Nice to meet you," he said, giving me a quick nod. "We're just stopping in to see if there's any mail."

"So, you moved into the old Katz place? Pretty house," Charlene said with one of her spellbinding smiles. Despite the arm slung over his young companion's shoulders, I could see him respond, just as all the other men on the island did, but the woman beside him kept her head down, as if she were a shy young child. I studied her surreptitiously. She had good bone structure — what I could see of it — and olive-colored skin, which made sense with her Italian surname. Her lips were thin, in contrast to her rounded cheeks and chin, and she wore her dark hair bobbed. When she noticed me watching her, she looked away, apparently uncomfortable with scrutiny. I wondered if that was the reason for the big glasses.

"It suits our needs, at least for the present," Gladstone responded to Charlene, smiling. I turned my attention to him, and noticed his somewhat bulbous nose was purpled by the broken capillaries that often resulted from a drinking problem. He was probably in his late fifties, and despite his expensive scarf and immaculate wool coat, he gave off an air of dissipation. I found myself wondering about their relationship. I had heard he was the young artist's agent, but didn't realize he had moved to the island with her. Was it possible that they were lovers?

"I understand you're quite a celebrity in the art world," Charlene said, smiling at the young woman.

"Yes, yes she is," Gladstone said, as if the young artist weren't standing right next to him. "That's why I've whisked her off to Cranberry Island. Found a house with suitable light and plenty of solitude. The paparazzi were making it impossible even to stop for a cup of coffee!" He paused for a moment, then asked again, "Is there any mail for us?"

"Let me look," Charlene said, turning to inspect the mail cubbies behind the counter. A moment later, she pulled out a large manila envelope, glanced at the address, and held it out to Nina. "Big envelope from New York for you," she said.

"Fan mail," Gladstone said quickly, reaching out and grabbing the envelope. The young artist made no move to stop him. He tucked it under his arm without looking at it. "Thank you; good to know things are being forwarded. Well, we must be off."

"Looking forward to the party tomorrow," Charlene said, and smiled at the woman in the hat. "Everybody's dying to meet you, Nina."

The artist gave a faint smile, but it was her agent who answered.

"Ah, yes," Gladstone said. "The big bash. Well, Ms. Torrone is not a fan of crowds, but we'll stop by for a while."

"Fernand would be disappointed if you didn't," I said. "So would my niece, Gwen

— she's working on a show of her own right now, and I'm sure she'd love the chance to talk to you."

"Right." Gladstone gave Charlene a last brief smile, then steered the young woman toward the front of the shop. "Thank you for the mail. I'm sure we'll drop by again soon." The door jangled behind them as they left.

"Now that's an interesting pair," Charlene said, watching them as they turned up the hill.

"Not a big talker, is she?" I asked.

"When does she get the chance?"

"Good point. Do you think they're . . ."

"Together?" Charlene shrugged one cashmere-clad shoulder. "Probably. He seemed very possessive."

"And a bit posh. Makes me wonder why they chose to move to Cranberry Island in the middle of winter?"

"It does seem odd," Charlene said. "Moving in summer would be a different story — although I would have guessed Martha's Vineyard would be more up his alley. Old money and expensive restaurants." She raised her plucked eyebrows. "Maybe there's a scandal."

"Like what?"

"I don't know. Maybe they're lovers, and

35

there's a huge age difference."

"Like that matters these days," I said.

"Maybe she's married. Or maybe *he's* married."

"I have no idea," I said. "I'd never heard of her before last week."

Charlene rubbed her hands together. Whatever their secrets were, I knew, they would not stay hidden for long. "I'll have to see what I can dig up."

I laughed. "If Nina Torrone moved here for privacy, she's going to be in for a surprise."

THREE

"Think they'll be wanting a boat?" The question came from the front of the store; we'd both forgotten about Eli. "They look like they could afford a nice one."

"I don't know, Eli." Frankly, I suspected that the odd duo would not find island life to their liking — and would probably be gone long before boating season. "But if they are," I said, "I know who I'll tell them to call."

"Speaking of calling, shouldn't you be calling in on the knitting ladies around now?" he asked.

"Shoot — I almost forgot!" I grabbed the basket, which I had left on the front counter.

"You're taking all of those with you?" Charlene looked aghast.

"Here," I said, pulling back the napkin. "Take a few. They'll never know."

Charlene took five and Eli took two more before, with a much-lightened load, I hurried back out of the store and into my van, trying to leave my worries about the mortgage company behind me. It didn't work, but it was worth a try.

It had started snowing again when I closed the van door behind me and hurried up to Claudette's front door. Next to the small, wood-framed house was the barn that operated as Eleazer's boatwright shop. It was closed up tight against the weather, but a variety of old boats still dotted the yard, looking like sleeping animals under their blankets of snow. A fierce gust of wind dashed snow into my face, and I huddled down into my coat as I rang the doorbell and waited for someone to answer.

It would be an understatement to say I was surprised when Edward Scissorhands answered the door. I took an involuntary step back before recovering my manners.

It wasn't really Edward Scissorhands, of course; not only was she a woman, but instead of long, silver blades, her fingertips ended in bitten-to-the-quick nails, and her face was free from scars. Still, she had the same waxy complexion, hollow eyes, and wild black hair as the character in the movie; the resemblance was uncanny. She was dressed in a black thermal shirt and a pair of holey gray sweatpants. "What do you want?" she asked, her voice high and suspicious.

"I'm, uh, here for the knitting group," I said, wondering if I'd somehow gotten the time or place wrong. "Is Claudette here?"

"Natalie? Is that you?" Claudette's voice floated from behind the woman at the door, and I relaxed. A moment later, my friend appeared, putting her hands gently on the woman's shoulders and steering her away from the door. "Come on in, Natalie," she said. "Dawn, dear, why don't you go back to bed?"

"Don't call me that," the woman said, her lower lip stuck out like a third grader's. She looked at me and narrowed her eyes.

"Natalie, this is my daughter-in-law. Dawn . . ."

"I said, don't call me that."

Claudette ignored her and continued on. "I'd like you to meet Natalie, the innkeeper I told you about."

"Why is she here?" The woman's voice was strangely childish. Petulant. I smiled at her, but it only made her frown deepen. "Are you sure she's not Patricia? Did you invite Patricia here?"

"She's part of my knitting group," Claudette said. "Why don't you go and lie down?

I'm sure you'll feel better in a little bit."

"Why did you invite Patricia here?"

"I told you, it's not Patricia. Her name is Natalie."

Dawn — or Edward, or whatever she liked to be called — gave me another suspicious look, then turned back to Claudette. "Can I have some hot chocolate?"

"I'll bring you some in a minute," Claudette said.

When the woman had shuffled away down the hall toward the bedrooms, I raised my eyebrows questioningly.

Claudette sighed. Although she still had the same solid bulk as she always had, she looked more tired than I'd ever seen her. I didn't know what was wrong with Dawn, but it was clearly a serious issue, and I could tell it was taking a toll on my friend. "I know, I know," she said. "That's why they moved here. My daughter-in-law's got a few . . . issues."

A few issues? That was putting it mildly, I thought. No wonder Claudette had taken over caring for the grandchildren. "I'm so sorry you're having to deal with this, Claudette," I said, reaching out to squeeze her pillowy arm. "Eli said things were rough. Is she getting treatment?"

"She is," Claudette said. "But it doesn't

40

seem to be working very well."

"What's going on with her?" I asked, but before Claudette could answer, I heard Emmeline Hoyle's voice. "Claudette, I need your help deciding what color to use next."

"Go ahead," I said. "I'll fix the hot chocolate." I wanted to give Claudette a quick break, despite Dawn's obvious distaste for me — but more importantly, I liked the idea of doing something I had some skill at. The yarn for the scarf I'd been working on had been knitted and unraveled so many times it looked like packaged ramen.

"No, no," Claudette said. "I've got it under control. Why don't you help Emmeline pick a color?" She smiled weakly and turned to head into the kitchen. I looked after her longingly, then took a deep breath before hanging my coat and scarf on the coatrack and heading into Claudette's cozy living room, my knitting bag slung over one shoulder and my basket in the other.

"Ooh, she brought goodies!" Emmeline said with a smile. She was dressed today in one of her vintage 1950s plaid housedresses, and her brown eyes, which had always reminded me of currants in a bun, were bright in her round, wrinkled face. In her lap was a ruffled thing that I knew was supposed to be a tea cozy, but looked more like

41

a yarn jellyfish.

"What's in the basket?" asked Maggie Brumbacher, looking up from the sweater she was knitting for her daughter, Emma. Maggie, with her blunt-cut red hair and frank, open face, was another island newbie; after her husband passed away from cancer, she had used the proceeds from his life insurance policy to move her small family to the island. I liked her spirit, and her decision to raise her children in a place with a strong sense of community, but I wasn't overjoyed with her decision to start a petition to oust the island's schoolteacher simply because her partner was a woman. Maggie had always been pleasant to me, but her chilliness — and her obvious disapproval of Sara's lifestyle — had kept the young teacher from attending many of our sessions.

"Candy Cane Chocolate Sandwich cookies," I told Maggie, and offered them around the room. Selene MacGregor, who owned Island Artists, reached for a cookie.

"So much for my diet," Maggie said. "Between the hot chocolate I've been guzzling and your cookies, I'm going to be wearing muumuus this summer!"

"Don't worry about it," said Selene, smiling as she adjusted her jeweled reading glasses. She was dressed in a flowing hand-knit sweater with shades of blues and greens that draped beautifully over her ample form. "A little extra padding helps keep you warm in the winter." Selene had a pile of amazing Fair Isle stitched hats and mittens beside her; she turned them out at a phenomenal rate. Like many of the other knitted items produced by the group, I knew she would sell them all this summer at the store.

Maggie took a bite and groaned. "These are amazing," she said. "Better than sex. Not that I can remember what that's like," she said. There was an awkward silence, and I found myself reflecting how odd it was that someone so open in some ways could be so narrow-minded in others.

"Natalie, you'll have to get us the recipe for these," Emmeline said, coming to the rescue. "They're delicious — and so Christmasy!"

"Thanks." I smiled at my friend, who had given me more than one of her own terrific recipes. When the plate had been passed around, I set the remaining cookies on the table next to Claudette's less exciting offerings. She had put her usual sugar-free snack out on the table: celery sticks and fat-free ranch dressing. I didn't understand how a woman who eschewed sugar and ate a diet composed primarily of rabbit food managed to maintain her substantial bulk. Another of the mysteries of life.

I settled into one of Claudette's comfortable overstuffed chairs, resolving to leave my mortgage troubles behind — at least for now.

I looked at Selene, who was finishing off a blue mitten. "What do you think of all the artists coming to Cranberry Island?"

She peered over her glasses at me. "It certainly can't hurt business," she said. "Although I don't think they'll be selling their work at our store. Still, it will get people onto the island, and they often browse while they're waiting for the boat." Island Artists was located on the pier, and got most of its business from day-trippers who browsed while waiting for the mail boat to dock.

"I hear Fernand's not too excited about it," Emmeline said, and glanced at me. "One of them — Zelda Chu — has been seen chatting with Murray Selfridge a lot lately."

"Uh oh," I said. I knew Zelda, whose art was rather avant-garde compared to Fernand's, was looking to establish a retreat center. If Murray got involved, we'd have a six-acre spa resort, a condominium com-

44

plex, and a subdivision of enormous houses.

"They've got to get anything through the board of selectmen," I said.

"Seen Ingrid lately?" Emmeline asked. "Maybe that's why she's been dodging the group. Guilt."

"She's not the only vote," I reminded her. "I can't see Tom Lockhart doing anything that's bad for the island."

"We'll see," Emmeline said, not sounding convinced.

"I heard Zelda asked you to put up her guests this summer," Selene said.

"We talked about it, but I haven't decided anything yet," I said.

"Gwen won't like that, will she?" Emmeline asked, her thin needles clacking in her lap.

"Gwen's got other things to worry about right now," I said.

"Like the show she's doing for that awful man," Selene said. "Herb Munger. I heard he's got her doing enormous oils."

"It's true," I said. "And she's not liking it much."

Maggie, who was working on a hot pink fuzzy scarf, tsked. "I heard he's a failed artist himself. He can't make art, so he's trying to be a bigwig by 'mentoring' others."

She put down her knitting to add the air quotes.

"Munger is clueless," Selene said. "I saw one of his exhibits this summer — it was terrible. He should stick to vacuum cleaners."

"Why do you think Fernand encouraged Gwen to take the opportunity, then?" I asked.

"Opportunity is opportunity," Selene said with a graceful shrug. "If her paintings are good, they'll find an audience — regardless of Munger."

"He only wants oils, though," I said. "Said that's what's selling."

"She should ignore him," Selene said, "and show her watercolors."

I sighed. "Wish me luck convincing her of that," I said.

"While you're doing some convincing, you think you might talk to Mr. Munger about his wardrobe?" Emmeline asked.

"Oh, I know. Those plaid pants . . ." Selene shuddered.

"What do you think of Nina Torrone's work?" I asked her. I'd looked at her paintings online out of curiosity. They had a definite energy to them, but they were too abstract for my taste. I preferred Gwen's delicate watercolors; I guess I'm a traditionalist.

"She's the real deal," Selene said.

"Do you think she'll stay on the island?" Emmeline asked, looking up from her tea cozy/jellyfish.

"She's only renting, for now," I said. "At least someone's finally in that house."

"It's a bad luck house," Emmeline said.

"What do you mean?" Maggie asked.

"It never stays occupied for long," Emmeline said, "and bad things seem to happen to the people who live there."

I remembered the web of murder and financial trouble that had plagued the house's former owner. I didn't know what had happened to the previous residents, but I couldn't argue that the Katzes hadn't had a terrific time of it — although it seemed that the house had little to do with their troubles.

"It seems odd that she would choose Cranberry Island. If I made that much money," Emmeline said, her needles clacking quietly as she added another row to the yarn jellyfish, "I would pick somewhere warmer. Maybe Hawaii!"

"I wouldn't," I said, glancing out the window at the snow-frosted scene outside. "It's a winter wonderland out there!"

"It is beautiful. And such a wonderful place to raise kids," Maggie added.

Emmeline grinned. "The thrill wears off after forty years, I'm afraid."

"Hopefully I'll be around long enough to find out," I said gloomily, thinking of the foreclosure notice.

As I pulled my wad of knitting from my basket and eyed it warily, Claudette appeared at the door. I turned my attention from it to her, thankful to have something else to focus on. She sat down next to me, looking like she wanted the overstuffed chair to swallow her whole. I reached over and patted her hand. "Eli mentioned things have been a little hectic around here," I said. "It's wonderful of you to help your son and his family this way."

Claudette looked defeated. "We do it for the children."

"Can we help?" I asked.

"We can bring dinners, help out with the children . . . whatever you need," Emmeline piped up.

"The children can come play at our house anytime," Maggie said.

"We're fine," she said quickly, then, in a slightly softer tone, "It's just . . . family stuff. I'll let you know if I need anything."

"We're here for you if you need us," I said,

and the other women in the room nodded, sympathy on their faces.

My old friend gave a sharp nod. "Well now, let's see how far you've gotten," she said with her typical crisp take-charge voice, and I sheepishly handed over my scarf nub. I hadn't worked on it at all since the last meeting, but Claudette didn't chide me, and we quickly settled into a pattern. I would knit two rows and somehow end up with half the stitches I started with. Claudette would help me unravel it and try again. Two or three rows later, we'd go through the same process all over again. I had been hoping that the activity would help take my mind off my mortgage worries, but instead, it was compounding my frustration.

"Has anyone met the new artist yet?" Claudette asked as I attempted to loop a few more stitches over my knitting needle.

"We saw her today," I said. "Down at the store. She came in to get her mail."

"What's she like?" Lorraine asked.

"Hard to tell; she didn't get a chance to say anything." I told the group about the young Nina Torrone and her overbearing agent.

"How old is she?" Maggie asked.

"She looks to be in her late twenties," I

said, thinking of her rounded cheeks and chin. "Her agent's older — in his late fifties, early sixties. He treated her like a little girl."

"Or the goose that laid the golden egg," Claudette suggested.

"Do you think they're . . . well, getting it on?" Maggie asked. Again, I cringed at the widow's bluntness. With her preoccupation with conjugal relations, I found myself thinking that maybe we needed to sign her up for match.com.

"Hard to say," Charlene said. "I am curious, though. For someone so successful, she's awfully meek."

"At least he knows art," Selene said.

"Unlike Munger," I said, under my breath.

"No wonder Fernand's green with envy," Emmeline said, shaking her head. "They both studied under the same artist, but she's twenty years younger and selling her paintings for millions while he's running art classes in a small town."

"But he gets to live on this island," I said. "And do what he loves." I thought of John, who spent hours creating beautiful driftwood sculptures. They would likely never pull in hundreds of thousands of dollars — or even thousands — but that was not why he spent hours in his workshop. I, too, would never get rich making cookies and cakes, but I loved doing it, and to be able to make my living on the island was worth more than millions to me.

"For you, that might be enough," Emmeline said. "But I don't think Fernand's ever been satisfied with the choices he's made."

"Gwen's never mentioned that he was unhappy," I said, attempting to loop the last crinkled red loop onto the needle and launching into my seventh row for the fifth time. I had been planning to get the scarf knitted in time to give to John for Christmas, but I was glad I'd kept the latest L.L. Bean catalog, just in case.

"I think he keeps it under wraps," Lorraine said. "But Tom ran into him down at the lobster pound a few weeks ago, after he found out this Torrone woman was coming to Cranberry Island. He had had a few too many glasses of port, and he was pretty open about his feelings regarding young, pretentious artists who gyp the public into paying millions for fingerpainting." Lorraine bit her lip. "At least that's the gist of what he said, according to Tom."

"Why is he throwing her a party then?" I asked.

Emmeline shrugged. "Maybe that's what artists do for each other."

"Poor Fernand. Should be an interesting

party," I said.

"Too bad the deputy won't be on hand to attend," Lorraine said. I had almost forgotten that he wouldn't be there; John's training wouldn't be over until the day after the party. "Sounds like we might need him."

"It's just a party. I'm sure everyone will be fine," I said, clumsily knitting a fat, loose stitch.

Unfortunately, I was dead wrong.

FOUR

The basket of cookies was empty, but the stunted nub of a scarf was no bigger by the time I packed up my knitting bag and returned to the inn a few hours later. Claudette had had to leave many times to deal with Dawn, who was evidently having some sort of emotional breakdown. We'd quietly speculated on what might be the problem, but no one had seen her enough to know. I was worried about Claudette, though; I'd never seen her so tired. I resolved to visit soon and talk to her privately; maybe she'd be more likely to accept help if I approached her that way.

As I rolled down the hill in the van, my other worries crept back in. I wouldn't be able to help Claudette at all if I didn't have an inn. Would Murray Selfridge snap it up if it went into foreclosure? I wondered. I knew he hadn't given up on his crusade to transform Cranberry Island into a resort town — and make oodles of money on the land he'd been quietly acquiring over the years. Banishing the thought of Murray owning the Cape Anne I had called home for the last three years, I gathered my knitting bag and hurried into the kitchen, where I checked the answering machine for a message from the attorney or the mortgage company. No one had called.

I pulled a pork loin out of the fridge and snipped some fresh rosemary from the pot I kept on the windowsill. Rosemary was one of the few things I missed about Texas; I had had three big bushes by my back door when I lived in Austin, and I was always going out to snip a branch for a marinade or a rub. The Mediterranean plant couldn't survive the winters in Maine, but it did reasonably well on a window sill — well enough to supply my occasional craving for pork loin with garlic and rosemary, anyway.

I pinched my fingers and ran them down the rosemary stalks, stripping the leaves, and chopped them, along with a few cloves of garlic, with a mezzaluna. As I rolled the crescent-shaped blade back and forth over the mixture, the pungent, delicious scents of garlic and rosemary perfumed the kitchen. I had cooked in this kitchen for three years, I realized. I felt more at home in this large, butter-yellow room with its big pine farm table and butcher-block counters than anywhere else in the world. I glanced out the window toward the mainland, silhouetted against the dark blue sky of approaching dusk. Was the attorney going to be able to work things out?

Or would I soon lose the home — and the community — I cherished more than anything?

I was putting the roast into the oven when the kitchen door opened and Gwen walked in. She dropped her bag with a thud and sank into one of the kitchen chairs, cradling her head in her hands.

My own worries took a back seat as I closed the oven door and sat down across from my niece. "What's wrong?" I asked.

"I don't know," she said tonelessly. I sat quietly, waiting. After a long moment, she said, "All right, I do know. Maybe I'm not cut out to be an artist."

Not cut out to be an artist? I couldn't think of anyone more suited to the profession. Talent, discipline . . . she had both in spades. "What happened?"

"Herb Munger came by the studio today. He hated my new canvases," she said. "I have to start all over again."

"What??? But the show's in less than a week."

"I know."

"What did he say was wrong with them?"

"He says I've 'lost the delicacy of my earlier work'," she said, adding air quotes. I could see her anger in the set of her jaw. "Well, when he tells me to paint oils on 3×5-foot canvases, of course they're not going to have the delicacy of a small watercolor!"

"Sounds reasonable to me. What does Fernand say?" I asked, scratching at the skin around my engagement ring absently. I was beginning to wonder if I was developing some kind of weird allergy to metal; I'd never reacted to jewelry the way I did to the ring John had given me.

"I don't know," she said miserably, the anger fading. "I didn't get a chance to talk to him. He's been locked in his office most of the time for the past week. Worried about that Zelda Chu woman, probably."

"Maybe you just need a break," I suggested. "You've been pushing yourself awfully hard lately."

She looked up. "A break? You're kidding. The show is days away, and I have no canvases. How can I possibly take a break?"

"What about all your other work?" I

asked. "The watercolors? The one you did of the dock is absolutely beautiful. And the piece you did for the inn brochure . . ."

"They won't work," she said miserably. "He told me they needed to be bigger."

"I don't understand. If he wanted big oil paintings, why did he ask you?" I foolishly wondered aloud.

"Maybe it was a favor to Fernand," she said bitterly. "Since obviously I suck as an artist." On that note, she pushed her chair back with a jerk and ran up the stairs, slamming her door behind her.

I sat staring after her, regretting my poor choice of words and wishing I'd known what to say. John would have a better handle on how to help her, I thought; as an artist, he understood the challenges better than I did. I picked up the phone to call him, but then put it back down. I didn't want to tell him about the mortgage problem yet — not until I had it worked out. No need to worry him on his trip to Portland.

With a heavy heart, I rinsed a dozen fingerling potatoes and tossed them with sea salt and olive oil, glancing at the Currier and Ives scene outside my window. Maybe a good dinner and a night of sleep would help Gwen. After all, things usually looked better in the morning. I hoped the same would apply for me, too; the mortgage worry was pressing on me like a load of bricks. I'd called the attorney's office twice more, but the receptionist had been less than helpful. And I was getting nowhere with the mortgage companies.

Outside, dusk was falling, and the world had softened to shades of blue and gray. Fat flakes of snow floated down, some of them sticking to the window briefly, then melting against the pane. It was a fantasy world outside — a perfect stage for the Snow Queen, or maybe the Sugar Plum Fairy. I'd always wondered what sugar plums tasted like; maybe I'd find a recipe and cook some up for Christmas, I thought idly. I was about to turn and reach for a pan when a flash of movement caught my eye.

I leaned forward, peering through the window. There was someone out there, walking among the trees.

Abandoning the potatoes, I crossed the short distance to the outside door and stepped out onto the stoop. The sharp, cold air pierced my thin sweater. "Hello!" I called.

No one answered, but I heard the sound of footsteps crunching through the snow and receding into the woods. I scanned the driveway; my truck was the only vehicle.

Whoever it was had come here on foot. I scanned the trees, but saw no other movement. "Hello!" I called again. Nobody answered. After a long moment, I stepped back inside and slid the dead bolt home, suppressing a shiver that had nothing to do with the cold.

Seal Point Road was lined with cars — or what passed for cars here on Cranberry Island — when I arrived at Fernand's gallery next evening with a tray of mini quiches. I closed the van door behind me and wrapped my scarf more tightly around my chin; fat white flakes were whirling down, covering everything in a thick blanket of white. Beautiful as it was, the snow was making getting around a real challenge; I was glad Ernie White, the only person on the island with a snow plow, had plowed the roads before the party. As it was, I hoped he would plow again before it was time to go home.

Fernand's studio and gallery, a yellow wood-framed house with lavender shutters and pale blue trim, had been decked out for Christmas with icicle lights and balls of colored lights that hung from the spruce trees outside like giant balls of sparkling yarn. Electric candles burned in the windows, reflecting warmly against the snow, and an enormous balsam wreath graced the door. I caught a whiff of cinnamon and apples, and felt my spirits rise despite the worry that had gnawed at me all day.

The inside of the gallery was just as festive as the outside, with softly glowing Christmas lights festooning the open rafters. Along with candles scattered around the well-stocked buffet (where I spotted what I hoped was an enormous bowl of lobster salad) and on the tables Fernand had set up around the room, they were the only source of light, and the warm glow was magical. My eyes were drawn to an enormous balsam fir in the corner, decorated with hundreds of lights and bright red glass balls. I took a deep, appreciative breath; I could smell the fresh scent of balsam mingling with the cinnamon and cloves of the mulled cider.

"Natalie! What did you bring?" Fernand wove his way through the crowd of islanders toward me, looking remarkably relaxed for the host of a big party. As usual, he was impeccably turned out, this time in a pair of slacks and a festive red sweater with a starched collared shirt peeking out. The light glinted off his steel-rimmed glasses, and his hands, as usual, still bore faint traces of paint. He peeked under the foil and groaned. "Tell me those aren't mini quiches."

"They are."

"I'll gain ten pounds!" he said in his clipped Canadian accent.

I grinned at him. "No you won't. You never do."

"From your lips to God's ears," he said.

I laughed. "Great party. Looks like the whole island's here."

"Everyone except the guest of honor," he said ruefully. "And John," he added. "Still at continuing ed?"

"He'll be back the day after tomorrow, but he's sorry to miss it," I said. "Where's Gwen?"

"She helped me set up," he said. "She's with Adam, talking with one of the gallery owners from Mount Desert Island. They're talking about doing a show in the summer — best time to do it, with the tourists in town. That girl is going places." He waved toward the far corner, where Gwen, looking radiant in a deep emerald dress, was smiling and chatting with a stout, graying gentleman. She looked better than she had in days; I hoped that meant she'd had a breakthrough today.

"How's the show coming together?" I asked.

"It's always stressful," he said, "and working in oils has been a challenge. I still think watercolors are her strength, but Herb Munger, for some reason, is insisting on oils. It's not a bad idea to experiment with different media, and she's coming along fairly well."

"That's not what I'm hearing at home. She thinks she needs to start over."

He waved the idea away. "She's got lots of things to show. Don't worry about it. I talked with Herb a few minutes ago," he said, indicating a tall man in plaid pants who was swilling down mulled wine in the corner. How anyone who would intentionally wear those pants could consider himself a judge of art, I had no idea. I planned to mention it to Gwen later. "He's not an ideal patron, but everyone has to start somewhere." Something in his expression made me hope she found a different patron sooner than later. "I'm trying to convince him to feature her watercolors."

"Are the oils that bad?" I asked.

He sucked in his breath. "She's still learning. It'll come."

Not encouraging.

"Anyway," he said, "I'm glad you're here. I'm just going to go put these on the buffet. If I were you, I'd get some of the clams

62

casino before they're all gone."

As he whisked the platter off toward one of the buffet tables along the back wall, I scanned the room. The lobstermen and their spouses were clustered in a corner by the window; I was happy to see Terri Bischoff and the new schoolteacher, Sara Bennett, among them, laughing at something Tom Lockhart, the tall, charismatic Cranberry Island selectman and lobster co-op chair, had said. Terri was looking good in dark slacks and a blue button-down shirt; Sara wore a red velvet dress with a sweetheart neckline that framed her heart-shaped face beautifully.

Gertrude Pickens from the *Daily Mail* was here, of course, flitting from person to person with a notebook and pen in her hand, as were the Winter Knitters, whose knitting needles, I was relieved to see, had been replaced by mugs of mulled wine and cider. Although I didn't see Claudette, her son Mark was there, alongside a sleek, dark-haired woman I didn't recognize.

"You made it!" I turned to find Charlene, dressed in a form-fitting sparkly red dress that set off her full figure to its best advantage. "And you even found a dress!" she said, looking at the rather plain green wool number I'd found in the back of the closet.

"Just about the only winter dress I own," I said, making a mental note to go shopping next time I made it to the mainland. "You look terrific!" I said.

"You like it?" she asked.

"New dress?"

"Nah," she said, "but it's stretchy, so I can eat. Speaking of eating, have you visited the buffet yet?"

"No, but I was on my way," I said. As we walked toward the groaning tables, I asked Charlene about the dark-haired woman next to Claudette's son.

"That's Dawn," she said. "Claudette's daughter-in-law."

"That's her daughter-in-law?" I asked. As I watched, the dark-haired woman tipped her head back into a laugh. With her black sheath dress and artfully applied red lipstick, she bore no resemblance to the wild-haired woman in sweats who had met me at Claudette's door just a day earlier. "Far cry from the woman at Claudette's yesterday. Her hair was out to here," I said, holding my hands about a foot from my head, "and she didn't even know her name."

"I know she has some psychiatric issues," Charlene said. "I'm not sure what, though."

"You wouldn't know it tonight," I said, still trying to square the slender, fashionably dressed woman with the hollow-eyed specter I'd seen yesterday. Her husband, a stout, fortyish man with a worried look on his pink-cheeked face, stayed close; there was a nervous quality about him, as if he were expecting her to break. She was engaged in conversation with Munger, the gallery owner who was torturing my niece. He appeared to be comfortable flirting despite his awful pants. I focused on Claudette's son Mark again. He looked as if he wanted to be anywhere but here. Claudette and Eli weren't in evidence; I guessed they were staying at home with the kids. Maggie hadn't made it to the party, either, I realized as my eyes swept the room. They were quickly drawn back to Dawn, though, as she tilted her head back into a tinkling laugh. "She's like a different person," I said.

"There's Zelda," Charlene said, pointing to a stout Asian woman in the corner. The artist was dressed in black, her silver hair styled in an attractive, asymmetrical cut. She seemed to be in deep conversation with Murray Selfridge, who, as usual, looked like he'd just come off the golf course at the country club, even though it was twenty degrees outside.

"And Murray," I said darkly. He was always plotting some big development on the island, and it made me nervous to see him conferring with Zelda. "Wonder what they're cooking up?"

"I'll have to ask Tom if they've talked to him about their plans at all," Charlene said.

"Natalie!"

I turned to see the sharp face of Gertrude Pickens, the *Daily Mail* reporter.

"Gertrude," I said, forcing a smile. The reporter had never been kind to the inn, and seemed always to be looking for a reason to give me more bad press. "How are you?"

"Better than you are, I hear," she said.

"What do you mean?" I asked frostily, feeling a trickle of ice water down my spine.

"I understand there's some trouble with a mortgage company," she said, with a predatory smile.

FIVE

My eyes flicked to Charlene, who shook her head almost imperceptibly, widening her eyes.

"Oh?" I said, as coolly as I could. "Where did you hear that?"

"I never reveal my sources," she said, poising her pen over her notebook. "Now, is it true that you just received a foreclosure notice on the inn?" she asked.

"I don't see how the inn's financial business is any business of yours," I said.

"Oh, so it *is* true," she said, jotting busily away.

"I didn't say that," I protested.

"What happened? Business dry up with the economy?"

"If you'll excuse us, Gertrude," Charlene said, grabbing my arm, "this is a social gathering, and we are on our way to the buffet."

"How long do you have to pay before the

bank takes over?" she called out as Charlene pulled me past her through the crowd. I felt my breath come in short spurts.

"Ignore her," Charlene said.

"I'd like to, but she's making it difficult. Maybe I should buy her a bullhorn for Christmas."

"She seems to be doing fine without it," Charlene muttered.

"How did she find out?" I asked. "You and I were the only ones there when we talked about it."

"Eli was there," she said.

"Eli? Do you really think he said something to someone?"

"Of course not. But who else would have known?"

I thought of Eli, who had been my friend since I came to the island. He hadn't said anything to me about the letter. Would he really tell Gertrude about the inn's financial troubles? I didn't want to believe it. But someone had said something. Which meant my private problems were about to become very public. As in front-page-of-the-local-paper public.

Charlene sighed. "Who knows how she found out? But now that she does, you can bet it'll be all over the island even before it hits the *Daily Mail*." She grabbed a paper

68

plate and handed it to me. "Eat. It'll make you feel better."

I had lost my appetite, but I took the plate anyway, glancing over my shoulder and half-expecting to see Gertrude standing behind me with her notebook. Instead, she was making a beeline toward the door; the local celebrity had arrived.

Nina Torrone was dressed much as she had been last time we met — right down to the sunglasses and the pillbox hat. Mortimer Gladstone stood beside her in a capacious double-breasted suit with a red scarf tossed artfully around his neck; it picked up the color of his nose capillaries quite well, I thought. His arm was slung protectively around the young artist, and there was something in the possessiveness that struck me as odd. A murmur traveled through the assembly of guests, and my eyes were drawn to Fernand. His eyes were narrowed; he looked almost as if he were trying to recall something. Then the expression was wiped clean, and he smiled and stepped forward to greet his guests.

"She really is young," Charlene said after polishing off a bacon-wrapped shrimp. "I can't believe she makes a half million dollars a painting."

"Have you seen any of her work?" I asked.

"I looked it up the other day. It's abstract stuff — nothing I'd hang in my living room." She reached for another shrimp. "You should eat a few of these before they're gone — they're really good."

"I will," I said, still watching Fernand, who was now in conversation with the pair from New York. Although Nina wasn't saying much; it seemed the agent was the talker of the two. Gwen sidled up a moment later, extending a slender hand toward the young artist. She took my niece's hand quickly, gave it a perfunctory shake, and then dropped it as if she'd been burned.

"Try the crab dip," Charlene said, handing me a chip laden with gooey, cheesy sauce.

"Just a second," I said, still watching. Fernand was speaking now, directing his comments to Nina. Gladstone's eyes darted to the side; then he stepped forward, directly between Fernand and Nina. Abruptly, he took her arm and guided her toward the buffet — and right into Gertrude.

"Gertrude Pickens, *Daily Mail*," Gertrude trumpeted, her eyes gleaming. "So exciting to have a celebrity on the island!" she cooed, loudly enough that I could hear her over the hum of voices. "What inspired you to retreat to the coast of Maine?" I moved

70

closer, leaving Charlene to the crab dip.

As always, Gladstone stepped up to answer the question. "Ms. Torrone appreciates solitude. And privacy," he said, stressing the last word.

"Will she be painting more canvases?"

"Of course," he said. "It's well known that she paints every day."

"I understand you have your largest show ever in New York right now, and that your paintings are selling very well." Gertrude directed the question at Torrone, but the artist simply tilted her head toward her agent. I wondered what her eyes looked like behind the dark glasses — and why the glasses were necessary when the sun had set three hours earlier.

"Ms. Torrone has become very popular," he said. "Now, if you will excuse me, my client is rather parched, and could use . . ."

"Her signature drink," Fernand said, appearing as if out of nowhere with a cocktail glass filled with a sickly greenish liquid.

"What's that?" I asked Charlene.

"I don't know," she said. "Maybe a Stinger?"

"A Stinger?"

"Brandy and crème de menthe."

"Ugh."

As Fernand presented the drink, Torrone's

smile faltered for a moment. After a quick glance toward Gladstone, who nodded, Torrone reached for the drink with a pale, well-manicured hand — the first thing I'd seen her do for herself — and said "thank you" in a voice no louder than a mouse's.

"Kind of you," Gladstone boomed. "Very kind."

"I would love a tour of your studio when you get it set up," Fernand said, again directing his remarks to Torrone. "Haven't seen you in what . . . a year? What are you working on now?"

"Top secret, I'm afraid," Gladstone said, putting a hand on Torrone's arm. "Now, if you'll excuse us, we're going to avail ourselves of your delightful buffet."

"My," Charlene murmured from beside me as the duo swept past us. "Aren't we snobby."

"How did Fernand know what she drank?" I asked.

"I don't know. Maybe he Googled it," Charlene said. "Oops. Better hide. Gertrude's coming your way again."

She steered me away from Gertrude and right into Gwen, who was standing in the corner by the door to the studio. Munger had moved on from Dawn and now had his arm around my niece. Something about it

72

reminded me of Torrone and her agent, and I had to resist the visceral urge to yank his arm off of her. He was telling her something, his mouth mere inches from her ear; her brow was furrowed. I looked for Adam; he was talking with Tom Lockhart, over by the drinks station.

"Gwen," I said. Munger looked startled and retracted his arm.

"Aunt Nat!" she said, looking relieved to see me. She stepped away from Munger. "I don't know if you've ever been introduced, but this is Herb Munger. He owns the gallery where I'm showing my paintings."

Munger put on a hearty, toothy smile and extended a meaty hand. I put mine out tentatively, and he shook it hard enough to rattle my teeth. "So good to meet you. Your niece is a talented young lady. Beautiful, too!" he said, winking at my niece.

"I know she's looking forward to the show," I said. "She's been working hard."

"Can't work too hard, though. All work and no play makes Gwen a dull girl!" He winked at her again, and gave her arm a squeeze. She smiled weakly and averted her eyes.

"I understand you're quite an entrepreneur," I said.

"They don't call me the vacuum king of

New England for nothing," he said, puffing out his polo-clad chest a little bit. I couldn't help noticing that a roll of fat hung over his Sansabelt waistband.

"Vacuum cleaners to fine art — it's quite a leap," I said. "What got you interested in art?"

"I wanted to take my expertise in trend-spotting and marketing and assist artists. They're often talented, but have no understanding of what the market really wants," he said.

"Like oils instead of watercolors?"

"Exactly!" he said. "I know it's been hard on her, but I think she'll appreciate it when she sees the payoff."

"I understand she's got to rework a lot, though," I said. "Wouldn't it make more sense to show her watercolors, too?"

"Too traditional," he said. "You just worry about your cakes and muffins," he said. "Fernand and I will get this little lady where she needs to be." He turned to Gwen. "Weren't you going to show me your canvases?" he said.

"Oh, yes," she said, sounding less than enthusiastic at the prospect.

"Well, then. Shall we head into the studio together?"

"Sure," she said, and reluctantly headed

toward the stairs.

"I'll come with you," I said, not wanting Munger alone with my niece.

"No, I'll come." Adam stepped up to our little group, and his presence made me relax. Gwen looked up at him with a relieved smile as the tall, dark-haired lobsterman slung a casual arm around her. Munger stepped away from Gwen. "You know, I really should catch up with Zelda and Fernand. Maybe later on?" he said.

"We'll be around," Adam said, and Munger drifted off, suddenly anxious to be away.

"I'd still love to see your paintings," I said.

Gwen groaned. "Let's not ruin the party."

I glanced over my shoulder at Munger, who was back to Dawn again. "Watch out for that one," I said to Gwen.

"You think?" Gwen asked.

"I do."

"Your aunt's right," Adam said. "Do the show, but keep your distance. I don't trust him."

"I can take care of myself," Gwen said.

"I'm not saying you can't," I said. "But it's better not to be in a situation where you have to, if you get my drift."

"Have you eaten yet, young lady?" Adam asked my niece.

"Not really," she said.

"Well, let's fix that," he said. He smiled at me. "Coming, Natalie?"

I glanced toward the buffet and spotted Gertrude. "Maybe later," I said. "I ate a lot this afternoon." As they headed toward the clams — and Gertrude — I scanned the room again. Torrone was in the corner, standing silently while her agent spoke with Zelda Chu. She held the drink awkwardly; it didn't look like she'd drunk much of it. I looked for Fernand; he was talking with Tom Lockhart, the head of the lobster co-op and one of the island's selectmen, across the room from Gertrude. I walked over to join them, hoping to have a chance to talk to Fernand about Gwen — and Munger.

"You'll let me know if they file plans?" Fernand was saying as I walked up.

"As soon as I hear anything," Tom said. He spotted me and smiled. "Natalie! I hear you're responsible for the mini quiches!"

"I am."

"They're terrific. How's business at the inn?"

"Doing just fine," I said, conveniently omitting the little issue of impending foreclosure. "I'm worried about Gwen, though. Do you mind if I steal Fernand for a moment?"

"Not at all. I'll be in touch," he said, and headed back toward the quiches.

"Everything okay?" Fernand asked, his brow furrowing as we drew away from the crowd, toward the corner.

"I'm not sure this show is such a good idea," I said. "Gwen hasn't been eating, she thinks she's a terrible artist . . . and I don't trust that gallery owner."

"I know," Fernand said. "I keep telling her it's just an opportunity to get her work some exposure. I tried to convince both of them that Gwen's watercolors would be perfect, but Munger disagrees with me."

"What do you know about him personally?" I ask.

"Why?"

"He seems awfully . . . flirtatious," I said.

"He's not married," Fernand said. "And he plays golf with Murray a lot."

"Not a ringing endorsement. Can you keep an eye on her for me?"

"I will," he said. "I'm going to make sure she shows some of her watercolors; they're really amazing, and I don't think Munger sees it. She's got potential with oils, but it's not a medium she's been working with for long. Don't worry," he said, putting a hand on my arm. "I'll be there to make sure she doesn't get derailed."

From what I could tell, she was already off the tracks, but I thanked him. "What's Munger's fascination with oils, anyway?"

"He fancies himself a trend-spotter," Fernand said, rolling his eyes.

"That's what Torrone and Chu work in, isn't it?"

"Yes," he said, and his eyes drifted to Nina Torrone, quietly standing next to Gladstone, who was deflecting questions from a curious islander.

"Did you know Nina before she hit it big?"

"Yes," he said. "At least I think I did."

"Has something changed?"

"Completely," he said.

Before I could ask another question, Zelda Chu strode up to us, oozing confidence. Her sleek asymmetrical hair — stylishly silver — high cheekbones, and high-fashion, fluttery black dress seemed out of place in the rustic setting. "Fernand," she said, thrusting out a hand.

"Zelda," he said. I could practically feel their hackles rising.

"Have you considered my proposal?" she asked, without even looking at me.

"Can we discuss this later?" Fernand asked, glancing at me.

"It's already been a month."

"This is not the time, Zelda," he hissed.

At that moment, Gertrude strode up, pad and pen in hand. "What a lovely party, Fernand. I understand you knew our guest of honor in New York?"

"Yes," he said tersely.

"I don't believe we've met," Zelda said, smiling at Gertrude. "I'm Zelda Chu."

"Gertrude Pickens," Gertrude said, and turned back to Fernand. "How did you and Nina meet?"

"We are all from New York," Zelda said before Fernand could answer. "She and Fernand briefly studied under the same artist, but we are colleagues. I'd love for you to come and visit my gallery someday. I'd be happy to give you a personal tour, and tell you about our plans for the future."

"Oh, how nice!" Gertrude said. "Do you give lessons, too? I've always wanted to learn to paint."

"We will be," Zelda said.

"You'll be offering art lessons?" Selene MacGregor of Island Artists had drifted up to the cluster of artists, looking like a vision in a purple chiffon dress. I took a step back, glad not to be the center of attention.

As Gertrude launched into a description of the art classes she'd taken in high school back in the 70s, I edged away, thankful that something had distracted the reporter from grilling me on the foreclosure issue. I wondered about the "proposal" Zelda had mentioned, though. Gwen hadn't said anything about it. Was she looking to partner with Fernand? If so, Fernand didn't look too enthusiastic about it. If he turned her down, would he hate me for agreeing to put up her retreat participants this summer?

Deal with that when it comes, I reminded myself. The mortgage catastrophe was more than enough to handle for now.

I glanced over toward Nina Torrone, who was still holding the cocktail glass Fernand had given her. It was almost full of the sickly greenish liquid; she'd hardly touched it. I found myself studying the young woman — very young, it seemed to me, to have studied with Fernand in New York. She seemed to be trying to take up as little space as possible. Her agent had positioned himself partially in front of her, as if shielding her. What had Fernand meant when he said she'd changed? A loud, tinkling laugh caught my attention, and I turned to see Claudette's daughter-in-law, holding court in a corner of the room. Both Tom Lockhart and Father Timothy, the island's new priest, were in animated conversation with her. Talk about completely changed . . .

"Did you escape Gertrude?" Charlene had

snuck up beside me with a plate full of mini quiches.

"For now," I said. "And I think Gwen escaped Herb Munger."

"That man gives me the willies," Charlene said.

"Me too," I said, glad to see that my niece was still with Adam, and well away from the tacky gallery owner. "I wish he'd stuck to vacuum cleaners."

"It's a good opportunity for Gwen," she said, popping another mini quiche into her mouth. "Besides," she said through a mouthful of egg and melted Gruyére, "it'll all be over soon."

"Fernand said he'll look after her, at least." I glanced over at her mentor, who had detached himself from Zelda and Gertrude and was pouring himself a glass of white wine.

"And John will be back soon," she said.

"Yeah," I replied, eyeing the bar. Maybe I could use one of those green drinks, too.

"What did he say when you told him about the notice from the mortgage company?"

"I haven't told him yet," I said.

"Better do it soon," she said. "Or else he'll read about it in the paper."

"Don't remind me," I said. I reached for

one of the mini quiches on her plate.

I was reaching for a second when there was the clink of a fork against glass. I looked up to see Fernand at the front of the room, preparing for a toast.

When everyone had quieted enough to listen, he put down his glass and smiled. "I wanted to take a moment to welcome one of the luminaries of the art world to our island. Welcome to Maine, Nina!"

Six

I looked at the young artist. Her olive skin seemed pale as she smiled and dipped her head.

"It is an honor to have you here with us," he said, "and we hope you will share your expertise with the many budding artists in our community."

Again, applause. Gertrude, I noticed, was busily scribbling in her notebook.

"I'd like to invite you to say a few words, Nina," Fernand said, looking at the young artist.

All eyes turned to Nina and her agent. It was hard to tell what she was feeling behind the enormous sunglasses, but she took a step backward, losing her balance and sloshing her drink on the floor. There was a murmur in the crowd as she steadied herself. Her agent whispered a few words to her, then strode to the front of the room to stand beside Fernand.

"Thank you so much for the warm welcome," he said in a deep, stentorian voice, as Nina, who had set down her glass and looked as if she'd like nothing better but to melt into the floor, smiled weakly. "It's been a lovely party, and you are all just delightful people — it is an honor. Ms. Torrone is currently in a deeply creative phase, and although solitude is a crucial element of that phase — all in service to a greater good — we are both very thankful for your generosity in hosting this party." He made an abbreviated bow and returned to Nina, who was still looking pale. And moist; the drink had left a dark stain on her dress. I watched the two of them together, trying to figure out what was going on. Fernand, too, was observing them, I noticed. His mouth was a thin line. Despite the throng of people, I could feel the tension in the room.

Conversation started slowly, and it was a couple of minutes before it returned to its previous hum. I was not surprised when, ten minutes later, Gladstone escorted his client from the gallery, citing her moistened wardrobe as the reason for their hasty departure.

"Weird," Charlene proclaimed as they disappeared out the door. "I think I'm glad I'm not a famous artist."

"Do you think she has vocal cords?" I asked.

"If so, they sure don't get much exercise," Charlene said. "Maybe she saves up all her self-expression for her paintings."

"Maybe," I said. Something about that duo bothered me. My eyes sought Munger, who was deep in conversation with another of my least favorite people — Murray Selfridge. The gallery owner's greasy hair shone in the dim light.

Torrone and Gladstone might bother me, I thought, but not as much as the former vacuum cleaner salesman.

I didn't see Gwen again until after breakfast the next morning. My niece looked more haggard then ever when she slumped down the stairs at ten.

"What's wrong?"

"Everything," she said. "My work. After you left, I showed the new paintings to Munger."

"Was Adam with you?" I asked, too quickly.

"No. Fernand was, though."

"I just . . . worry," I said.

"Anyway, it doesn't matter. He didn't like any of them."

I poured her a cup of coffee and put one

of the blueberry muffins I'd baked that morning on a plate for her. "I'm sure they're better than you think. Besides, Fernand told me he thinks you should show some of your watercolors, too."

She didn't answer, but sat down and picked at her muffin. I'd never had to live with a teenager, but I was starting to get a feel for the experience. Gwen might be twenty-one, but she was acting more like thirteen. Or even twelve.

When she pushed the plate away after eating almost nothing, I grabbed her coat and handed it to her.

"What?"

"We're going to Fernand's," I said. "I want to see these 'terrible' paintings. I never got a chance last night."

"But . . ."

"No argument. Let's go."

After a moment's delay, she slid her arms into her coat and followed me out to the truck. "I'm warning you. They're awful," she said as I revved the engine.

I didn't bother responding.

The gallery looked clean and windswept when I pulled the van up outside of it a few minutes later. A light blanket of snow covered the tire ruts left by the partygoers last night, glittering in the sunshine.

Gwen fumbled with the keys as I waited, shivering in the cold wind off the water. When she pushed the door open, I was surprised at the mess. The spell cast by the Christmas lights was gone; in the harsh morning light, the place was a wreck. Dirty plates and platters were scattered over the long buffet table, cups and napkins littered the floor, and there was a sour smell of spoiled food.

"Maybe we should help him clean up," I said.

"I'm surprised he didn't do it last night," Gwen said. "He's usually totally on top of things."

"Hung over, maybe?" I said, checking my watch. "It's only ten."

"Maybe."

I followed Gwen up the stairs to the studio, which took up the whole second floor and was lined with north-facing windows. Since the party had been limited to the gallery, this room was clean and spare, with three easels set up and several canvases leaning against the back wall. Framed by the glass was the tip of the mainland, gray and white with snow, and a stretch of steely blue water tipped with whitecaps.

"Here they are," she said, gesturing to a wall covered in brightly painted canvases. I blinked, surprised. The work looked ama-teurish, nothing at all like the finely ren-dered, almost translucent paintings I'd come to expect from Gwen.

"This is my best one," she said, pointing to one that featured a childish-looking boat against a too-blue sky.

"They're quite a departure from your earlier work," I said awkwardly. She was right; they weren't as good as her normal work. I felt a wave of frustration toward the gallery owner who was pushing her into a direction she clearly wasn't comfortable go-ing.

"I knew you wouldn't like them," she said, her beautiful face crumpling into tears. "They're awful."

"They're not awful," I said, trying to sound convincing. "They're just not what I'm used to." On the opposite wall were a few of her watercolors. They looked like they had been done by a different person. "I like your original work better . . . you've worked on your technique for years, and I think they're absolutely stunning."

"Really?" She looked at me with swollen eyes.

"Really. Fernand wouldn't have taken you on if he didn't agree with me. Can you use these for the show? Just while you're figuring out the other medium?"

"Munger told me they're too small," she said. "They won't sell."

"I don't think so at all," I said. "And what does he know? Did you see the pants he had on last night?" I asked, playing my trump card.

"True," she said, sulkily.

"Besides, who cares how big they are? Art comes in all sizes. And if he really wants big paintings, why can't you just try a few larger watercolors?"

"That's what Fernand suggested, but when Munger wanted oils . . ." She sighed.

"Let's go talk to Fernand," I said. "He knows what he's doing."

She sighed. "Okay."

Fernand's house was painted the same yellow as the studio, and was tucked into the trees next door. We tromped up the steps, shaking the snow off our boots. When Gwen knocked, the door swung open; it was ajar. "He mentioned you had to jiggle the handle to get the door to latch," Gwen said. "He must not have closed it properly last night."

We stepped inside. There was a light dusting of blown snow on the wood floor of the front hall.

"Fernand?" Gwen called, still standing at

89

the doorway.

When there was no answer, we entered cautiously. The open door had chilled the house, and I kept my coat zipped up as we walked through the small, sparsely furnished rooms. Unlike the gallery next door, the downstairs was as neat as you would expect from a tidy man, with framed original art in every room. "He hasn't made coffee this morning," Gwen observed as we walked into the kitchen.

"How do you know?"

"Usually he keeps a carafe of it on the counter, but it's still on the shelf."

I was starting to get a bad feeling. Maybe he'd had too much to drink last night, I told myself. Still . . .

"Stay here," I said. "I'm going to check upstairs."

"But . . ."

Without waiting for her to answer, I climbed the steps. They creaked ominously, and despite the sunshine pouring in through the windows, the house felt suddenly very wrong.

There were three doors on the second floor, but I didn't have to try any of them to know where Fernand was.

A long finger of blood oozed from the nearest door, which was half-open. Lying on the floor, a knife in his hand, eyes staring sightless at the ceiling, was my niece's art teacher.

I took a step back and covered my mouth with my hand.

He lay in a pool of his own blood, his wrists slashed open.

SEVEN

It was a shocking scene. Fernand was still wearing the same red sweater — only parts of it had been stained dark with blood. My mind refused to process what I was seeing. How could Fernand — Fernand, who had mentored my niece for years, who had shared so many dinners at my kitchen table, who was such a huge part of this — how could he be gone? I'd never see those blue eyes glint behind their wire-rimmed glasses again, I realized, feeling sick.

I tore my eyes from the body, searching for a note — for some explanation of why he had taken his own life. It was incomprehensible that he could have done such a thing to himself — to Gwen, to all of us — without some explanation.

There was nothing, though, but a half-finished glass of a cloudy amber liquid. A quick sniff of the glass confirmed my guess: it was Scotch, Fernand's favorite tipple.

Had he been drinking it to fuel his courage — or had it been the depressive effects of the alcohol that spurred him to his death? Either possibility was too awful to consider. My heart felt leaden in my chest as I realized I would likely never know. Fernand, who was such a vital part of our little island community, was gone forever.

I stepped away, unable to look at my friend for another moment, and wiped at the tears that had welled my eyes. I dreaded telling Gwen, but knew I had to.

"What's wrong?" Gwen asked me when I came down the stairs, feeling the muffin I'd eaten earlier churn in my stomach.

"Honey, I'm so sorry," I said, touching her shoulder. "Fernand's gone."

She stared at me blankly. "Gone?"

"I'm afraid . . ." I swallowed, hating to say the words. "It looks like he killed himself."

Her face drained of color, and she let out a long, moaning wail.

"I'm so sorry, sweetheart," I said, and folded her into my arms as she sobbed. We stood there for a long time before she pulled away. I looked at my niece's tearstained face and tried to get my mind in gear. It would be hard to stay in the house — not with Fernand so close — but we needed to be here until the police arrived. I had to call the police, I realized, my mind working slowly, still processing the shock. But I didn't want to do that where Gwen could hear me.

"Why don't we get you to the gallery?" I said, and put an arm around Gwen, walking her over to the larger building. I settled her into a chair and stroked her hair, telling her I'd be right back, then hurried back to the house.

I dialed the mainland police — a number that I had unfortunately memorized — feeling numb as I told them what had happened. They took the details, told me not to touch anything or leave the premises, and promised someone would be there within an hour. I was missing John, I realized as I hung up the phone — and not just because I craved the comfort of his strong arms around me right now. I hadn't realized until now how much I relied on his ability to take charge when tragedy struck. Which had happened all too often these past few years.

I tried to reach Adam, but could only leave a message; he was likely miles offshore, and even if I had a radio with which to contact him, it would likely be at least an hour before he could be back on the island.

After hanging up the phone, I stood in the too-quiet kitchen, feeling a sharp pang of loss. The empty blue coffee carafe, the mugs lined up in a neat row on the shelf by the window, waiting to be filled — Fernand would never use any of them again. He liked his coffee black, I knew — he'd often teased me about my milky "lattes" — and had a weakness for my cinnamon rolls. I sometimes sent a few for him with Gwen when she headed out to the studio. Just last night he was joking about gaining ten pounds, but today he was gone. He'd never eat another cinnamon roll again. He'd seemed happy last night, at the party. Was it all an act?

Or had something happened at the party last night — or after it? What could be so catastrophic that it would drive Fernand to take his own life?

My heart ached for my lost friend as I walked down the hallway to the front door. The cold, sharp air felt refreshing after the heavy atmosphere inside the white and blue house.

I found Gwen in a corner of the gallery, hugging knees to her chest and rocking back and forth. She looked up at me with eyes swollen from crying.

"How did he do it?" she asked.

"A knife," I said, sitting down next to her and putting an arm around her bony shoulders. "He slit his wrists." As I spoke the words, the image blossomed in my mind. Fernand's limbs flung out like a doll's, wrists gashed open, the Exacto knife lying in his open palm. And the blood. It was everywhere, soaking into the floorboards, spattering the white dust ruffle of the four-poster bed. I shook myself involuntarily, as if I could shed the memory.

"No," she said, shaking her head wildly. "He wouldn't have done something like that. He wasn't depressed. He had been dating someone for months and it was going well; I think they were planning a trip to Italy in the spring. The show was just around the corner, he had plans to expand the retreat center . . . it doesn't make sense." She ran her hands through her hair, making the tangled curls look as if they were standing on end. "Was there a note?"

"I didn't see one," I said. "But they don't always leave a note." I sighed. "I just don't know, honey." It didn't make sense to me either, but I knew what I'd just seen. "Nobody ever knows, really. Maybe having Nina Torrone here set him off."

"Why?" she asked.

"Maybe because of her success," I said. "I don't know. Maybe because he was in love with her, and she was with another man."

Despite her tears, she snorted. "He was gay, Aunt Nat."

Scratch that, then. I had wondered, but never confirmed it. "Okay, maybe he broke up with someone," I said. "Or someone broke up with him."

She shook her head vehemently. "He would have told me if something like that had happened. I'm telling you, Aunt Nat, it doesn't make sense. Everything was going well. His sales were increasing, he was going to expand the summer art school . . ."

"He wasn't bothered by the new art retreat?" I asked. "Apparently Zelda made him some kind of an offer. She was asking him about it last night."

"I didn't hear anything about an offer." Her eyes were swollen and red, and her voice was rough from weeping. "And of course he was bothered by the new retreat, but why would he kill himself over that now? He's known about it for months."

"He did seem pretty happy last night," I concurred, remembering his smile when he greeted me. "You were here longer than I was; did something happen after I left? Did you notice a change in mood?"

She shook her head. "Nothing. He was in good spirits."

I thought of the open front door. From

the snow that had drifted into the front hall, it must have been open for several hours. "I guess it's possible someone might have killed him," I said, "but what's the motive? What would he have that would be worth killing for?"

"I don't know, but I know that's what happened," she said, tears streaking down her cheeks. "He wouldn't have killed himself."

If only John were here, I thought for the hundredth time since Gwen and I had arrived at the gallery. "We're getting ahead of ourselves here. Let's see what the police have to say," I said.

"The police?" Gwen asked, pulling me out of my reverie. "You mean that idiot Grimes? He thought Polly killed herself, too," she said, echoing my own thoughts. She drew up her knees and hugged them more tightly. "I wish John were here."

"Me too," I said, thinking I needed to call him as soon as possible. John would want to know about Fernand, although I knew it would be a blow. They'd become good friends these last few months. And, I thought with a sick feeling in my stomach, I needed to tell him about the mortgage fiasco. Why did it always have to be bad news? I wondered.

We sat together, not speaking, listening to

the wind moaning through the eaves, for what felt like an eternity, but was probably only forty-five minutes. Then there was a bustle of voices, and a knock on the door that dispelled the feeling of emptiness. The police had arrived, and the loneliness was eclipsed as Detective Penney, a briskly efficient woman who gave the impression of having everything under control, questioned both of us while her team cordoned off the house.

The only good thing about it was that Detective Grimes wasn't with them.

"I can't believe he's gone," John said. I could hear the sadness over the phone, and ached to give him a hug.

"I know," I said. "It just doesn't seem possible that he was so vibrant last night, and now . . ."

"What did Grimes say?" he asked.

"It wasn't Grimes," I said, cradling the phone to my shoulder as I shredded the leftover pork roast for green chile stew. I always craved hearty, comforting fare after a death, and the succulent pork stew, along with a basket of cornbread, would fit the bill perfectly. Adam had arrived shortly after we returned to the inn, and he and Gwen had been in the parlor by the fire ever since.

I hoped preparing one of Gwen's favorites would tempt her to eat.

"Not Grimes?" John asked. "Who was it, then?"

"A woman named Penney. She seemed very efficient, and didn't start looking at us as potential murderers. It was rather refreshing."

"I don't know her. Did she say anything about how she was classifying the death?"

"Not a word. She asked who had been at the party last night," I said, putting the last of the pork into a stockpot and reaching for a can of green chiles, "and what we found — and touched — when we got there." I took a deep breath. "Gwen doesn't believe it was suicide. He didn't seem suicidal last night, but I guess something might have happened after I left the party."

"It doesn't seem right to me, either," John said. "But sometimes people can surprise you."

"One strange thing is that the front door was open when we got there."

"In this weather?"

"I know." I turned on the water to rinse my hands; the engagement ring was itching again, and had turned my skin a greenish black. I scrubbed at it with soap, then dried my hands. The black was gone, but the skin was red and slightly inflamed.

"Did you tell the detectives about the door?" John asked, recalling me to the conversation.

"Of course," I said, giving the ring a twist.

He was quiet for a moment. "Where did you find him?"

"Upstairs, on the bedroom floor." I looked down at the potatoes on the cutting board and the sharp edge of the French chef's knife, and was reminded of the gleaming blade in Fernand's hand. "It was awful — blood everywhere. I don't know if I'll ever forget seeing it."

"Not the bathtub?"

"No, he was on the bedroom floor," I said, confused by the question. "Why the bathtub?"

"People who are serious often use water to make sure they bleed out."

"Ugh." I looked at the pork in the pot and shuddered. "Sounds like pig butchering."

"Sorry," he said. "I didn't mean to be graphic. I'm sure they'll check his computer and see if he was researching suicide. Although I just can't imagine it."

"Me neither," I said. "Maybe Gwen's right, and it wasn't. Remember Polly Sarkes?"

"Of course I remember her," John said.

My former cleaning helper had turned up dead with a gun in her hand, and although the police thought it was suicide, it had turned out to be murder. "We need to wait until we have all the information before we jump to conclusions, though. Maybe the new relationship didn't work out . . . there's likely to be an e-mail about it on his computer if that's the case."

"I know, I know. It's just . . ." I sighed as I poured the green chiles over the shredded pork.

"We can't do anything now, Nat. Let's let the detectives do their work. I'm sure they'll follow up and do due diligence."

"Speaking of due diligence, how's class?" I asked, glad to change the subject.

"Interesting," he said. "Some of the time, anyway. Not a whole lot of drug trade on Cranberry Island, so I'm not sure how relevant this particular course is."

"I hope not at all," I said.

"It's a nice change of pace, and it's interesting subject matter, but I'm looking forward to being home." He was quiet for a long moment. When he spoke again, the professionalism had faded, and I could hear the pain in his voice. "It's going to be hard with Fernand gone, though. I still can't believe it."

I felt my heart contract — both at the thought of Fernand, and at the mention of home. With the shock of Fernand's death, I had temporarily forgotten about the foreclosure notice I'd gotten in the mail yesterday. Not to mention Gertrude's questions last night. I checked my watch; there was still time to make some phone calls. It was on the tip of my tongue to tell John about the mortgage problem, but something held me back.

"Will you still be home tomorrow?" I asked. When John came home, I could show him the letter in person. Heck, with my luck, he'd be able to read it in the local paper. Although last night's tragic events would likely bump news of the inn to the back page.

"Absolutely," he said. "I can't wait to give you a hug. And Gwen. Tell her to hang in there for me."

"I will. Adam's with her now."

"Good." He hesitated, then added, "I hate to bring this up right now, but I talked with my mother today."

"Oh, really?" I asked, feeling my hackles rise. We had visited her home in Boston over Thanksgiving, and I'd gotten the distinct impression that I was not the bride she'd envisioned for her handsome son.

"She's announced she's coming to visit," he said.

I stifled a groan. The last thing I needed was Catherine, whose eating regimen made the Pritikin diet look epicurean, hovering and critiquing everything I said — not to mention everything I cooked. Still, she was my future mother-in-law. The thought made me shiver. "When?"

"Within the week," he said. "I figure we'll put her up in the carriage house."

"For how long?" I asked, dreading the answer.

"She's planning on staying through Christmas," he said.

"What?" I had barely managed four days with the woman, and that was before my friend had died and foreclosure notices started popping up in my mailbox. Two weeks was more than I was prepared to face right now.

"Let's talk about it when I get there tomorrow," he said. "My next class starts in five minutes, and I've got to run. Give Gwen a hug for me, and tell her I'll help her figure out what to do for the show when I get back."

"But . . ." I said.

"We'll talk tomorrow, sweetheart. Take care of yourself. Love you."

"Love you too." I hung up and arranged the root vegetables on a cutting board. My kitchen was cozy and comforting, with Biscuit curled up in her favorite warm spot and a snow-frosted tableau out every mullioned window, but it wasn't enough to dispel the thoughts that haunted my mind. Catherine's impending arrival was the least of the many worries that plagued me. I looked at the scarred pine farm table where Fernand had shared so many meals and late-night glasses of wine with us over the last year with a deep sense of loss. I would miss his sharp wit and sense of humor. I'd even miss the discussions of art that lasted until so late I finally gave up and climbed the stairs, knowing John would eventually make it up after me. Although I knew all about his art, I knew little about his personal life, I realized. Until Gwen told me, I didn't know he was gay, and although I knew his family hailed from the area, I'd never heard him mention them. What a shock it would be when they heard the news, I thought. I chopped the potatoes and onions with a heavy heart, wiping my eyes with the back of my hand. Not all the tears were from the onions.

Fernand would be missed — but his death opened up other questions. Questions I didn't like to think about, to be honest. Such as, what would my niece do now that he was gone? Would Zelda Chu be willing to take Fernand's place as her mentor — and would Gwen even consider it?

And if Gwen did decide to stay, would there still be an inn for her to live at?

I put the rest of the ingredients into the pot, wiped my eyes with the backs of my hands, and composed myself before heading into the parlor to check on Gwen and Adam.

Although I didn't yet have a Christmas tree, the inn's biggest room was festive and cozy, with a fire roaring in the fireplace, pine boughs on the mantel, and a bowl of my Christmas potpourri scenting the room with cinnamon, cardamom, and cloves. Gwen and Adam were sitting on the couch together, talking in low voices.

"Sorry to interrupt," I said quietly, "but I hope you'll stay for dinner, Adam. I'm making green chile stew."

Adam turned and smiled at me with warm, intelligent eyes. It was easy to see what Gwen saw in him; not only was he handsome, but he was witty, kind, and generous. I hoped my sister would look past what she considered his "blue-collar" profession and see how much joy he brought her daughter — he'd done more to calm Gwen in a half hour than I'd managed the entire afternoon.

"I'd love to stay," he said, sounding more like an Ivy League student than a local lobsterman. Which made sense, since he'd gotten his degree from Princeton before taking up lobstering. (The degree currently resided somewhere in the deep waters just off Cranberry Island, where he'd pitched it after he got his lobstering license.) "As long as this young woman promises to eat," he continued, giving Gwen a hopeful look.

"There'll be cornbread," I offered.

Gwen gave a shuddery sigh. "I'll try. You haven't heard from the police?"

I shook my head. "I just got off the phone with John, though. He'll be back tomorrow, and he'll look into things for us."

She lifted her chin. "They're going to say it's suicide, and they're going to be wrong."

"Let's not jump to conclusions," I said. "We'll know soon enough."

Gwen let out another long sigh and I retreated to the kitchen, glad I could leave her with Adam, who was better comfort than I could be right now. Biscuit meowed plaintively at me from in front of her empty food bowl. I refilled it with dry kibble, which did nothing to stop the meowing —

evidently my plump ginger tabby had been hoping for Fancy Feast, not dry nuggets — then retrieved the foreclosure notice from the drawer I had tucked it into. Just looking at it brought a fresh jolt of near-panic. I took a deep breath and forced myself to think.

There was nothing I could do about Fernand, but I had to do something about this foreclosure notice. If I couldn't reach the attorney who had managed the closing, I could still contact the new mortgage company again. They claimed they'd paid off the existing mortgage; if that was true, they must have a record of the wire transfer.

After being transferred six times, I finally ended up talking with someone who could help me.

"Do you have a record of the wire transfer?" I asked.

"Yes," he said, and I felt a surge of relief.

"So it *was* wired to the mortgage company." If I could show them the proof of the wire transfer, they would have to retract the foreclosure threat.

"Actually, no," he said. "It was wired to an attorney in Bar Harbor."

My stomach clenched. "How long ago?"

"Looks like that was back in September," she said.

"Can you e-mail me a copy?"

"Of course," she said. "Is there anything else I can do to help you?"

"Yeah," I said, gripping the phone. "Is there anything I can do if my attorney skipped town with the money?"

"I'm afraid I can't help you with that," she said.

I didn't think so.

EIGHT

After slipping the corn muffins into the oven, I noticed my answering machine was blinking, and I realized I hadn't called Charlene. I didn't need to listen to the messages to know who they were from; instead, I picked up the phone and dialed the store. My best friend picked up on the first ring.

"Charlene. It's Nat."

"I called you three times already. Don't you check your messages?"

"It's been a busy afternoon. I'm sure you heard about Fernand," I said, feeling tears well in my eyes. "I'm sorry I didn't call earlier; it's been an awful, awful day."

"I heard about Fernand," my friend said, her voice soft with compassion. "I'm so sorry you had to find him."

Not for the first time, I wondered how news traveled so fast — and how Charlene always seemed to know it.

"It was a real shock," I said, glad to have

someone to talk to. "We went over there to look at some of Gwen's paintings, and I found him on the floor of his bedroom."

"Suicide, I hear?"

"His wrists were slit, so that's what it looks like. There was no note, though, at least not that I could see."

"Poor Fernand," Charlene said. "What a shock — I never would have guessed he'd kill himself." She was quiet for a moment, and I could hear the buzz of voices in the background: doubtless the islanders exchanging theories on what had happened at Fernand's. "Do you think he was upset over that Torrone woman?" she asked in a low voice.

My heart ached in my chest. "To be honest, I have no idea what he was thinking, and neither did Gwen — she doesn't believe he killed himself, and I can see her point. He seemed fine last night." The more I thought about it, the more it didn't make sense. "Did you see anything happen after I left the party?"

"You mean, with Fernand and Torrone?"

"Or Fernand and anyone," I said. "Suicides are usually depressed, aren't they? Not thinking about the future."

"That's my understanding," she said.

"But he was talking about gaining weight

when I saw him. Not something you'd need to worry about if you were planning on ending things in a couple of hours."

"Maybe it was his goodbye party," Charlene suggested. "A way to see everyone before he left."

"Why throw it in someone else's honor, then?"

"I don't know, Nat." She sighed. "I'm sure John'll be able to give us the skinny," she said. "And you've got other things to worry about, anyway — like keeping your inn."

The inn. My stomach dropped like an elevator in free-fall at the reminder. "That's another thing. The mortgage company wired the money. The attorney didn't forward it to the old company."

"What? He must have made a mistake!"

"I don't think it was a mistake, Charlene. I think he may have taken all my money and skipped town."

"No." Charlene breathed. Hearing my always-unruffled friend's response made my predicament feel somehow more acute. "What are you going to do?"

"I don't know," I said.

"Well, I do," Charlene said, and the confidence in her voice made my spirits lift a little bit. "We know where the attorney's office is. We're going over there tomorrow," she said. "And we'll sit in the lobby until the receptionist gets in touch with him."

"Okay," I said, trying to make myself breathe. "Okay." It was a start, anyway.

"Have you talked with John?"

I swallowed. "About Fernand, yes."

"And the mortgage?"

"No," I confessed. "I haven't told him."

"Why not?"

"I . . . I don't know."

"Well, if the attorney has taken your money and skipped town — I'm not saying that he has, but as you said, it's a possibility — it might be nice for the police to know, don't you think?"

"God, I feel so stupid."

"Stupid? He has a good reputation, and he's done more transactions than anyone else in town. What's there to feel stupid about?"

"You're probably right," I said half-heartedly.

"I am right. And I promise we'll get this sorted out, Nat."

"You think?"

"I know," she insisted. Her confidence was comforting. "Well. Now that we've got a plan for your financial issues," she continued, "how are you and Gwen managing? Are you okay?"

"Adam's here with her. I'm making us green chile stew for dinner — hoping it will entice her to eat something."

"Is that the one with the pulled pork and the potatoes and that yummy sauce?" she asked. I could almost hear her drooling.

"And cornbread."

"How much do you have?"

"Enough for four. I'll set another place at the table," I said, smiling for the first time that day.

Misery loves company.

The pork stew was delicious, reminding me of Texas despite the snow whirling down outside the window. In Austin, I often served it with homemade corn tortillas, but I didn't have masa on hand, so I had made cornbread muffins instead, and managed to pack away four of them. As always, the act of putting ingredients together and feeding people — including myself — had been soothing. Gwen might lose weight under stress, I reflected as I placed the warm, sweet-smelling cornbread muffins in a basket with a clean towel, but I had a rather frustrating habit of picking up anything she dropped. And then some.

The green chile stew had the perfect mix of heat and rich flavor, matched by the counterpoint of the moist muffins, but the conversation was less than stimulating. For much of the evening, the only sound in the kitchen was the clink of spoons and chewing — and an occasional plaintive meow from Biscuit, who was still hoping for something better in her food bowl. Adam and Charlene each made it through two bowls and a handful of muffins, but Gwen just picked at her food. Charlene did her best to keep the conversation rolling, but it was challenging with the two elephants in the kitchen with us: Fernand, and the uncertain future of the inn.

It wasn't until Adam and Gwen retreated to the parlor that Charlene and I were able to talk freely. As I cleared the table and began putting together the batter for Gwen's favorite muffins — Lemon Blueberry Ricotta — Charlene deposited herself in one of my chairs with a tin of fudge. The kitchen light caught the sequins on the shoulders of her candy apple red sweater. Combined with the green eye shadow, the sweater made her look like an attractive elf.

"I wasn't going to show you this, but thought you should know," she said, retrieving a copy of the *Daily Mail* from her capacious cloth bag.

I set down the flour canister and picked

up the paper. The article was buried on page five, but it was definitely there. "Local inn faces foreclosure."

"How can they print this?" I asked, feeling my stomach turn over. "It's totally unsubstantiated."

"She found the record at the county clerk's office," Charlene said, brushing a crumb of fudge from her sweater.

"It's in public records?" I groaned. "I can't believe this is happening."

"At least it's not a top news item," Charlene said. "And it's only the local paper; most of your customers don't subscribe to the *Daily Mail.*"

"Let's talk about something else," I said.

"Like your future mother-in-law's impending arrival? Or Fernand's death?"

"It's hard to choose," I said gloomily as I measured out flour.

"I found out that Fernand did have words with someone the night he died, you know," Charlene said.

"Who?"

"The gallery owner," she said. "The one with the awful pants. Fernand argued that Gwen should show her watercolors, but the guy was adamant that oils were selling better, and that's what he commissioned."

"Not exactly a motive for murder," I said,

zesting a lemon. "He also had a rather snippy exchange with that Chu woman. Told her she was cheating the people who registered for her courses." Charlene raised a tweezed, penciled eyebrow. "That might be a little more promising."

"What would she gain from killing him, though?" I asked as I zested a second lemon into a bowl. The fresh citrus fragrance gave my spirits a lift, perfuming the kitchen

Charlene shrugged. "More business?"

I shook my head. "It doesn't seem like it would be enough. Although at the party, I did hear her ask about a proposal she had given him. She said 'we': I don't know who else would have been involved."

"I know she and Murray Selfridge have been meeting lately," Charlene said. "I assumed it was about her new retreat plans. Maybe the proposal had something to do with that."

"I meant to ask, but I never had a chance."

"Have you asked Gwen?"

"Not yet, but I will."

"It's certainly worth looking into," Charlene said. "People do desperate things for money."

I measured the ricotta into a bowl and reached for the butter. "Gwen said he was dating a guy from Bangor. I wonder why he wasn't at the party?"

"Fernand's always been private about his personal life," Charlene said.

"That's certainly the truth. I didn't know he was gay until Gwen told me yesterday."

Charlene blinked at me, the green frosted shadow sparkling in the kitchen light. "Really, Natalie?"

"I know," I said. "I'm just oblivious."

"Even Maggie figured it out," Charlene said. "Heard her complaining about it last night, while she drank his champagne. Tania babysat for her, and she was making the most of it; Tom Lockhart had to give her a ride home." She leaned back in her chair, putting her legs, which were encased in tight blue jeans, up on the corner of the table. "Do you have any more of that fudge handy?"

"I've got one more tin," I said, retrieving a green and red tin from the counter and setting it in the middle of the table. We both took big pieces. I closed my eyes, letting the rich chocolate fill my senses. The slight bitterness of the walnuts was a perfect counterpoint to the creamy sweetness. Comfort food: just what I needed. I turned back to my muffins with the taste of chocolate suffusing my mouth. "So," Charlene said as I licked the last bit of chocolate from my thumb. "We should probably find out what was going on with Fernand's mystery man in Bangor. Does Gwen know who it is?"

"I haven't asked," I said as I put the bowl in the mixer and turned it on low, adding in two eggs as the beaters whirled. "With the shock . . . I haven't wanted to upset her. Besides, it's not clear if there's foul play."

"It doesn't hurt to ask a few questions," Charlene said.

"We don't even know what the police think yet." I added the lemon zest to the ricotta/butter/egg mixture, inhaling the tart sweet aroma.

"Does it matter what they think?" Charlene said. "Honestly, Nat. What's their track record been so far?"

"Less than stellar," I admitted.

"Gwen's pretty convinced, and lord knows the police have been wrong before," she said. "I'd love to know who inherits the gallery."

"That's one option we don't have to investigate." I folded the dry ingredients into the batter. I'd store the mixture in the fridge and add the blueberries in the morning, I decided. "We should probably find out about the will, though."

We were both quiet as I stretched plastic wrap over the bowl and slid it into the refrigerator. The talk of wills brought us both back to Fernand — and what had happened to him.

"How did he do it?" Charlene asked in a quiet voice.

"What do you mean?" I asked, reaching for another piece of fudge.

"How did he die?"

The image of Fernand on the floor bloomed in front of me again as I told Charlene, "He slit his wrists with an Exacto knife."

She sat up straight. "An Exacto knife? Wouldn't you think a butcher's knife would be a better choice?"

"I can't even think about this right now," I said, biting into another piece of fudge. But there wasn't enough chocolate in the world to make my problems go away. "I don't know if I'm going to have an inn, I don't know what's going to happen with Gwen, I haven't told John about the foreclosure notice . . . Even my engagement ring is itching."

"It's itching?" Charlene reached for my hand and inspected the ring. "What's this black stuff on your finger?"

"It's from the ring," I said miserably. "It was his grandmother's."

"Gold shouldn't do that," she said. "Will

you take it off so I can take a closer look?"

I twisted it off my finger and handed it to her. She inspected the inside of the band, and held the diamond up to the light. "Have you had a jeweler look at this?"

"Why?" I asked.

"There are no marks on the inside of the band, and there should be."

I took it back and looked at the gleaming metal; it was smooth. "What does that have to do with my skin itching?"

She sighed. "I hate to say it, but it may be that the ring isn't gold. That would explain the black marks on your finger; you're reacting to the metal."

"And the diamond?"

She shook her head. "I don't know, but if it isn't real gold . . ."

I reached for another piece of fudge and jammed it into my mouth, chewing mechanically. Fernand's death, the attorney, John's ring . . .

Was nothing in my life what it seemed?

I woke long before the sun rose the next morning — not that I'd slept much. My mind kept turning things over and over — even picking up one of Susan Wittig Albert's *Darling Dahlias* mysteries didn't help take my mind off my worries.

Leaving the bed to Biscuit, who burrowed under the covers I had just vacated, I headed downstairs and brewed a pot of French Roast coffee, sipping at it as I cracked eggs into a bowl and whipped them with a little bit of milk. I'd put them in the fridge and toss them in the pan when I pulled the muffins out of the oven, I decided.

The sun was just cresting the pines behind the inn when I finished, making the snow-frosted world outside the window sparkle. I had preheated the oven, but now, tempted by the pristine white outside the window, I turned it off, put plastic wrap over the bowl of batter and tucked it back into the fridge, then pulled on my boots and winter coat.

The cold, fresh air was a tonic. I breathed deep, thankful for the privilege of enjoying this winter morning — after decades in too-warm Texas, fresh snow always made me feel like a kid again. As always, the fresh snow muffled the world, giving it a soft stillness broken only by the soft crunch of my boots in the snow. This morning, I chose the forest path.

The snow had made my familiar world into a magical place. The pine trees were frosted with white, their tips adorned with small, translucent icicles that sparkled like

Christmas lights where the sun caught them. The deciduous trees formed a delicate tracery above me, like the ceiling of a Gothic cathedral. A set of snowshoe hare tracks cut across the path in front of me, and I found myself wondering where the elusive animals lived; I'd seen their tracks, but never spotted one. How did they survive the long winters on the island?

The enchanted landscape lifted my spirit as I moved deeper into the woods. One of the lovely things about living on a small island, I thought, was that you never really could get lost; you didn't have to worry about keeping your bearings, because if you kept walking, you'd end up at the shoreline or a road before too long. In the silence around me, however, it was hard to imagine that there were any houses anywhere on the island. Even the inn, which was such an enormous part of my life, seemed like a distant dream.

Lots of dreams were in jeopardy right now, I thought as I jumped over a frozen brook. The inn, of course. Gwen's art career. And even, I admitted to myself, my future with John.

I'd taken the ring off last night, and although I didn't miss the itching, its absence nagged at me. As I tramped through the snow, I found myself asking the question I'd been avoiding these last few months: Did I really want to get married?

I'd come up here to forge a life of my own; I hadn't been looking for a relationship. After the wedding, John and I would be together all the time, working on the inn together — probably even living there together, sharing the rooms above the kitchen. Already, we'd had some differences in opinion regarding improvements to the inn — even things as simple as menu choices, which had always been completely under my control. There would be much more of that in the future — and as equal partners, we both had to be willing to compromise.

Provided there was an inn, that was; there still was the issue of the attorney to deal with. And I hadn't been comfortable sharing that with John — another thing that worried me.

Was I really ready to give up that independence, and commit to sharing my entire life with another person? Already, I'd found myself holding back from John. I hadn't told him about the mortgage issues, and now there was the issue of the ring. I unconsciously rubbed the space under the glove where the ring should have been, feeling an uneasiness in my stomach.

He'd be back today. I pushed myself up the slope, comforted by the rhythm of my boots in the snow. The sky was brilliant blue between the bare branches above me, and as I crested the hill, a small bird — one of the island's few feathered winter denizens — flitted through the trees, disturbing a tuft of snow as it landed. I would address both issues with John today, I resolved, pausing at the top to catch my breath. I would show up at the attorney's office — and if I couldn't get the answers I needed, I would use my meager savings to hire another one.

As I started down the other side of the hill, another hunch settled on me like a heavy blanket of snow. Fernand's death had been a shock, but now that the truth of it was settling in, something about it was bothering me — something beyond the tragic loss of my friend. The open door, the lack of a note, the suddenness — the messiness of it, even — all of it felt wrong. Gwen had been right. There was something fishy about it.

In fact, the more I thought about it, the more out-of-character the whole thing seemed. Fernand would have recoiled at the thought of his blood staining his meticulously finished floors. He wouldn't have left the gallery strewn with dirty plates and platters of food. And most of all, he would have left some explanation for Gwen, who he knew would have been devastated.

The more I thought about it, the more I found myself reaching a new conclusion: someone had murdered Fernand LaChaise two nights ago. And until the killer was caught, every single one of us — including my beloved niece — was at risk.

As the thought crystallized, I found my steps slowing, until I was standing quietly in the snow-frosted world, the only sound my heart pumping in my chest.

Gwen was alone in the inn, I realized. I hadn't thought to lock the door when I left. She had told me she thought Fernand was murdered — which might be enough to make someone want to shut her up for good. Had she told anyone else?

It didn't matter who she'd told, I knew with a sick certainty. I'd already mentioned her suspicion to Charlene, which was as good as putting it on the front page of the *Daily Mail.*

The beauty of the still morning shattered as I turned and began running, my boots churning up the snow as I retraced my steps to the inn. The bird I had admired just a moment ago tweeted in alarm and flew up into the sky as I passed, slipping and sliding down the hill. The odds that someone would slip into the inn and kill Gwen early in the morning were small . . . but Fernand had been killed overnight, too. Had I locked the door last night? Was it possible that someone had snuck in while we slept?

Panic fueled me, and despite the cold, sweat slicked my skin under the winter coat. The walk out had seemed to take no time at all, but even running, it seemed to take forever to get back.

Finally, I caught a glimpse of the inn's gray painted siding and blue shutters through the trees ahead. My breath was coming in short spurts, my chest tight, but I spurred myself on, running as fast as I could through the snow until I tripped on a hidden root and went sprawling into the snow.

I pushed myself to my feet, using a nearby tree for support, then jerked my hand back in horror.

Dangling from a tree limb was a crudely made cloth doll with gray buttons for eyes. A loose mop of brown yarn served as hair, and the mouth was marked with a crooked red line. Dirty yellow stuffing spilled out where someone had slashed at it with a knife, and around its neck was a noose.

NINE

Brown hair, gray eyes . . . I stared at the thing for a moment, then tore my eyes away and focused on the inn.

Terrifying though they might be, voodoo dolls weren't my main concern right now. Knife-wielding murderers with unfettered access to my niece were higher on the list.

I closed the gap to the inn in seconds, throwing open the kitchen door. "Gwen!"

"What?"

She was sitting at the table, wrapped in a pink bathrobe, with a coffee cup in her hand.

I sagged against the open door in relief. Biscuit waddled forward, taking a few tentative steps toward the great outdoors, then sniffed at the cold air and changed her mind, retreating to the radiator.

I pushed the door closed and peeled off my snow-crusted gloves.

"Are you okay?" Gwen asked.

"I was worried the murderer might have come while I was out," I said, sliding the dead bolt home. "I was stupid and didn't lock the door."

Gwen blinked at me, still looking half-asleep. "But we never lock the doors."

"That needs to change," I said, thinking of the gruesome doll I'd found swinging from a branch. "And I don't want you over at the gallery by yourself."

"You believe me, then? About Fernand not killing himself?" she asked, sitting up straight in her chair.

I nodded. "I can't say for sure, but my instinct is telling me you're right. And if there's a killer on the island, we need to take precautions."

"And find out who the killer is," Gwen said.

"That would certainly be helpful," I said, taking a deep breath and turning the oven back on.

Now that I knew my niece was safe, my mind turned to the awful doll hanging in the trees outside the inn. I had seen someone out there a few days ago; had it been the person putting up the doll? If so, both the snow and my hike had likely ruined any tracks that might have remained.

"You look like you've seen a ghost," Gwen said.

"Not exactly," I said.

"What, then?"

I pulled out a muffin pan and began tucking muffin wrappers into the cups. "Someone left a nasty doll hanging from a tree outside."

"Like a Barbie doll?"

I tucked another muffin wrapper into its cup and shook my head. "More like a voodoo doll." I shivered, glancing at the window; I wanted to take it down as soon as possible, but not before John had had a chance to look at it.

"Creepy."

"It had gray button eyes. Brown hair, too."

"Do you think it's supposed to be you?"

"I hope not. It had a noose around its neck and had been slashed up by a knife."

Gwen put down her cup so fast the coffee sloshed out onto the pine table. "Why?"

"I don't know," I said as I removed the plastic wrap from the bowl of batter and grabbed a bag of blueberries from the freezer.

"Do you think it's the murderer?"

"If the murderer is hoping the police rule it a suicide," I said, "I can't see how hanging up a doll would help."

I folded in two cups of frozen berries, then scooped the first dollop of creamy, blueberry-studded batter into a muffin cup.

"Maybe it's a warning of some kind," Gwen said.

"If it is, I don't know what it would be warning me away from," I said.

"Investigating Fernand's death?"

"I doubt it. I think it may have been put up before Fernand died." Which made no sense at all.

Gwen shivered, and hugged her thin frame. "When is John coming home?"

"This afternoon," I said, using my finger to wipe a stray drop of batter from the muffin pan. "He should be back on the 1:00 mail boat."

"Good," she said. "I'll feel safer with him here."

I would, too, I thought.

"What am I going to do about painting, though? If I can't go to the studio alone, how am I going to get anything done? I still have that show coming up."

I thought about it. I could join her, but really didn't want to spend all day sitting in the studio with nothing to do. Besides, I had to get to the mainland and track down my wayward attorney.

"What about working here?" I asked as I

131

filled the last cup. "We could set up one of the guest rooms for the time being. John will be back this afternoon, so you'd have someone here with you."

"The Crow's Nest has a nice northern exposure," she said, a thoughtful look on her face.

"We'll just move the bed out of the way and put a drop cloth down," I said. "That way I can keep tabs on you." And make sure she ate regular meals, too, I thought to myself.

"I guess we could try it," she said, not looking entirely convinced.

I plowed ahead despite her hesitation. "We'll drive over and pick up your canvases as soon as the muffins are done," I said. "I have a few questions to ask you, anyway." As if on cue, the oven beeped to tell me it had come to temperature, and I slid the pans onto the middle rack.

Within minutes, the comforting smell of baking filled the kitchen. I popped a CD of Christmas carols into the player, then washed the mixing bowl in the sink. There might be a murderer on the island, a wacko was leaving threatening dolls in the trees outside the inn, my engagement ring appeared to be fake, and there was an excellent chance I'd have to drain my bank ac-

132

count fighting to keep the inn, but somehow, with my niece sitting at the table and "Hark the Herald Angels Sing" filling the kitchen, I felt a faint glow of hope.

John was the first one off the mail boat, and despite my worries, my heart skipped a beat at the sight of his tall, lanky frame and sandy blonde hair. I met him as soon as he stepped out onto the dock, and he pulled me into an enormous bear hug. I closed my eyes and inhaled his familiar, woodsy scent. Despite my worries about the inn, the ring, and our impending nuptials, I felt something inside of me open up as he held me in his arms.

"I've missed you." He kissed me on the top of the head, and his voice was almost a low growl.

"You're not allowed to leave anymore," I said. "Everything's gone south since you left."

"South. Not a bad idea. Maybe I'll do my next continuing ed in Florida, and you can come with me."

"We'd have to teach Gwen to inn-sit," I said. Provided Gwen was still here. And provided there was an inn to sit for. The reminders of my current situation made me feel hollow inside. There were too many things we had to discuss . . . but not right now.

"Let's get you back home," I said. Holding my hand, which even under the glove felt naked without its ring, John walked with me to the waiting van. As he slung his overnight bag into the back seat, I said, "Gwen's painting in the Crow's Nest — just to be safe. I didn't want her at the studio alone." In fact, I hadn't been comfortable leaving her to go to the dock, but she'd insisted on staying.

"They've ruled Fernand's death a suicide," John said.

My heart sank, but I wasn't surprised. "Who did you talk to?"

"The detective you told me about. Penney."

"So she's not investigating."

He shook his head. "No need, as far as she's concerned."

"Did they find a note anywhere?" I hadn't seen one, but it was possible he'd put it somewhere else.

"No," he said. "They're running a toxicology report, but he'd evidently been drinking."

"There was a glass of scotch on his dresser," I said.

"Which supports the suicide theory," he

said. "Alcohol is a depressant, and the holidays can be a hard time for people. Evidently Fernand was estranged from his family; when they got in touch with his mother, she said she hadn't spoken with him in ten years."

"I wonder why?"

"Could be his lifestyle," John said.

I presumed John meant the fact that Fernand was gay. Which evidently everyone but me had been aware of. "It's hard to believe parents would disown a child because of his sexual orientation," I said. "I assume that's what you mean."

"It happens a lot," he said. "But I'm speculating; I don't know what caused the rift."

"Even so, it had been ten years — not exactly a fresh wound. And he'd just had a huge party," I said. "He hardly seemed isolated to me."

John shrugged. "Jealousy over a younger artist's success?"

I glanced over at him. "Whose side are you on?"

"Just being devil's advocate, Miss Natalie. If you and Gwen are convinced, we'll look into it. I'm just telling you what Detective Penney will say if you ask her to reopen the case."

135

I gripped the steering wheel hard. "Can you convince her to change her mind?"

"Only if we can come up with some evidence," he said. "Why is Gwen so sure it was murder?"

"She thought he was too excited about things going on in his life to commit suicide. He seemed in good spirits to me, too; even said something about watching his weight. You wouldn't think a person who was about to commit suicide would be worried about that kind of thing."

"Maybe he got bad news after the party."

"That's what I told Gwen, but my instinct tells me she's right. I don't see him as the suicide type."

He sighed. "Well, we'll see what we can find out." He reached over and squeezed my shoulder. "And see if we can keep both of you safe in the meantime."

Something inside me relaxed. I hadn't realized until now how much John's calm, solid presence comforted me. "Speaking of safe . . ." As we turned onto the narrow, curvy road that led to the inn, I told him about the awful doll I'd found.

His voice was calm, but his words were clipped. "Did you touch it?"

"No."

"Good," he said. "I'll bag it when we get home."

"It had been there a few days — there was snow on it. And I saw someone out there a few days ago, right where I found the doll."

"It sounds like a threat," he said. "Have you done anything to make anyone angry at you?"

"Not any more than normal," I said.

He sighed. "You are a trouble magnet, aren't you?"

"Seems that way," I said. "Although at least I'm still here."

"Which is a happy stroke of luck," John said, reaching over and squeezing my hand. "Any other unpleasant news?" he asked.

"Actually, now that you mention it, there is," I said, trying to decide which thing to bring up first — the foreclosure notice, or the ring.

"Uh oh. Let's have it."

I took a deep breath and decided I should get the mortgage fiasco off my chest. The sooner I told him, the better I'd feel. "Remember how I refinanced the inn a few months ago?" I said, cringing as I spoke.

"What about it? Did you miss a payment?"

"No. The new company wired the payoff funds to the attorney, but it looks like he never paid off the original note."

"So . . . you still have two mortgages?"

"It's worse than that," I said, taking a deep breath. We crested the hill above the inn. The gray cape was nestled below us, a comforting puff of smoke drifting from the chimney, a red-bowed wreath on the front door, the windows glowing warm and yellow in the gray afternoon. "The original mortgage company sent me a foreclosure notice. And the attorney is out of town and can't be reached." I stared at the inn, realizing with a powerful wave of emotion exactly how much I treasured the gray-shingled inn — and the life it had allowed me to build. It didn't seem possible that soon it might all belong to somebody else.

"He took off with the money?" John's voice was low and steady, but I could sense he was upset.

"It looks like it," I conceded, feeling that too-familiar hollow sensation in the pit of my stomach. I told John everything I'd learned. "The foreclosure notice made the local paper, thanks to our friend Gertrude at the *Daily Mail*," I concluded.

"Natalie." John was very still beside me; I could not bear to look at him. "How long have you known about this?"

"Two days," I said.

"Two days???" He ran a hand through his hair and let out a long breath. "Why didn't you tell me?"

I felt sheepish. "You were involved in your class, and I didn't want to worry you."

"Didn't want to worry me?" I turned to look at him, finally. The hurt and anger in his green eyes felt like a physical blow. "Natalie, we're going to be married in a few months. We're supposed to be a team."

"I know," I said. I looked away from him and pulled into my parking space outside the inn. "I'm sorry. I just . . . I was embarrassed. Ashamed that I'd made such a bad decision."

He put his hand on my shoulder. I jabbed my foot at the parking brake, feeling tears well in my eyes.

"You hired an attorney to run the closing. This is not your fault. You are a victim of a crime." He sighed. "Why didn't you tell me? I'm supposed to be your partner. Your best friend."

"It doesn't change the fact that I did something that might cause me to lose everything," I said, shame and guilt welling in me. "Because of this stupid refinance, you could lose your home, too. The carriage house, the workshop . . ."

John squeezed my shoulder, then touched

my cheek. I turned my head to look at him, feeling a stab of remorse at the mix of compassion and hurt in his eyes.

"Whatever happens, we're in it together," he said quietly.

As much as I'd thought about wanting to keep my independence, hearing John say he was in it with me, no matter what, felt like climbing under a down comforter on a sub-freezing night.

"Have you had any luck reaching the attorney?" he asked.

"He's skiing in Colorado, and isn't taking calls. Charlene and I are going over this afternoon to strongarm his receptionist into getting him on the line."

"I doubt you'll have luck with it — I'd be surprised if he wasn't in Rio by now — but it's certainly worth a try. We need other legal representation, though," John said. "And you need to report this to the police. The sooner, the better."

"Didn't I just do that, Mr. Deputy?" I asked, surprising myself by grinning.

He laughed, lightening the heavy feeling that had fallen over us. "Let's get inside where it's warm, and we'll figure out the rest." As we got out of the van and hurried toward the kitchen door, he asked, "Any other unpleasant surprises?"

"I'll save them until after you've had a cup of hot chocolate to warm up," I said. I knew from experience that winter trips on the mail boat could be bone-chilling.

He turned, overnight bag slung over one shoulder, and cocked an eyebrow at me. "You're kidding, right?"

"Of course," I said, twisting the ring on my finger. Despite what John had said about telling him everything, I didn't have the heart to bring it up.

As I poured cocoa and sugar into a pan filled with creamy whole milk, John sat down at the kitchen table and reached over to pet Biscuit.

"So," he said, as the plump tabby arched her back under his hand, "where's this doll?"

"Near the base of the forest trail," I said.

"Are you sure it's recent? It could have been put there some time ago."

"It didn't look weatherworn," I said. "And I saw someone out there a couple of days ago."

"Who?"

"I don't know — I just saw a person through the kitchen window. They came on foot, though, and not down the road."

John stood up and grabbed a plastic bag from under the sink, then walked over to the coat hooks.

"What are you doing?" I asked.

"Checking it out," he said.

"What about your hot chocolate?"

"I'll be right back," he said. "Where is it again?"

"It's about twenty yards that way, on the forest trail," I told him as he opened the door. I watched as he tramped through the snow, following my tracks. The look on his face when he returned a few minutes later was grim. "You didn't tell me it looked like you," he said as he peeled off his snow-crusted boots. The doll was in a bag in his hand; I shivered, remembering it.

"I wanted a second opinion," I said. "The yarn hair and button eyes were a bit vague."

He raised a dubious eyebrow at me. "Gray eyes and brown, bobbed hair? Who else fits that description?"

I shrugged. "I guess you're right."

"It's recent," he said. "Whoever it was used the path you used, probably. How far did you go on the trail?"

"Across the creek, and then to the top of the hill."

"We'll retrace your steps and see if we see any footprints leading off the trail."

"I doubt you'll see much. We've had snow since it happened."

"I know," he said. "But it's worth looking at."

"Hot chocolate first," I said. "You must still be freezing from the mail boat. And those tracks — or what's left of them — aren't going anywhere."

He glanced out the window. "Any snow forecast?"

"None," I said.

"I guess it can wait," he said. "For a quiet island, there's a whole lot going on."

"Hope you don't want to go back to the peace of the big city," I said.

"With you here?" He reached for my hand. "Never."

By the time we finished our second mugs of hot chocolate, we'd put together a game plan for the foreclosure problem, and decided we would definitely house Catherine in the carriage house when she arrived, but were coming up empty on potential suspects in the case of Fernand. Neither of us had any idea who might have wanted to kill him, and the more I thought about it, the less likely it seemed to be. "Let's go see Gwen," John said, pushing his mug away. "I want to see what she's doing for the show." He stood up and stretched, then walked to the dining room door. I found myself admiring the way his shoulders moved under the green flannel shirt as I followed him. He stopped at the door, turned, and enveloped me in another hug.

"I've missed you so much," he said. "I love having you to come home to every day."

"Even if we lose our home?" I asked.

"Shh," he said, putting a finger to my lips. "We're working on that. And home is anywhere you are, anyway."

He kissed me then, and if I hadn't had to meet Charlene, I might have stayed in that doorway all afternoon. "We should probably go check on Gwen," John said when we both came up for air.

"Yeah," I said, halfheartedly.

Reluctantly, we parted, but held hands as we climbed the stairs to the second floor of the inn.

"Have you seen her new work?" he asked.

I nodded.

"What do you think?"

"Just between you and me," I said in a low voice, "they're not terrific. The oils aren't nearly as good as her watercolors, which makes sense, because it's a new medium. The problem is, she's decided she never should have been an artist in the first place."

"What's she going to do if she's not doing

art? Join Adam on the lobster boat and haul traps?"

I couldn't imagine my slight, fashionable niece in bright orange waders and covered in salted herring, but he was right; there weren't a plethora of options on the island. "I don't know," I said. "With Fernand gone, I'm afraid she may leave the island."

"Just because Fernand's gone doesn't mean she can't still paint," he said. "Zelda Chu might be willing to take her on."

"She views Zelda as public enemy number one, I'm afraid." I sighed. "What will I do if she leaves?" Not only had I come to depend on her help, but I had come to depend on her being part of my life. Although she was my niece, I had come to love her like a daughter.

"We'll deal with that if it comes, Natalie. We have enough on our plates already; no need to add more." He squeezed my hand as we arrived at the door to the Crow's Nest. I could already smell the oils.

I knocked, but no one answered. "Gwen?"

Silence.

Glancing at John, I opened the door.

Gwen was gone.

TEN

"She was here when I came to get you," I said, staring at the empty room. A canvas with a few smears of deep blue pigment was the only sign of my niece.

"Maybe Adam came to pick her up," John said.

I hurried downstairs to the phone and dialed Adam's number. His voice mail picked up on the second ring. I left a message and hung up, then looked at John. "What do I do now?"

"I'm sure she's fine," he said. "Maybe she left something at the studio, and went back to get it."

"I told her not to go there alone," I said as I picked up the phone and dialed the studio a second time. I let the phone ring ten times before hanging up, feeling my stomach clutch. "Let's drive over there," I said.

"You're supposed to meet Charlene in

thirty minutes," he reminded me.

"If we don't make it, we'll take the next boat over," I said. "The attorney can wait."

"I can drop you off at the pier and call you when I know . . ."

"No," I said. Cell phones were sketchy at best on the island, and I didn't want to wait all afternoon for news. "Let's go."

It was a short drive to the studio, but it seemed to take forever. The clouds had broken, and the sun glistened on the fresh-fallen snow, giving the island a fairyland appearance, but the beauty was lost on me; I was too worried about Gwen.

"Relax," John said, sensing my tension. "I'm sure she's okay. Maybe she walked down to the store. Or maybe she had the music on too loud, and didn't hear the phone."

Despite his assurances, I had barely pulled up outside of the studio before John was out of the car and trying the doorknob. When it didn't turn, he began hammering at the door. I felt my heart contract. Finally, the door opened, and my niece appeared, her jaw set and a streak of blue paint on her cheek.

"Gwen!" I said as I slammed the van door behind me. "What are you doing here alone? I called twice, and you didn't pick up."

"Sorry, Aunt Nat — I must have forgotten to turn the ringer on. But I'm glad John's here."

"Why?"

"I know Fernand didn't kill himself," she announced, her eyes gleaming. "I found proof."

John glanced at me, and I gave him a barely perceptible shrug. "Let's go inside where it's warm, and then you can tell us," he said to Gwen. In our haste to get to the studio, neither of us had remembered our coats.

"What did you find?" I asked when we'd shut the cold air out behind us. I wrinkled my nose. The gallery smelled of spoiled food; I made a mental note to come with a few islanders and clean it up sometime in the next few days.

"Remember how you said he'd used an Exacto knife?"

"Yes," I said, shivering as I remembered the bloody blade.

"Well, it wasn't one of his," she said. "Come look."

I followed her through the gallery to the studio. She led me to Fernand's easel, which was at the far end of the room. A large unfinished watercolor was taped to a board leaning against it; a row of canoes, reds,

148

oranges, and vivid yellows, lined up next to a brilliant blue lake. The colors seemed to glow on the paper, the translucence giving the whole work an airy, light quality. He had even captured the reflections of the trees in the water. I leaned closer, marveling at his ability to take such an uncontrollable medium and make it obey his wishes. He'd taught much of that precise technique to Gwen . . . but would no longer.

"I have to agree with you," John said as we admired the painting. "That doesn't look like the work of a depressed man."

"That's not what I wanted to show you, though." I turned and looked; she was holding an open blue case. There were three slots for knives and a half dozen for blades; each of them was filled. "His knives are all here," she said.

"He was very organized," I said, not getting what she was showing me.

"Exactly. My knives are all accounted for, and we're the only two painting in here."

"You're saying the knife Natalie saw him with didn't belong to him," John said.

Gwen nodded. "Exactly. Which means the murderer must have brought it with him. Or her."

I mentally ran through my list of suspects. It was rather short, and at the moment, there were no women on it. Or anyone at all, really.

"Are you sure he didn't have any in the house?" I asked. "Most artists have multiples of things like knives and brushes." I knew I had more spatulas than I could shake a stick at — and not all of them lived in the same drawer.

"He just did a purge and gave all his excess equipment to an art school in Bangor," she said firmly. "There weren't any other knives here."

"Even in the house?" John suggested.

"He kept everything here. His home was his home, his studio was his studio."

"It's certainly something to think about," John said. "I'll mention it to Penney when I talk to her." His green eyes swept the windows along the back wall of the studio. "Did you or Fernand ever go down to the shore?"

"Not since the weather turned cold," Gwen said.

"It looks like there are footprints out there," he said, pointing to a series of indentations in the windswept snow. Goosebumps rose on my arms as I walked closer to the glass. "They seem to go to Fernand's house," I said. "And they haven't been snowed over."

"Did you notice any footprints on the day you discovered Fernand?" John asked.

"No," I said, "but I didn't think to look."

"Let's go check it out now," he said.

Gwen and I followed John out the gallery's front door, shivering in the wind. There was a path shoveled from the gallery to the road, and from the gallery to the house. If anyone had come this way, there weren't any footprints to show for it.

"What about the back door?" Gwen asked.

"It's off the kitchen, isn't it?" I asked.

Gwen nodded. We all looked at the foot of snow between us and the back yard. Since none of us was wearing boots, and two of us didn't even have coats, traipsing through it to the back of the house was not an enticing prospect.

"I'll go," John said. "If there is evidence, the less it's disturbed, the better. You two head into the gallery."

I would have argued, but with the north wind slicing through my thin flannel shirt, I agreed.

I had started picking up paper plates and throwing them into a half-filled trash bag when John returned.

"What did you find?" I asked.

"There are tracks," he said. "They lead to the kitchen door." He looked at Gwen, who was helping me with the cleanup. "Did Fernand ever use the back door that you know of?"

"No, but most of the time we're in the studio when I'm here."

"How many sets of tracks are there?" I asked.

"I think I can identify one coming in, and one going out. Same person, by the size of the prints."

"Or one going out and one coming in," I said. "The problem is, whose are they?"

"Fernand has a spare pair of rain boots in the storage closet," Gwen said. "At least we can compare footprint size."

"Good thinking," John said.

"I'll go get them," she said, and scurried to the closet, returning a moment later with a pair of black rubber boots.

As John exited the gallery a second time, I began scraping the old food from the serving dishes into a plastic bag, wishing it were warm enough to open a window — or that there was an exhaust fan. When the door opened again, the blast of cold air was welcome; it was icy, but at least it was fresh.

"Well?" I asked, not sure what response I was hoping for.

"Whoever it was," he said, "it wasn't Fernand. The prints are several sizes larger."

"The police have to believe us now," Gwen said, hope in her eyes. "The boot size, the knives . . . they'll reopen the case for sure."

"The thing is, if the murderer came through the back door, why was the front door open?"

"That's presuming there was a murderer," John reminded me.

"Surely they'll at least reopen it!" Gwen said. "They've got to!"

"I can't promise that they will," John cautioned her, "but at least we've got some evidence now that supports your theory. I'll call Penney as soon as we get back to the inn." My fiancé glanced at his watch, and then at me. "We're late," he said. "You may miss the boat."

"The mail boat?" Gwen asked. "Isn't the grocery order coming here?"

"I've got some business on the mainland," I said. No need to worry Gwen.

She eyed my flannel shirt. "You're going to freeze without a coat."

I realized she was right. Standing outside for a few minutes was one thing; standing outside on a boat for thirty minutes without a coat was a ticket to hypothermia. "Shoot. I left it at the inn," I said, "and it's too late to go back."

"Borrow Fernand's," Gwen suggested.

I looked over at the coat rack by the back door; sure enough, Fernand's black parka hung on the last hook, closest to the door. I didn't like the idea of wearing a dead man's coat . . . but I liked the idea of crossing the water without any coat at all even less.

"Are you sure it's okay to wear it?" I asked John. "I'm not messing with evidence, or anything?"

"It's not a murder investigation, remember?"

"Not yet," I corrected him.

"It's fine," he said.

I took the coat gingerly, as if it might bite me, and slid my arms into it. The coat still held the faint scent of Fernand's cologne, and I felt a pang of loss. How could Fernand be gone, and his coat still be here, waiting for him? Death was so unfair.

Bar Harbor was a shadow of its summer self — in August, cars lined the streets of the quaint downtown, but today, all but two spaces were empty, the verdant trees bare of leaves. A strong wind rolled up off the water, slicing through Fernand's thick parka as we hurried up Cottage Street. Warm light glowed in Sherman's, the local book and general store; I planned to go stock up on books before returning to the island.

John had offered to go with me, but I told him it was more important to stay with Gwen. Besides, I had my best friend along for moral support.

On the trip over, as we huddled in the wheelhouse to avoid the wind that swept over the water like a polar blast, I'd told Charlene about the footprints and the open front door, and asked if anyone had seen a boat coming to or from the island the night of the party.

"I don't know, but I'll ask around. It's weird — why wouldn't they come to the gallery? That's where the party was."

"That's part of the reason it's so suspicious. I'm thinking maybe whoever it was came later — after the party."

"Or before," she said. "Also, if the killer — assuming there is one, that is — came through the back door, why was the front door open?"

I shrugged. "Another mystery."

"Too many mysteries, if you ask me," she said. "As much as I hate to think of Fernand ending his life, it's better than the alternative." She shivered under her hot pink parka. "I don't like thinking there's another murderer loose on the island."

"But if the murderer had to take a boat to

155

get to Fernand's, chances are whoever it is doesn't live on the island."

Charlene sighed. "Well, maybe there isn't a murderer, but there's somebody nasty on Cranberry Island."

"What do you mean?"

"Somebody cut up Muffin and Pudge," she said.

"Oh, no!" I hated to hear of anything bad happening to Claudette's goats, who spent most of the summer moving around the island chained to a tire that was supposed to keep them out of people's flowerbeds. Problem is, the tire didn't work. "I know they're a nuisance, but they're such sweethearts, and Claudette's got a lot on her mind right now. She must be crushed to lose them."

"They didn't die," she said. "At least not yet; it's still touch and go."

I shivered. "Who would do such a thing?"

She snorted. "Ingrid just put in an order for six more rosebushes. Maybe she decided to do a preemptive strike." Selectwoman Ingrid Sorenson was an avid gardener who lived just down the street from Claudette, and she'd fumed for years over the goats' annual rampage of her carefully tended rosebushes.

"I don't see her as the slice and dice type," I said.

"You never know," Charlene said darkly.

"Well, I hope they find out who did it — and that the goats pull through. Claudette's got enough on her plate."

"I know," Charlene said. "Caring for those kids, and then dealing with the daughter-in-law . . ."

"She's an odd duck, isn't she?"

"You're telling me. She was as normal as could be at the party at Fernand's, but when she came into the store yesterday, she looked like she'd escaped from a mental asylum. Kept asking about someone named Patricia."

"She called me that when I first met her. Do you know what's wrong with her?"

"Not a clue," she said. "I don't think Claudette does, either; I called to let her know Dawn looked like she needed some help, and Claudette hurried in to take her home as fast as she could. I've never seen her looking so tired. She's aged ten years since her family moved up to the island."

"I wish she'd let us help," I said as the wind whistled by us. Garland hung from some of the shops, and it swayed in the wind.

"All we can do is keep offering," Charlene

said, as we hurried past the shuttered shops and empty streets.

The attorney's office was only a few blocks from the main street, on the bottom floor of an old wooden house with large porches. Charlene and I hurried through the door, relieved to be out of the cold, and were surprised to see a red-faced man haranguing the receptionist, who was cowering behind her big wooden desk.

"When will he be back?"

"Not until next week," she said.

"That's not good enough." His face flushed deep red. I found myself thinking it was a good thing we were on the mainland; we weren't too far from the hospital in case he keeled over with a heart attack. "I just got a foreclosure notice from the original mortgage company today."

The receptionist's voice trembled. "I'm sorry, sir, but I don't know anything about it."

"You did, too?" I asked, stepping forward.

"Who are you?" the man barked at me. His red necktie was knotted so tight a good half inch of flesh protruded over his college, and his head looked swollen.

"I'm another of Lloyd Forester's clients," I said. "I got a foreclosure notice in the mail yesterday."

He swung back to the receptionist without acknowledging what I'd told him. "When will he be back?"

"He's supposed to be in on Monday."

"That's a week from now!" he bellowed. "I need this resolved immediately!"

"I'll e-mail him and let him know . . ." the young woman said, her voice high and reedy.

"No," the man said. "You'll call him right now, and if he doesn't answer, I'm hiring another attorney and suing his ass!"

"Did you refinance a property with Forester?" I asked.

He turned to glare at me. "And who are you again?"

"I'm Natalie Barnes. I own the Gray Whale Inn on Cranberry Island, and I think we may be in similar circumstances."

"My circumstances are none of your business." He turned and shook a fat finger at the young woman behind the desk. "Tell that yellow-bellied snake he hasn't heard the last of me!"

Eleven

He stormed out of the office, slamming the wooden door behind him, taking any hope I might have had that it was a technical error with him. I looked at the young woman, who appeared to be attempting to merge with the potted ficus in the corner.

"Has this happened a lot lately?" I asked.

"He's the tenth one this week," she said, looking pale. "I can't reach Mr. Forester. I don't know what to do. And he was supposed to leave me a paycheck, but he didn't." There were tears in her eyes. Despite my anger at the attorney, I felt sorry for her; she didn't know what her boss was doing. And what he was doing, I guessed, involved sitting on a beach in the Caribbean, sipping a drink he'd bought with my payoff money.

Charlene must have had the same thought; she looked at me and said, "Uh oh."

I felt my stomach contract. "When did he

leave town?"

"Two weeks ago," the receptionist said. "He said he'd be checking in, but I haven't heard from him."

"What do we do now?" I asked Charlene, feeling a pit open in my stomach.

"Engage other representation?" she suggested.

"Wonderful." I turned to the receptionist and asked her to contact us if she heard anything, told her I hoped she got a paycheck soon, and then I headed out into the cold with my best friend trailing me.

"Not good," I said to Charlene as the door closed behind us and we turned into the wind.

"No, it's not. Maybe we'll get better news at the jeweler."

"Here's hoping," I said, as we hurried down the street.

We'd gotten half a block when Charlene looked back, then tugged on my jacket. "Is that who I think it is?" she asked, pointing across the street.

As we watched, the man, who was wearing an expensively cut wool coat, crossed the street and hurried toward the attorney's office. It was Murray Selfridge.

"Interesting," I said. "Do you think he got a foreclosure notice, too?"

161

"I haven't seen anything come through the post office," she said, "but it may have come when Tania was working." I knew she'd be keeping a lookout from now on, though.

It was two blocks to Island Jewelers; as much as I wanted to stay and see how long Selfridge stayed at the attorney's office, it was too cold to linger, so we pressed on. After the frigid wind, the warm interior was a welcome change. The smell of dust and glass polish filled the air of the old store, whose proprietor, who always looked like Santa Claus to me, stood polishing a display case filled with Maine tourmaline.

"What can I do for you ladies today?" he asked.

"I was hoping you could take a look at a ring I received not long ago," I said.

"What seems to be the problem?" He set aside his polishing cloth and adjusted his glasses.

"It's supposed to be an antique," I said, "but I seem to be having a reaction to it."

"Let's take a look," he suggested, reaching for his jeweler's loupe.

I yanked off my glove and tugged at the ring. Despite the cold, the skin around the gold band was inflamed, making it hard to pull off.

Charlene grimaced at the greenish black ring and the red, chafed skin on my finger. "That looks nasty."

The stout jeweler picked up the ring and inspected it. His eyes, I couldn't help noticing, were suddenly less twinkly. "No markings on the inside of the band," he said.

"I thought that was strange," Charlene said. "Isn't there usually at least a carat mark?"

"Usually," he said, "but not always." I clung to that faint ray of hope as he held the ring to the light and inspected it with the jeweler's loupe. I held my breath, praying that it was just some strange chemical reaction.

The jeweler looked up at me over the rims of his glasses. "I'm sorry to say, but this is not a diamond."

I let out my breath slowly, feeling deflated.

"And the band — is it gold?" Charlene asked.

He shook his head sadly. "I'm afraid not. That's why your skin is reacting."

I felt as if he had punched me in the stomach. "Crap."

"I wish I had better news," he said as he put the ring on the counter. I grabbed it, shoving it deep into the pocket of the parka.

"Thank you for your help," Charlene said.

"If you're in the market for a real antique," he said, "I have a few you might be interested in."

"I'll think about it," I said, retreating to the doorway, anxious to be out of the small store. Cold as it was, I was glad when we were back on the street.

Charlene squeezed my arm through my coat. "You need a drink."

"I need a pastry," I corrected.

"Let's go to the Corner Bakery," she said, and I let her guide me to the cozy bakery on a side street. The smell of fresh-baked muffins permeated the small shop, and Charlene quickly rustled up two hot chocolates and two chocolate croissants, then installed me at a corner table near the frosted window.

"Don't blame John," she said as she set down the golden pastry in front of me. I took a bite mechanically, barely tasting the rich dark chocolate encased in buttery layers of pastry. I was glad Bess, the owner, wasn't at the shop today; normally I loved catching up with a fellow foodie, but today, I wasn't up for much more than licking my wounds.

"What am I going to tell him?" I asked. "If I wasn't allergic to it, I'd just wear it, and say nothing. But that's obviously not an option." I glanced down at my swollen, discolored finger and sighed. I reached into the pocket of Fernand's coat for the ring, and pulled out a folded piece of paper.

"What's that?" Charlene asked.

I unfolded it. It was blank, except for a couple of lines of Fernand's neat handwriting. Again, I felt the sharp stab of loss.

"There's a web site address," Charlene said. "And a street address." She pursed her lips. "The address looks familiar, but I can't think from where."

"The street address? Or the web site?"

"The street address," she said. "I wish I could remember . . . I see so much mail, though, it's hard to keep track." She sighed. "Still, it might be worth looking into the web site when we get home," she said. "Could be nothing, but it might have something to do with what happened. What does John think about Gwen's murder theory?"

"He's willing to consider it, at least. Particularly after what Gwen found this morning." I told her about Gwen's Exacto knife discovery.

"Weird," she said, shivering. "But I keep trying to think — who would have wanted to kill him?"

"The only possibility I can come up with is Zelda Chu," I said. "She was pushing him

165

to do something about a proposal, and he kind of blew her off the night of the party."

"The way I hear it, she wasn't too worried about competition from Fernand. If anything, it was the other way around."

"I know," I said, gloomily, taking a sip of the warm, buttery hot chocolate. "But I think she wanted the property he had. I don't know if she wanted it enough to commit murder, though." I took another sip, but even the sweet, thick chocolate wasn't enough to dispel my dark mood. "Gwen is convinced someone killed him, but I'm having a hard time coming up with anyone who might have a motive."

"Maggie isn't big on gay folks," Charlene pointed out.

"Yeah, but why would she murder Fernand? It's an awfully weak motive. If anything, you'd think she'd want to get rid of the person who's teaching her children."

"She is; she's circulating that petition, remember? And I heard she's considering homeschooling now," Charlene said.

I shook my head, exasperated. I'd never understood why people got so riled up about homosexuality.

"Back to Fernand, though. Has anyone gone through his files, or his computer?" Charlene asked.

"Not that I know of," I said, folding the paper neatly and tucking it back into the parka pocket. "I think they only do that if it's considered a crime scene."

"Might be worth checking out," she said. "Maybe a spurned lover?"

"Gwen tells me he was dating a man in Bangor, and it was going well."

"Maybe they broke up."

"Who knows?" I said.

"If you fire up his computer, you might have a better idea."

"Maybe Gwen and I will go over there tomorrow," I said. "But in the meantime, I still have the mortgage and the ring to deal with."

"Ah, yes. The brass ring. Didn't John's mother give it to him over Thanksgiving?" she asked. "Maybe she had it cleaned, and the jeweler substituted a fake one."

"You can ask her when she gets here," I said dully, taking another bite.

"What?"

"She's coming for Christmas."

Charlene groaned. "Well," she said, "at least you'll get to ask her in person, instead of over the phone."

"Something else to look forward to," I said.

"On the plus side, you don't live a dull

life!" Charlene licked her spoon and gave me a half-hearted smile.

I never thought I'd say it, but at that moment, the thought of a dull life was pretty appealing.

It was almost dark by the time Charlene dropped me off at the inn. We'd caught the last mail boat back to the island after splurging on books at Sherman's; I had Lea Wait's latest mystery, and Charlene had snapped up a few more of the romances she'd become addicted to. Again, my stomach clenched as I looked at the shingled Cape with the glowing windows.

How was I going to figure out the mess with the mortgage company if the attorney had skipped town?

"Good luck telling John about the ring," Charlene said, reminding me that the missing attorney wasn't the only problem.

"Should I tell him tonight?"

"It's going to bug you until you do," she said. "Clear the air, I say."

"We'll see how it goes," I said, dreading the idea of telling John the antique ring he had given me was a fake.

"Call me if you need to," she said. "I'll be up late reading." She patted the bag of books.

I turned and waved as I opened the door to the kitchen, then recoiled as a wave of foul air blasted through the door.

"Hello?" I called, breathing through my mouth as I closed the door behind me and shrugged out of Fernand's coat.

A rattling sound caught my attention; a pot was steaming on the kitchen stove. I rushed over and lifted the lid, then recoiled. Someone had started steaming cabbage, but the pot had run out of water, leaving a foul-smelling burnt residue on the bottom.

I grabbed the pot and headed for the door, throwing it open and depositing the smelly load on the bottom step. The heat of the pot made the snow sizzle and hiss on contact. I closed the door behind me and took a deep whiff of the kitchen. The smell was still unbearable; even Biscuit had fled, abandoning her post on the radiator. Since the main windows were covered with storm windows, I opened the door to the back patio, then pushed through the swinging door into the dining room. A cold wind gusted into the kitchen, and I shivered.

"John? Gwen?" I called, pushing through the swinging door into the dining room.

"Natalie! Is that you?"

My future mother-in-law appeared like a specter in the doorway to the parlor.

TWELVE

Her skeletal frame was dressed impeccably in a Talbot's twin set and knife-creased slacks, her platinum blonde hair shellacked into a chin-length helmet. "I . . . I didn't expect you so soon!" I said, lamely. Burnt cabbage in the kitchen . . . I should have known.

I was acutely aware of my flannel shirt and jeans as she stepped forward to give me a perfume-scented air hug. "I called from the mainland, but you weren't here, so some nice gentleman in a very smelly pickup truck gave us all a ride to the inn." She sighed. "I may have to give those clothes to charity. Anyway, I was just talking with one of your guests in the parlor," she said. "Since no one was here when I got here, I started dinner. I should probably go check on that cabbage . . ."

"I took care of it already," I said quickly. "But we don't have any guests. The inn is empty until after Christmas."

She blinked in surprise. "But you've got two. Frederick came over on the same mail boat as I did," Catherine said. "There's a young lady here, too; she checked in right after Frederick."

"What?" How was I going to feed two guests? And why hadn't they made reservations?

"The young lady went to her room, but Frederick and I have been enjoying the fireplace. Here, let me introduce you," she said.

I followed her into the parlor, where an equally neatly dressed young man with short-cropped brown hair stood, hand extended. Despite his polite smile, his face looked drawn, and there were circles under his eyes. "I'm sorry I didn't call ahead and make a reservation. A young woman named Gwen checked me into a room when I arrived, and Catherine has kept me company ever since."

"No problem," I said, trying to think fast. What was I going to feed this young man? I could manage breakfast, but I hadn't shopped for guests. I suddenly remembered the extra pan of lasagna I'd tossed in the freezer a month ago, with just such a situation in mind. I also had a few loaves of frozen French bread and plenty of salad makings, which would make a perfect hearty dinner for a cold night. I glanced at my watch. "It's 5:30 now — I can have dinner ready by 6:30, if that would work for you."

"Oh, no need, darling," Catherine said. "I put some cabbage on to steam."

"Um, there was a little problem with the steamer," I said.

She sniffed. "Is that what that smell is?"

I nodded. "I've got a lasagna in the freezer I can heat up, though."

She sighed. "Well, it's not on my diet, but I suppose a little lasagna won't hurt. It's turkey and low-fat cheese, right?"

"Pork sausage and full-fat Provolone, mozzarella, and Parmesan, I'm afraid."

She gave me a rueful smile. "Ah, well. You really should think about installing an elliptical, or maybe a treadmill — with all those high-calorie goodies you're always making, your guests need it! I'll just have to do a bit longer walk tomorrow. Can't let myself go to seed!" She patted the concave space under her ribcage where most people's stomachs resided. It was only a couple of weeks, I told myself. I could survive that, couldn't I?

"Lasagna sounds just fine," Frederick said.

"Terrific," I replied, hoping my other

mystery guest felt the same way. "What brings you to Cranberry Island in December?" I asked.

He swallowed. "I'm here because of Fernand," he said.

Of course, I realized. The wan face, the shadowed eyes . . . "I'm so very sorry," I said. "We're reeling from the shock as well; he was a good friend. Are you related to him?"

"I'm . . . or, rather, I was . . . his boyfriend," Frederick said.

My mother-in-law said nothing, but I stole a glance at her; her smile seemed to have turned a bit brittle. The only thing I could think to say to Frederick was, "Oh, you poor thing."

"I've come to make arrangements," he said, looking shell-shocked.

Of course he looked shell-shocked. Putting a loved one's affairs in order when you've just lost him or her unexpectedly was a terrible, terrible chore. "I'm happy to help however I can," I said. "There's a small church on the island, and I'm sure Father Timothy would be happy to take care of the service. We can have the reception here, if you'd like."

"Thank you," he said. "It's all just so sudden, and so . . . so horrible." His eyes began to well with tears. "I don't know where to start."

"We'll get it figured out," I said, resisting the urge to hug him. "I know my niece will want to talk with you," I said. "Gwen — the young woman who checked you in — she was very close to Fernand."

"Oh, yes," the young man said, recognition sparking in his eyes. "Gwen. He mentioned her many times. He was very proud of her; he said she had a lot of promise."

"Please mention that when you talk to her," I said. "She's taken Fernand's loss hard."

"I would love to meet her," he said. "Maybe she can give me some insight as to why . . ." he trailed off. "We were planning to visit Florence in the spring. Why would he do something like this? He never even told me he was depressed, and now . . ."

He shook with sobs, and even though we'd only just met, I reached out and hugged him, patting his back until the sobs subsided. "I'm sorry," he said, finally, pulling away and swiping at his eyes.

"It's okay," I said. "Gwen doesn't understand either. In fact, she has a theory that someone else . . . well, that things aren't what they seem."

Frederick's eyes widened. "Do you

mean . . ." He paused. "But it doesn't make sense. Who would want to . . . to kill Fernand?"

"I don't know," I said. "I was hoping maybe you could give us some ideas."

He shook his head, still looking stunned by the idea. If Frederick had wanted Fernand out of the way, I thought to myself, he was a very good actor. Had Fernand put Frederick in his will? I wondered. Or was the relationship still too new? Despite Frederick's apparent distress, I thought it might not be a bad idea to find that out. Even if he hadn't been seen on the mail boat, there was always the possibility that he had taken a small boat over. I glanced at the clock on the mantel. "Unfortunately, I have to get dinner underway, but maybe this evening we can talk some more. Gwen should be here, too."

I excused myself to the kitchen, leaving Frederick and Catherine in the parlor. I hoped the news that Frederick was gay wouldn't keep her from being friendly; I sensed he needed the human contact right now. I checked the ledger at the front desk and determined that Gwen had put our other mystery guest into the Lupine room. The name gave me a start: Irene LaChaise.

The door was on the first floor, at the end

175

of the hallway. I hurried down the hall and knocked quietly. The door opened to reveal an attractive woman in her late thirties with cropped red hair and blue eyes that reminded me painfully of Fernand's.

"I'm sorry to disturb you, but I wanted to let you know about dinner."

She blinked at me. "What about it?" Her accent was the same clipped Canadian as Fernand's, but without the warmth.

"I'll be serving at 6:30 in the dining room," I said.

"Oh. Thanks." She began closing the door.

"Wait," I said, before I thought about what I was doing. She paused and looked at me expectantly. "I noticed your last name is LaChaise. You must be here because of Fernand."

A small furrow appeared between her eyebrows. "Yeah. I came to make the arrangements."

"How are you related to him?"

"I'm his sister," she said.

"Ah." I waited for her to volunteer more, but she didn't. I wanted to tell her about Frederick, but decided it was probably not my place to do so. "We were very fond of your brother. His death is a loss for all of us; my niece in particular was very close to him."

"Thank you," she said.

There was an awkward silence into which I wanted to interject several questions. I finally broke it by saying, "Well, I'll see you at dinner, then."

"Great."

The door shut before I'd taken two steps down the hallway. Either Irene was very closed, I thought, or the rift in Fernand's family had extended beyond his relationship with his parents. I wondered how she'd feel about her brother's boyfriend staying at the inn — and planning to take care of his funeral arrangements. Again, my thoughts turned to Fernand's will. Did Irene know about the boyfriend — and was she worried he was going to change his will to disinherit her? I didn't know how much money Fernand had in the bank, but I knew he owned his oceanside property free and clear. As I walked down the steps, I got another whiff of cabbage, and was reminded that my future mother-in-law was still in the parlor. I unconsciously rubbed the raw place on my finger where I had worn the fake engagement ring — she hadn't noticed I wasn't wearing it yet, but would she say anything when she noticed it? And how was I going to talk to John about it?

After checking the Crow's Nest — no

Gwen, unfortunately — I headed back downstairs, steeling myself for another encounter with my future mother-in-law. I put on a smile as I turned the corner at the bottom of the steps. Frederick and Catherine were still sitting in the parlor, and I was pleased to hear them speaking in low tones. I smiled at Catherine, making a mental note to thank her later for her compassion, as I swept past them into the kitchen, glad to have a cooking task to keep me occupied.

The kitchen was cold, but at least it smelled better than it had when I got home. I opened the freezer, glad I'd made an extra pan of my favorite rustic three-cheese lasagna last week, and turned on the oven. Then I dug in the fridge for two heads of lettuce, a colorful bunch of radishes, some green onions, and a carrot. As I washed and sliced the vegetables — I knew Catherine would barely touch the lasagna, so I was planning on making an extra-large salad — I glanced at the clock. I needed to call Father Timothy to warn him of the situation with Fernand's sister and boyfriend. Maybe, I thought as the French Chef's blade sliced through a creamy-colored radish, I could also ask his advice about my mother-in-law — and the fake "antique ring." And I still needed to figure out something to do about the mortgage company.

The oven beeped, telling me it had come to temperature, just as I finished slicing the pile of vegetables, which looked like bright jewels against the wooden cutting board. After sliding the pan into the oven, I picked up the phone and dialed the priest's number.

He wasn't home; I left a message, then set to work tearing up a head of lettuce. As I put the last leaves into the salad spinner, the door opened, and Gwen and John walked in.

"How'd the painting go?" I asked.

"Same as usual," Gwen said, and then wrinkled her nose. "What's that smell?"

"John's mother was making a healthful snack," I said drily.

My fiancé groaned. "Sorry about that. She just kind of turned up."

"There are two other rooms full now, too," I said.

"So Gwen tells me." John sniffed the air. "Cabbage?" he asked. "Or brussels sprouts?"

"Cabbage," I told him. "Only she forgot to check on it, and the water evaporated."

"Burnt cabbage. The smell of my childhood," John said ruefully.

"Are you going to be okay for dinner?" my niece asked. "I know we weren't expecting any guests."

"I've got lasagna in the oven. Thanks for checking them in though, Gwen." I took a deep breath. "The man, Frederick, is Fernand's boyfriend."

Gwen's eyes widened. "The one from Bangor?"

"He's here to make arrangements. So's his sister, unfortunately."

"I recognized her name," Gwen said, "but didn't want to pry."

"Well," John said. "That should make for some interesting dinner table conversation."

I sighed. "I left a message for Father Timothy; maybe he can help them figure it out." I glanced back at my niece. "Fernand told his friend about you; he said he'd like to talk to you."

She bit her lip. "Really?"

I nodded. "Maybe after dinner. He's in the parlor with Catherine right now."

"I should probably go say hello," John said reluctantly.

"I'd join you, but I've got to make salad," I said, relieved to have an excuse. I was thinking I might pop the cork on a bottle of wine, too. With the evening I had ahead of me, I could use a bit of liquid courage.

"Are you sure you've got dinner under control?" Gwen asked, lingering at the base of the stairs.

I nodded. "I'll pull out a coffeecake and make oatmeal and egg soufflé for breakfast," I said. "I don't have fruit, but I'll call in an order tomorrow morning."

"My mother won't like it," John said.

"I have yogurt and frozen fruit; that will have to do," I said, thinking that if she was going to show up unannounced, Catherine was going to have to take what she could get. I glanced at Gwen, willing her to go upstairs. I needed to talk about the mortgage issue with John — and the ring — but didn't want to bring up either subject with my niece in the room.

"Before I talk with Frederick, I think I'll run up and take a shower," Gwen said. "See if I can get some of this paint off my hands."

"How's the painting going?"

"Don't ask," she said, scowling, and disappeared up the stairs.

When we heard her door slam overhead, John turned to me. "Any luck on the mortgage issue?"

"The attorney skipped town two weeks ago, and can't be reached. The receptionist hasn't gotten her paycheck. There was another man there who was in the same

181

boat as me."

"What was his name?"

"I don't know; he was too busy yelling at the poor receptionist to give me details."

"We need to find out who else is being foreclosed on," he said. "And we need to get another attorney ASAP. It sounds like fraud; we need to interview the victims."

"I saw Murray Selfridge, too. He went into the attorney's office after I'd been there."

"I've heard they're friends. Do you think he could be in trouble, too?"

"He owns a lot of property," I said.

He sighed. "I'll file a report tomorrow, and see if we can track down who else might be affected." He glanced at the door to the dining room. "In the meantime, I'd better go say hello to my mother."

I knew John struggled with his mother, who had never forgiven him for following his artistic impulses rather than following his father into medicine. Although he had forged the life he wanted, it was not the life she had envisioned for him. Even the news of his gallery show in New York — and the article in the *Times* that had accompanied it — had not been enough to appease Catherine Quinton. I gave my fiancé a hug, feeling the tension in his body. He handled her well, but it wasn't easy.

"Good luck," I said, feeling both guilty and relieved that the need to serve dinner in an hour gave me a good excuse to stay in the kitchen while he greeted his mother. He grimaced and straightened his shoulders, then pushed through the door to the dining room.

With my mind still on John, I checked on the lasagna, which was looking melty already — I loved the recipe, which called for Provolone and fresh mozzarella studded with chunks of Italian sausage and sprinkled liberally with Parmesan cheese — and pulled an emergency loaf of French bread from the freezer, wrapping it in foil and tucking it onto the rack below the lasagna pan.

With the salad made and everything else in the oven, I sat down at the kitchen table with my binder of recipes to plan the menu for the rest of the week and make a grocery list. I didn't know how long Frederick and Irene would be staying, but for now, I decided to plan three days of meals. Comfort food was definitely in order. After some deliberation, I settled on juicy pork tenderloin in an Asian glaze, with mashed sweet potatoes and bok choy in oyster sauce for sides. For the other nights, I'd make a hearty coq au vin and a comforting beef stroganoff. If Catherine objected, she was welcome to raid the fridge. I grabbed a pen and paper and jotted down the ingredients — I had honey and soy sauce for the pork, but could use a knob of fresh ginger, along with beef, boiler onions, and some mushrooms. I added two dozen eggs to the list, as well as bacon and sausage and some fresh fruit. For breakfast, I'd make oatmeal for Catherine, and a cheesy egg soufflé for everyone else, along with some coffeecake. If I felt like it, I might whip up a batch of muffins tonight.

Despite all of the problems swirling around me, it felt good to focus on food, I realized as I scanned my list; planning meals pushed everything else out of my head. As much as I'd looked forward to a week without people at the inn, it was a comfort to have people for cook for. Even if, I thought as I returned the binder to the shelf, two of them were bereaved, and the other was my future mother-in-law.

When I pushed through the door at 6:30 with three plates of salad on a tray, my guests had arranged themselves at three separate tables. Evidently the news of Frederick's relationship with Fernand had cooled relations with Catherine — her nose was buried in a book — and Fernand and Irene, who were back to back a few tables apart, were still strangers. At least for now.

Irene was gazing into her laptop when I set the salad down. I glanced at the screen — it was a listing for probate attorneys — before she quickly closed the computer up. "Thank you," she said, looking up at me with those uncannily familiar eyes. I deposited the salad and moved away toward Frederick, who smiled weakly and didn't pick up his fork, instead continuing to gaze moodily toward the flashing lighthouse in the distance.

"Are you sure you don't have anything other than lasagna?" Catherine asked, glancing up from her book as I deposited the salad.

"Leftover green chile stew," I told her.

"With chicken?"

"Pork, I'm afraid."

She made a little moue with her thin lips. "Perhaps just another salad for me, then. In fact, why don't I join you in the kitchen?"

"Sure," I said, feeling myself tense as she stood up, salad plate in hand, and marched over to the kitchen. I headed back into the kitchen after her, hoping John finished whatever he was working on soon; after a quick visit with his mother, he'd excused himself and gone back to the workshop to put the finishing touches on the piece he'd been working on for most of a week. "You don't seem to have too many guests," Catherine said as she deposited herself at my big farm table. Biscuit, who had finally deigned to come back downstairs, eyed her suspiciously from her radiator perch.

"This is usually the slow season," I pointed out.

"I don't know how your business survives, being out here in the middle of nowhere," she said. "My husband always wanted to come here in the summers. Sometimes I wonder what John might have become if he didn't fall in love with this place as a kid."

I glanced up at her as I sliced tomatoes. "He's turning into a very successful artist, you know."

"I know," she said, but she waved one hand as if swatting away my words. Her green eyes — the only similarity I'd seen between Catherine and her son — fixed on me. "Can I help you, dear?"

"No," I said, too quickly. "I've got it."

At that moment, Gwen appeared on the stairs, her wet hair pulled up into a loose bun. She wore jeans and a wraparound sweater, and appeared to have put on a bit of makeup. She looked better than I'd seen her in days.

"You look terrific," I told her.

"Thanks," she said, and her eyes strayed to the dining room door. "I think I'll save saying hello to Frederick until after dinner," she said. "What can I help with?" she asked.

I mentally reviewed the menu and realized I had forgotten dessert. "Shoot," I said. "I totally forgot dessert."

"Oh, I don't need any," Catherine said.

"I know you don't eat sugar, but the other two guests could probably use some about now," I said, adding a few sliced cucumbers to her salad and then sprinkling oil and vinegar over the top.

"Want me to warm up a few crepes and make some whipped cream?" Gwen asked.

"Great idea," I said, thankful for her quick thinking. What would I do if she left the island? I pushed the thought from my head and focused on the task at hand. "I still have some of the chocolate sauce I made last week, too. If we heat that up, it will be perfect."

"Don't make one for me," Catherine said, then glanced out the window. She had shredded her napkin, and was tearing it into tiny bits. "Where is my son?"

"He's down in his workshop. He'll be back soon."

She tore another piece of napkin into bits. "I don't understand what he sees in that old wood. His father used to collect it, too — I used to throw it out when he wasn't looking." She crossed her thin arms over her chest. "He's more like his father than me, I'm afraid."

Thank God, I thought, but kept my mouth shut. Gwen raised an eyebrow at me. I shrugged, added a few crumbles of goat cheese to the salad and crossed over to the table.

"What happened to your finger?" Catherine asked as I set down the plate.

"What do you mean?"

"It looks horrible — did you drop something on it?"

As I glanced down at the reddened skin on my finger, the back door opened, and John walked in, bringing a blast of cold air with it. "Still smells in here," he said.

"Here he is, now!" I said, hoping to get her off the topic.

"What about your finger, Natalie?" Catherine asked

"I . . . I burned it," I said, tucking my hand behind my back. "Gwen, I think the crepes are in the bottom drawer of the freezer."

"You burned yourself?" John's green eyes

darkened with concern.

"It's nothing," I said, giving him a look that meant "We'll talk later."

It didn't work, though. "Let me see." John reached for my hand. "I want to show my mother the ring, anyway."

Well, might as well get it over with, I thought. "Uh . . . the thing is, I seem to be reacting to it. Something about the metal."

"I never had any problem with it," Catherine sniffed.

"Let me see," John said. Reluctantly, I offered my hand. He took it in his large, capable ones, and as always, I felt a shiver of desire. He touched the tender skin with his finger. "It looks like it's reacting with your skin. But gold shouldn't do that!"

"That's the thing," I said, thinking I might as well get it out on the table. "I took it to a jeweler today to ask about why it might be turning my finger black, and, well . . ." I stole a glance at my mother-in-law, who was twisting the napkin around between her hands. "It's not real gold," I blurted out.

THIRTEEN

"What?" John looked at me, then turned to his mother.

The napkin was twisted into a tight ball, but she said, "Nonsense. You must not have gone to a reputable jeweler. Your grandmother gave me that ring: it's 24-carat gold with a 3-carat stone."

"It's not a diamond, actually," I said, dully. John looked stricken. I reached for his hand. "I'm sorry."

"But Mother," he said. "That can't be right. You had it appraised."

"Of course I did," she said, nodding fiercely. "The jeweler must be wrong."

John's eyes narrowed. "But her skin is reacting. You've never had trouble with gold before, have you?"

I shook my head.

"And the jeweler said the diamond's fake. He checked it with a loupe?"

I nodded, thankful he was asking yes or

no questions.

He was still holding my hand in his. "Nat, where is the ring?"

"It's upstairs," I said.

He turned to his mother. "Did you take it somewhere to have it cleaned? Is it possible they made a copy and gave you a fake one?"

"I . . . I don't know. It's possible, I suppose," she said. "Maybe that's what happened." She had abandoned the napkin and was pulling her twinset tight around her body, as if it could protect her.

John sighed. "We'll have to check it out. But in the meantime . . ." He turned to me. "I am so sorry, Natalie. I'll find you another ring."

"But the mortgage . . . we can't afford it!" I said without thinking.

Catherine's thin eyebrows shot up almost to her blonde hairline. "Mortgage troubles?"

Gwen, whom I'd forgotten was there, put down the jar of chocolate sauce with a loud thunk. "You're not going to lose the inn, are you?"

"No, Gwen, no," I said, hoping I wasn't lying. I cursed myself. "Snafu with the refinancing," I said dismissively. "It'll be squared away soon."

The timer went off on the oven; I was thankful for the distraction. "Lasagna's done," I said. "We can talk about all this later."

I hurriedly plated two giant squares of lasagna, added bread to two baskets, and loaded them on a tray to take to the dining room. I pushed through the swinging door just in time to hear Irene spit out, "So you're the reason he was planning to change his will!"

I took an involuntary step back, colliding with the swinging door and almost dropping the lasagna. Irene towered over Frederick, who had gone pale.

"He never spoke to me about a will," Frederick said.

"Yeah, right," Irene said, her pale face deep red. She glanced at me, then shook her shoulders and smoothed her hair back. "We'll talk about this later," she said, shooting Frederick a look of pure venom before stalking back to her table.

I walked over to Frederick's table with the lasagna. He had barely touched his salad. "Do you want to keep that?" I asked.

"It doesn't matter," he said, looking as if Irene had slapped him. Who knew: maybe she had? I actually found myself looking for finger marks on his cheek.

"I'll leave it, just in case," I said. "We've

got chocolate crepes for dessert," I said, giving him an encouraging smile. "Be sure to save room!"

He smiled weakly — just a twitch of his mouth — and I moved away, feeling bad for him. If he was lying about the will, he was an excellent actor. But I had to admit the will talk added substance to the homicide theory.

Irene's face was still flaming when I got to her table, and her breath was coming in short spurts. She had cleaned her salad plate of all but the onions, and I picked it up before placing the warm plate of gooey lasagna in front of her.

"Do you have wine?" she asked.

"Red or white?" I asked, with misgivings. The last thing I needed was a drunk, angry guest.

"Red," she said.

"I'll bring a glass," I said, not wanting to give her the option of a bottle, and turned back to the kitchen. At least I'd have an excuse to come back and make sure she wasn't threatening Frederick again.

When I walked into the kitchen, John had joined his mother at the table with a plate of lasagna; I wasn't worried about the lack of help, as I knew that meant he'd take care of the dishes, which was my least favorite part of cooking.

"Well, the secret's out," I said as I pulled a bottle of Chianti from the small wine rack in the pantry, glad to have something to talk about other than the fake ring.

"What do you mean?" Gwen asked. She was standing at the stove, stirring a small pot of chocolate. Already, the dark, sweet smell was perfuming the kitchen, replacing the sour stench of cabbage. I glanced at my future mother-in-law; she'd looked up from her salad and was paying close attention. Since I saw no reason to exclude her from the conversation, I forged ahead.

"Irene just accused Frederick of being the reason Fernand wanted to change his will." I pulled the corkscrew from a drawer and fitted it over the top of the bottle.

John cocked an eyebrow. "Whoa. What's this about a will?"

"First I've heard of it, too," I said. "Where does sis live?" I asked Gwen.

"She wrote down a Portland address," my niece said.

I looked at John and twisted the corkscrew. "It's not too far, then."

"Too far for what?"

"For her to have come and killed her brother," I said. "She could have taken a boat over after the party and slit his wrists."

"One potential problem with that. Are her feet bigger than Fernand's?" John asked.

"Why?"

"Because if you think she came by sea, she must have worn some real clodhoppers. The footprints behind Fernand's house were enormous."

"She could have landed somewhere else," I said, pulling the cork with a pop. I mulled over the options as I filled a glass with the dark red wine. "Or come over on the mail boat and hidden. After all, the front door was open, not the back."

"Unlikely, but possible," John said. "We can ask if anyone saw someone resembling her."

"I'll talk to George tomorrow," I said.

"You think this man was murdered?" Catherine said. "I had no idea this island was so unsafe!"

"Fortunately, we have a deputy on the premises," I said to reassure her. She glanced at her son, but didn't look comforted. "There's another problem, though," I told John. "I've been thinking about it. How would you get Fernand to sit still long enough to slit his wrists?"

"Drugs would do it," John said.

"Any word back on the toxicology report?"

"I asked about that today. They're work-

195

ing on it now," he said. "I also passed on the information about the knife set, and the footprints to and from the house. I told them I thought it was a suspicious death."

"What did Penney say?"

"She's not inclined to change the cause of death."

"Of course not."

"That's why I called her supervisor," he said.

I paused near the dining room door, glass in hand. "You what?"

"Her supervisor is the one who ordered the toxicology report."

I looked at John in surprise.

"Fernand was a friend," John said quietly. "If he was killed, I want the killer brought to justice."

"Detective Penney's not going to like that," I said.

He shrugged.

"John," Catherine said. "I had no idea you were so involved with the police!"

"He's terrific," I told her, with a wink at my fiancé. "Back in a sec — need to drop this wine off and make sure there hasn't been another murder."

Catherine giggled nervously as I pushed through the swinging door. To my relief, both guests were in their own seats, and there was no blood in evidence.

I put the glass down in front of Irene and asked how the lasagna was.

"Fine," she said crisply. I glanced at Frederick; he hadn't touched his plate, and was gazing out the window. Could he really have killed his lover? I found myself looking at his feet and wondering if they were bigger than Fernand's. Maybe I could check his shoe size while I was tidying his room, I thought. Or show his picture to the mail boat captain along with Irene's. I should probably surreptitiously snap photos of both of them. Another thing to worry about.

To think I'd moved to Cranberry Island for the quiet life, I thought as I headed back into the kitchen.

It seemed like hours before John's mother decided to retire for the night, leaving John and me alone in the kitchen at last. We hadn't had time to get the carriage house ready for her, so Gwen had put her in one of the second-story bedrooms. As soon as the swinging door closed behind her, John set down the bowl he was drying and took my hands in his.

"I'm sorry about the ring," he said. "I had no idea it wasn't real. We'll go pick out another this week."

"Let's hold off on that," I said, "until we get this mortgage thing taken care of." My stomach wrenched at the thought of the mortgage; time was running out, and although John had made a few calls, we had made no substantive progress on resolving the matter. I pushed the thought aside and smiled up at John, telling myself that at least one issue had been resolved — or at least broached. "But thank you for saying so. I was so nervous to tell you."

"No need," he said. "I want there always to be honesty between us." He brushed a strand of hair from my cheek. "How long have you known?"

I shrugged. "The metal has been bothering me for a few weeks, but I only knew for sure today. Speaking of honesty, your mother didn't want to talk about it too much, did she?"

"No, she didn't. There's something different about her," John said. "I can't place it."

"It's odd that she's here at all — much less early. She's never had much interest in the island in the past."

"No," he said. "She only came because my father and I loved it here. Something's going on with her. I hope she's not ill."

"She looks the same as always," I said. "Very healthy."

"If it's early stage cancer, or heart disease . . ." He sighed. "It will come out soon enough, I suppose," he said. "It always does. In the meantime, though . . ." He put his arms around me and kissed me, and all the problems of the week dissolved as I melted into him.

"I think we should go upstairs," he murmured into my ear.

"With pleasure," I said. We had taken two steps toward the staircase when there was a loud smacking sound at the door.

We jerked apart. "Go into the dining room," John ordered me, his voice almost a growl as he switched into his protector mode. I headed toward the swinging door to the dining room as he closed the gap to the kitchen door. I pulled open the door, but peered around it as he stood beside the exterior door and reached for the doorknob.

He pulled it open with a jerk, and I caught my breath.

The bottom of the door was splattered with what looked like fresh blood.

"Hey!" John yelled, and then disappeared through the door, leaping over the steps into the snow.

My heart rose to my throat, and I ran to the open doorway. The blood was everywhere, along with fragments of green latex, staining the stone steps and the snow. I peered into the darkness — if there was a moon, the clouds were too thick to see it, and the night was pitch black. John had vanished into the darkness, but I could hear a thrashing noise in the snow.

"John?" I called. He didn't answer. What if the person who had thrown the blood-filled balloon was armed? What if John got lost in the dark? What if . . .

I pushed those thoughts aside and tried to think logically. He wouldn't get lost if I followed his tracks with a flashlight. And if he needed help . . .

Without thinking further, I grabbed a knife from the knife block and a flashlight from the drawer next to the phone. Then I threw on a jacket and headed out after him, trying to sidestep the pooling blood on the step.

"John!" I called as I trained the flashlight on the tracks in the snow and hurtled into the night. As I followed the footprints into the trees, I realized that the light made me vulnerable if the prankster had doubled back — and that running through snowy woods with a knife in my hand was not the wisest idea. I couldn't think of a better plan, though — and wanted it handy if I needed it — so I pointed it outward, hoped I wouldn't trip on a tree root, and kept going.

The tracks followed the same path through the forest that whoever left the doll had traveled. As I pushed through the snow, I wondered if it was the same person. And whether John had caught up with him. Or her.

"John!" I called again, my voice shrill in my ears, yet muffled sounding, dampened by the blanket of snow. I couldn't hear anything above the crunch of my sneakers as I ran.

I followed the tracks up the hill, my lungs burning in my chest, terrified for John. On I went, though my legs felt leaden, and my shoes and jeans were filling with snow; I could feel the icy cold against the skin of my calves as I pushed through the snow.

Finally, I crested the hill. As I hurtled down the path, though, my foot slid, throwing me off balance. I struggled to right myself, but still fell hard, my hands instinctively going out to protect me. The knife slipped from my hand, the edge slicing into my palm, as I tumbled into the snow and continued to slide down the slope, stopping only when my shoulder slammed into the trunk of a fir tree. An avalanche collapsed on top of me.

I lay there stunned for a moment, the pain of the cut stinging, the cold taking my breath away. Then I flailed to my feet, shook myself off, and retrieved the flashlight, which was glowing beneath about a foot of snow. I scanned the snow quickly for the knife, my body shaking from cold despite the jacket. I couldn't find it in the churned-up snow. Giving it up for lost, I kept going, focusing on John, trying not to think about what I'd do if I found him in trouble.

I made it down the rest of the hill without incident, but with no sign of my fiancé. I ran until I couldn't run anymore, and limped until the trees ended and the path died into the road.

There was no sign of him.

"John!" I called, my heart about to explode from my chest.

"Right here."

Relief flooded through me. I waved the flashlight around, trying to find him; he was standing about twenty yards down the road, next to a person.

I hurried over, training the light on John's companion. Who was it?

"Are you okay?" I asked warily.

"I'm fine. But why are you out here? You could have been hurt."

I ignored the question. "Who's this?" I asked, training my flashlight on his companion's face. She held up a gloved hand and flinched away. "Sorry," I said, and dropped the light.

"This is Nina Torrone," John said. "She was out for a walk. She saw someone head down the road a few minutes ago, running."

I was dying to shine the light on her face again — it was the first time I'd seen her without those enormous sunglasses — but resisted the urge, instead peering at her through the gloom. She had high, arched eyebrows, but I couldn't tell much else. "I didn't mean to shine the light in your eyes; we just had a scary incident at the inn. I'm sure John told you what happened."

She shrugged. I slowly moved the flashlight so that it was near her boots; they were caked with snow. Was it all from the road? It had been plowed recently, so it had to be from somewhere else. The forest path, perhaps?

"A bit late for a walk," I said.

"I like to walk at night," she said in a small voice. "No one bothers me."

"Where's your agent?" I asked.

"He is asleep," she said. "He doesn't like

me to go out."

"Why not?"

She hesitated, then said, "Paparazzi."

"On Cranberry Island? In the middle of the night? In winter?"

"Nat." John put a hand on my arm.

"Sorry. I guess it must be a hard habit to break." I turned to John. "Any sign of our vandal?"

"I'm afraid whoever it is is long gone," John said. "I twisted my ankle at the end of the path. Nina told me that whoever it was had a good head start, and I can't run anymore."

"Who do you think it was?" I asked.

He sighed. "I wish I knew." He turned to Nina. "I'm sorry we had to meet at the dead of night, but I'm glad I ran into you. I've always admired your work."

"Thank you," she said. Even in the darkness I could sense her tensing up.

John must have sensed it, too, and kept his voice warm and casual. "There are a few of us on the island, if you ever feel like getting together with a few artists for a drink, or dinner at the inn. Zelda Chu is opening a gallery here. Fernand would have loved to talk with you; it's a shame he's not here."

"Yes. The party was lovely," she said in her small voice. It was still tight, though —

I could tell she was uncomfortable with the idea of getting together with others. Was it because of her agent? Or had she always been reclusive?

"You and Fernand met in New York, didn't you?" I asked.

"I'm sorry," she said. "I have to go. Mortimer will be wondering what happened to me."

Abruptly, she turned and fled, the beam of a penlight marking her progress. John and I stared after her; neither of us made a move to stop her.

Now that she was gone, the pain in my hand and the cold of the snow suddenly seemed to intensify. I shivered, and John turned to me. "You're freezing."

In a low voice, I said, "Do you think Nina Torrone was the one we were chasing through the woods? Her boots were covered in snow."

"Odd time of day to be out for a stroll," he replied. "But she wasn't breathing hard. If it was her, she's in terrific shape."

Unlike me, I thought, still catching my breath.

"Next time I tell you to stay home," John continued, "please listen to me. Whoever is doing this has it in for you; don't hand them the opportunity on a silver plate."

"I thought you might need help," I said. "Or at least a light."

He sighed. "Let's have a look at the prints, then."

I handed him the flashlight.

"Why is it sticky?" he asked, then realized it was slicked with blood. "Natalie!"

"It's just a cut," I said.

"How did you cut yourself?"

"I grabbed a knife from the block before I came to look for you. When I tripped, it cut me — and I lost it."

"You came after me with a knife?"

"I was worried you might be in trouble," I said.

He shook his head and sighed. "We'll look for it tomorrow," he said. "Show me your hand."

I held it out, and he trained the flashlight on it. "I'm going to put some butterfly bandages on this when we get home. You just can't stay out of trouble, can you?"

"You're the one who went bolting out the door," I pointed out.

He stroked the edge of my hand, then gathered me into his arms, kissing my forehead, then my lips. "I couldn't bear it if anything happened to you."

"Likewise," I said, hugging him tightly as a cold wind whipped off the snow, cutting through the layers of fabric. Despite the warm feeling in my heart, it was still cold. My body shivered violently, and John released me. "We've got to get you home," he said, flashing the light on the stirred-up prints. "But I don't want to disturb the tracks anymore than I already have. Are you up for the long way?"

"If we have to," I said.

He glanced up at the sky. "I hope it doesn't snow tonight; I want those prints fresh tomorrow morning. Let's get you home so I can put you in a hot bath and take care of that wound."

He put an arm around me; despite the lack of a jacket, I could still feel his warmth — and steered me toward the inn.

"Do you think it might have been Torrone?" I asked as we walked in the darkness, following the bobbing light.

"It is a bit suspicious that she happened to be out here," he said, "but why would she threaten you? She's barely even met you."

"I don't know," I said, "but there's something strange about her. She sure didn't want to get together with anyone else. And to walk after dark to avoid the paparazzi on Cranberry Island . . ." I shook my head.

"Maybe she's creatively blocked," he said.

"Maybe that's why they came up here. Sometimes success can do that to an artist."

"Maybe," I said. "But that doesn't explain why her boots were caked with snow."

He hugged me closer. "Why do you always seem to draw trouble?" he asked.

"I don't know," I said, snuggling into John. We walked together in darkness for a while, the only sound the crunch of our boots in the snow. "What will we do if we lose the inn?" I asked quietly, broaching the question that had been nagging at me all day.

"We won't," he said.

"I hope you're right," I said.

"We'll hire an attorney. If I need to pay the $15,000, I will; I'd like to see if we can get the attorney to waive those fees."

"It was my mistake," I said. "I can't ask you to pay for it."

"We're in this together, remember? You've worked way too hard to lose everything because of a crook." He pulled me closer. Although I was determined not to take him up on his offer — it was my mess, and I needed to clean it up — I felt something inside me relax knowing he viewed himself as my partner. For better and for worse.

"In the meantime," I said, wanting to

change the subject, "what do I do about the stuff on the steps? I know it's evidence, but I don't want to upset Gwen. Or the guests."

"I'll take a sample and a picture," he said. "Then we'll clean it up."

"Who do you think is doing this?"

"It might be worth mentioning at your knitting group," he said.

"Or to Charlene," I said. "If someone's annoyed with me, she'd be the first to know." I thought about it. "I just can't think of anything I've done that might have made someone mad."

"I don't know, Nat. You have mangled a lot of yarn," he said.

I laughed for the first time in a week.

Thankfully, the rest of the night passed without incident, and I was not exactly torn up about it when John told me I should lay off the knitting until the wound had partially healed. John took a sample of the red sticky stuff on the door; it did appear to be blood, although I didn't want to speculate on whose. After I scrubbed the door and the steps and sprinkled them with salt, I was thankful for the warm bath John had drawn for me. When I was clean and warm, I bur-rowed into his arms, relishing the feeling of being embraced as I fell asleep — and try-ing to forget that the alarm was set for 6:30

and that my future mother-in-law would be facing me over the breakfast table.

It was still dark when I stumbled down to the kitchen the next morning, thankful I'd come up with a plan the night before. John came down a few minutes after me; as soon as it was light, he headed out to the forest trail. The sun was high in the sky by the time he tramped up the steps to the kitchen.

"Any luck?" I asked John as he closed the door behind him. I was stirring grated cheddar cheese into a bowl of eggs for the soufflé.

"I found the knife, at least. Not hard to find — there was blood everywhere."

"What about the prints?"

"We muddled up most of them, but I got a few."

"The same as the ones at Fernand's?"

"Smaller," he said, "but I got a logo." He showed me the shot on his digital camera.

"Timberland," I said. One of the most popular boot brands on the island. "Well, that narrows it down."

"It's a start," he said. "And maybe we can figure out a shoe size."

"Was that on the sole, too?"

"No, but I measured the print," he said. "I'll let the mainland police know about it this morning."

"They're going to get tired of hearing from you," I said as I poured the cheesy mixture into a soufflé dish and tucked it into the oven, where I'd put a pan of water to heat. "First Fernand, then the attorney, and now this . . ."

"What attorney?" I turned around to see Gwen at the bottom of the steps.

"Nothing you need to worry about," I said. With everything else going on, the last thing she needed to think about was the prospect of the inn closing. Besides, John had offered to step into the breach, so it really wasn't anything to worry about. At least that's what I kept telling myself.

"What's that?" she asked, pointing to the sandwich bag in John's hand.

I looked at John, who nodded. "Someone threw something at the back door last night. It may be the same person who left the doll."

"You're being threatened," she said.

"It's just a nuisance," I said. "Nothing to worry about." I glanced at her, and realized she had combed her hair and put on a bright sweater — even a touch of makeup. "You look great," I said.

"Mind if I borrow the truck?" she asked. "I'm going to meet with Zelda Chu this

211

morning." She walked over and grabbed a banana from the counter.

"I thought you didn't like her."

"She's not Fernand," she said, and I saw a spasm of emotion pass over her face, "but she is an artist, and she paints."

"Good for you," I said, thankful to see her moving in a positive direction. "You're welcome to the truck, if you're careful," I said. "As long as I can run down to the pier at noon and pick up the food order."

"I should be back by ten, if that's okay." She pushed a stray strand of hair from her face and tucked the banana in her pocket.

"What about Fernand's studio?" John asked.

"I imagine whoever inherited it is going to sell it," she said. "If Zelda buys it, maybe I can keep painting there — I'm hoping she'll agree to mentor me."

"She doesn't work in the same medium," I pointed out. "Or even the same style."

"I do oils now too," Gwen reminded me. "And at least she's got connections."

"It's too bad Nina Torrone is so unfriendly," I said.

"Talk about different styles — she's completely abstract!" John pointed out. He smiled at Gwen. "You know you can always share the workshop with me."

"Or the Crow's Nest," I said, even though it was one of my highest-earning rooms. If it meant keeping Gwen, it was worth it.

"Thanks, you two." She gave John a wan smile, then looked at me. "Are you sure everything's okay with the inn?"

"Nothing you need to worry about," I said.

She glanced at the clock over the kitchen door. "Why don't I go ahead and set the tables? I'll be back this afternoon to help with the rooms."

"Thanks," I said.

"Three, right?"

I sighed. "If we can convince Catherine to stay in the dining room."

"I'll tell her we need a referee," John said.

"Catherine as a referee? God help us," I said.

Gwen hadn't returned by the time Frederick appeared in the dining room. He sat by the window again, and although he was dressed stylishly in a blue cashmere sweater and khakis, he looked as if he hadn't slept in days.

"Can I get you a cup of coffee?" I asked.

"Sure," he said. I filled his cup, then headed for the kitchen for sugar and cream. As I placed them on his table, I felt a pang of sadness for him.

"I heard you had words with Irene yesterday," I said.

"She's going to cut me out," he said.

I said nothing, wondering if he was talking about the will.

"She called the priest. Since I'm not family, I'm not allowed to do the memorial service."

"I'm so sorry," I said, feeling my heart ache for him.

"I'm going to the house, though," he said, lifting his chin. "One last time. I have to say goodbye."

"Do you need someone to go with you?" I asked softly.

"You knew Fernand, didn't you?" he asked, looking up at me.

I nodded. "I can give you a ride over after breakfast, if you'd like. It's a long walk in this weather." I glanced out the window. Although it wasn't snowing, it was overcast, and the wind was howling off the water.

"Thank you," he said.

"Will ten-thirty work?" When he nodded, I promised I'd meet him in the parlor after I got the dishes together. "I've got Winter Knitters later on, but I should have enough time to get you there and back." I gave his plate a pointed look. "You should eat; I know Fernand would want you to keep up your strength."

He made a noncommittal noise, and I drifted back to the kitchen, wondering about his "cutting out" comment. Was he only talking about the priest? Or was he talking about Fernand's estate, too?

When I walked out a few minutes later with the egg soufflé, Irene had arrived, looking smart in a black pants suit with heels. Clearly these folks hadn't spent much time on Cranberry Island in winter, I thought, looking down at my practical flannel-lined jeans and thick Aran wool sweater. I shook my head at the heels; I hoped she wasn't walking to the church in those. As an innkeeper, I felt obligated to offer her a ride — but then felt as if I was being a traitor to Frederick.

I filled her coffee cup and scurried back toward the kitchen, thinking that things were much easier when my guests didn't want to kill each other.

"Natalie!" my future mother-in-law said when I stepped into the kitchen, looking perfectly turned out in black slacks and a cranberry red twin set that made her look very pale. "My, you're looking tired this morning. Did you not sleep well?"

"Thank you," I said. *You're looking cadav-*

215

erous yourself, I thought but didn't say.

"Is there coffee?" she asked.

"Right here," I said. "Could you do me a favor, this morning?"

"What is it, dear?"

"Would you mind eating in the dining room, and keeping tabs on the guests? Emotions are running pretty high right now."

"I can imagine," Catherine said, pursing her lipsticked lips. "He's a nice man, but if I were her, I wouldn't be pleased if my brother's male lover were trying to horn in on my inheritance."

FOURTEEN

I blinked at her. "What?"

"Fernand's sister seems to think he was considering writing a new will," she said.

I glanced at the swinging door to the dining room and thought of Frederick, subjected to both Irene and Catherine. "On second thought, maybe it would be better if you stayed here with us," I said.

"Oh, Natalie. I know when to keep quiet," she said. Before I could respond, she was through the swinging door and striding across the dining room.

John's eyes met mine. "We may have another murder soon," I said, half-joking.

"Murder? Or self-defense?" John asked.

"Just check on them from time to time, please. Better yet, maybe you could keep your mother company in there." I gave him a pleading look.

"But you need help in here," he said. "Your hand . . ."

"Is fine," I said. I had covered the butter-fly bandages with a large latex bandage, and it was holding up well. "You can do the dishes when they've gone upstairs."

He groaned. "Is it too early for a shot of rum in my coffee?"

"Yes," I said, grinning. "Maybe you can ask her what happened to her grand-mother's ring."

"That'll make for some terrific conversation."

"Better than talking about lovers and wills," I pointed out. "Now, go."

With another deep sigh, he followed his mother into the dining room, and I busied myself in the kitchen.

Thankfully, everyone survived breakfast, and John took care of clean-up while I fed Biscuit — wet cat food, to her delight — and excused myself to take a shower. When I came downstairs at 10:30, the truck was back in the driveway, but I didn't see Gwen; I wondered how her meeting had gone. I wanted to go check the Crow's Nest, but Frederick was waiting for me in the parlor.

"I can't wait to get this over with," he said as I walked in. I glanced at the staircase and decided I'd check on Gwen later.

"Do you have a key?" I asked.

He nodded.

"Let's go, then," I said, and headed for the front door with Frederick in my wake.

As I headed to the van, I found myself glancing around, looking for other things out of place — another voodoo doll, maybe, or another splatter of blood. My eyes lingered on the steps to the kitchen door; I could still see tinges of pink on the crusted snow. Whose blood was it? I found myself wondering again, then pushed the thought away.

"How long were you and Fernand together?" I asked as we settled ourselves into the front seats of the van.

"About a year," he said.

"I didn't realize you had come to visit."

"I was only here a few times. We tried to keep things quiet," he said. "Smaller towns can be very conservative."

I thought of the petition Maggie Brumbacher was circulating about the elementary school teacher. Yes, they could. "You're from Bangor, right?" I asked.

He nodded. "But I was planning on moving here with Fernand. In the spring."

"It was pretty serious, then."

"Yes," he said, and it came out as a sob.

"I'm so sorry, Frederick," I said, and reached out to touch his shoulder.

"I just can't believe he would have done something like this," he said.

"I know," I said. "It was a shock to all of us." The van crested the hill. The wind had torn the snow from the branches, and the sky was a leaden gray. "Did he mention being depressed at all?" I asked.

He shook his head. "Not that I heard. I told you, his business was growing, he was happy in his work . . . and I think he was happy in our relationship. He'd just set up a trip to Florence for us. He wouldn't have done that if he wasn't planning to be there." He looked at me with something like desperation in his eyes. "Would he?"

"It doesn't sound like it," I said. "If you visited, though, I'm surprised I haven't run into you before — it's such a small island. Did you take the mail boat to get here?" He hadn't made the island gossip circuit, but enough tourists visited the island that it wasn't entirely surprising.

"Sometimes," he said. "But more often I took the dinghy. Fernand would take it over to the mainland and leave it for me if I was coming in too late for the mail boat, like when I had to drive in from Bangor after work. I didn't like to do it — usually he came to get me — but if he had a class or something, or I wasn't sure when I was going to make it in, we'd do it that way." He shivered. "I'm not a boat person."

We pulled up outside Fernand's house, and I cut the engine. Frederick sat quietly for a long moment, while I waited. "I'm ready," he said finally.

"Do you want me to come in with you?" I asked.

"If you don't, you'll freeze," he said. He turned and looked at me with reddened eyes. "You found him, didn't you?"

"Yes," I said, and found myself hoping they had cleaned up. "Why don't I go upstairs and make sure everything's okay before you go up there?"

"It happened upstairs, then," he said, looking pale.

"Yes," I said quietly.

He nodded, and I followed him to the front door, the icy wind biting through our clothes.

The heat was on, thankfully, and the house smelled of cleaning products, which I took to be a good sign. I glanced at Frederick; he had gone ghostly white. Again, I thought to myself that he was either a terrific actor or he had really cared for Fernand. Had he come over on the dinghy and killed Fernand? If so, why? Was it because Fernand had changed the will in his favor? Was he having financial troubles? I found myself glancing out a window toward the water. Where was Fernand's dinghy, anyway?

"Why don't you sit in the kitchen?" I said, taking his arm and steering him away from the staircase. "I'll be right back."

I left him at the kitchen table while I climbed the stairs, praying that the police had cleaned up. I breathed out a sigh of relief when I saw that the floor gleamed once again. The dust ruffle was missing from the bed, but other than that, there was no sign of what had happened here. I hurried back downstairs to Frederick.

"It's fine," I said.

"Where did you find him?" he asked, looking up at me with tortured eyes.

"It doesn't matter," I said. "I want your memories of this house to be good ones."

"How can they be?" he asked, but did not press me for details. "Do you want me to come with you?" I asked.

"No," he said, his voice hoarse. "I have to do this alone." He pushed the chair back with a scraping sound and slowly walked down the hallway toward the stairs.

As I sat at the kitchen table, wincing at the thought of what Frederick must be experiencing, my eyes were drawn once again to the coffee carafe that Fernand would never use again. I felt restless, sitting and waiting. And it occurred to me that if he had been murdered, the clue to his death might be here, in the house. And I was sitting in the kitchen, doing nothing.

I started to get up, then stopped myself. It felt wrong to pry.

But if I was bringing a murderer to justice, wouldn't it be justified?

I knew Fernand's office was in the next room. I debated it for a few minutes, but then decided to at least take a look at it.

Listening for the sound of Frederick's footsteps on the stairs, I slipped through the doorway at the end of the kitchen into Fernand's office.

Like every other room in the house, it was tidy, with signed original artwork on the walls and gorgeous views of the water. The desk was antique cherry, with a laptop placed in the center and a beautiful lamp crafted of metal and seaglass in one corner. In the other corner was a neat stack of papers. The top page was a printout of a *New York Times* article on Nina Torrone. After a moment's hesitation, I picked it up and leafed through the stack; below were several other articles on Torrone, from papers around the country. Was that how he knew what her favorite drink was? I wondered. Why was he so fascinated with the artist? I picked them up and leafed through them. Each article was accompanied by a picture of Torrone. Evidently sunglasses were her trademark; in all four images, the top half of her face was obscured by them. In one, she held a cigarette in a paint-stained hand. There was one picture of Torrone with her agent; the image showed him in the background as she apparently held forth, cocktail glass in one hand, cigarette in the other, with a fellow artist. Her body language in the picture was open and confident; very different from the woman I had met the other day. Was it because of the alcohol? Her hands were those of a working artist; like Gwen's, they bore streaks of paint. Was this image an alcohol-fueled anomaly? Or had something happened to make her change?

And more importantly, why was Fernand so interested in her that he had printed multiple articles? It did smack a bit of obsession, a thought I found disturbing. Had he really killed himself out of jealousy? Was he secretly in love with her — and was that why he died? I glanced through the articles again. They talked about her bold style, and the rising prices of her artwork, which had been selling for less than $50 apiece just a few years earlier. Fernand had visited New York several times over the past decade, Gwen had told me. Had he known her there?

I leafed through the rest of the papers, pausing when I spotted one from an attorney in Bangor. It was dated two weeks ago. "The documents you requested have been prepared. Please call our office to schedule an appointment."

Had he, though? I looked around for a calendar, but found none. With yet another twinge of guilt, I opened the top drawer of the desk. Nothing but pens and envelopes neatly lined up. I searched the other drawers, but before I could finish, I heard Frederick's footsteps on the stairs and hurried back to the kitchen, wishing I'd had just a few more minutes.

"Are you okay?" I asked as Frederick shuffled down the hall.

"I've said my goodbyes," he said. "Now I just have to arrange the service."

I bit my lip. "Have you spoken with his sister?"

He nodded stiffly. "He hadn't been in contact with her for a decade, but the police notified her first."

"What about his parents?" I asked.

"They disowned him," he said bitterly. "I imagine they won't be attending his memorial service."

"I'm sorry," I said, again feeling sadness for what Fernand must have gone through. And what Frederick was going through now. He stood in the kitchen, looking as if he were adrift at sea. I needed to get him out of here, I realized. "Do you need to look anywhere else?" I asked gently.

"No," he said. "I've done what I came to do." I wondered what that was, but didn't ask. There was bitterness in his voice when he spoke again. "Do you know I found out about Fernand in the newspaper? Nobody called me. And now I have to convince the priest to let me help with the service."

"I'm so sorry. Frederick. I think Irene believes she's going to organize it."

His face suffused with color. "How would she know what Fernand would have wanted? It's ridiculous."

I didn't know what to say. He was right. But there was nothing I could do about it. "Why don't we drop by the rectory on the way home?" I asked. "I hope you don't mind; I called Father Timothy yesterday to let him know the situation."

Frederick turned to look at me. "What did he say?"

"Nothing," I confessed. "I left a message."

Frederick sighed, his eyes sweeping the room. Like mine, they lingered on the coffee cups, and the empty carafes. The house felt empty without its vibrant owner. "Let's go," he said. "I can't bear it anymore."

I couldn't either.

Frederick locked the door behind us as we left. "I won't be needing this again," he said, his voice hollow, and shoved the key into his pocket. As we drove to the rectory, I braved a question. "Did Fernand say anything about Nina Torrone coming to the island?" I asked.

"He mentioned he was having a party for her," he said. "I was hoping to be invited, but he told me it wasn't time. We were going to be moving in together over the summer, though, so I don't know what he was so worried about. People were going to have to find out sooner or later."

"Whose idea was the move?"

"Both of us," he said, too quickly. "Someone was harassing him. I told Fernand if I were here, maybe whoever it was would realize he was in a relationship, and would lay off."

"Harassing him?" I asked, surprised by this piece of news. "He never said anything about that to me. Did he tell you who it was?"

"It was a man on the island," Frederick said. "Fernand never told me who it was, but he showed up drunk several nights. I think he left notes, too . . . Fernand never told me what was in them, though."

"I had no idea," I said. It opened up a line of possibility I hadn't considered before. Had Fernand been killed by a frustrated admirer?

"Of course you wouldn't have known," Frederick said. "Fernand wouldn't have said anything. He thought people didn't know he was gay."

"I didn't," I admitted. Although evidently I'd been the only one on the island.

"He was very quiet about it. You never know how things like that will go over in small communities."

"The local teacher seems to be doing okay," I said.

"Really? I thought someone had started a petition about her," he said.

"Well, mostly okay," I said. "Let's get back to this admirer, though," I said, anxious to change the subject.

"I know things escalated recently," Frederick said. "Fernand said he'd gotten a lot of phone calls. The guy would just call, and call, and call."

"And you don't know who it was?"

"He wouldn't tell me." Frederick turned to me, and a light seemed to go on in his eyes. "Do you think . . ."

"I don't know," I said. "It's certainly a theory."

"I hate to suggest it, but maybe, if we go back, we might be able to find out. Maybe if Fernand had caller ID, we could get a number."

"Maybe we can go this evening," I said. "If we can find some evidence of who was calling, it might be enough to get the police to investigate." I watched him, looking for a flicker of fear, but he seemed genuinely excited. I was on the verge of telling him about the footprints I'd seen behind Fernand's house, but decided against it. I still didn't know Frederick very well.

"We're here," I said as we pulled up outside the rectory. "I'll walk up with you."

"Thank you," he said.

Father Timothy answered the door when I knocked. He was an older man with a shock of bright white hair and a kindly face. I introduced Frederick; he didn't blink an eye when I explained their relationship.

"I'm so very sorry, my son," the priest said in his comforting, gravelly voice. "Come in

229

and have a cup of tea."

I shot Father Timothy a grateful glance. He'd only been on the island a few months, but his presence was a real addition to the community. "Can you drop him off at the inn when you're finished?"

"Of course," he said as I headed back to the van. I was glad Frederick wasn't going to be alone — and hoped Father Timothy could find a way to help balance Fernand's service. As I backed out of the rectory driveway, I glanced at the clock on the van's dash. I'd forgotten Winter Knitters was meeting this afternoon, I realized. I wanted to go — I was curious if anyone knew anything about the person leaving nasty surprises on my doorstep — but I dreaded the knitting.

Maybe I'd use the cut on my hand as an excuse to sit and eat cookies.

By the time I got back to the inn, I had just enough time to take care of the rooms before making it to Winter Knitters. I hadn't had time to bake, but I found some molasses snap cookies in the freezer. Gwen walked in as I was digging in search of a second bag.

"How did it go with Zelda Chu?" I asked, glancing over my shoulder at my niece.

"Okay," she said. "She really likes my watercolors, and offered to give me a few pointers on the oils."

"Wonderful!" I said, finding the second bag and closing the freezer door. "Did she offer you studio space?"

"Yes," she said, "and she's willing to mentor me."

"That's great," I said. "Her art is very different from yours . . . is that going to be a problem?" After seeing how Gwen had tied herself in knots trying to please Munger, the plaid-clad gallery owner, I was concerned. Again, I felt a wave of sadness that Fernand was gone.

"She's the only option I have right now," she said, her shoulders slumped.

"What about the mainland? There are a lot of artists in this area," I said. "I want to make sure you have the right mentor."

"I don't know, Aunt Nat," she said, twisting her hair between her fingers. I wished I knew what to tell her. Maybe I'd ask John to talk to her again. "By the way, she wants me to ask if you've thought about the retreat offer."

"Are you okay with it?"

She sighed. "I feel like a traitor for saying so, but there's no point in saying no."

"Why a traitor?" I asked, searching for a

231

tin for the cookies.

"She was Fernand's enemy," Gwen said. "In fact, I think she wants to buy his gallery."

My antennae pricked up. "Oh, really?"

Gwen nodded. "She's planning to expand her program. Maybe run the retreat in connection with one of the New York universities."

"That must be the proposal she was asking Fernand about at the party," I said. "He didn't seem too jazzed about it."

"That was probably it," she said.

Was the promise of potential waterfront property a motive for murder? It seemed like a long shot to me; after all, how would you know if the property's heir would be any more likely to sell? Unless Zelda and Fernand's sister had been in collusion . . .

Too far-fetched, I decided.

"Anyway, I'd better go and get to work," my niece said as I stared into the distance, cookie tin in hand. Her words brought me back to the task at hand.

"What are you doing?"

"I have to take the canvases over to the mainland tomorrow. It's time to start framing them."

"Will you be alone?"

"Adam will be there," she said.

"Good." I didn't like the idea of her being at the studio alone. "It sounds like you have enough paintings, then."

"I guess." She shrugged. "I don't know how good they are, but they're done."

"Take the watercolors, too," I suggested.

"I'll think about it," she said, and pushed through the door into the dining room. I glanced at the clock; I knew John was taking the doll and the wool to the mainland today, and talking to Detective Penney about his suspicions regarding Fernand's death. I'd have to ask about the case — and the doll — when he got back that evening.

I closed the tin on the cookies and grabbed my cleaning supplies, since I had volunteered to do room clean-up today. I headed toward Frederick's room first; since he was at the rectory, I knew I wouldn't be disturbing him. I knocked out of habit, then let myself in with the skeleton key.

FIFTEEN

Although his appearance was neat, his room was messy, with clothes strewn everywhere. I tidied quickly; despite the clothes draped over the counter and heaped on the floor, there wasn't much work. There was a bottle of scotch in the bathroom, on the corner of the counter. I thought again of the glass in Fernand's room, and the footprints leading to and from the water. I hurried to the wardrobe and picked up one of Frederick's shoes. He was a men's size 11; I'd have to compare it with what John had found. I didn't want to believe Frederick had done it, but I couldn't rule it out, either.

When I got to Irene's room, she was gone, too. I hoped she hadn't decided to visit the rectory, I thought as I closed the door behind me and set down my cleaning supplies.

Like her brother, Irene was very tidy. Although she hadn't made her bed, her clothes were neatly hung in the wardrobe, and her toiletries and medicines were lined up on the back of the counter. Two of them were prescription medications: Xanax and Ativan. She must suffer from anxiety, I thought to myself. Interesting: I wouldn't have guessed it from meeting her. The laptop was gone, but on the cherry desk was a short stack of papers. I resisted the urge to page through them, but was surprised at what lay on top of the stack.

It was a punch card for the Cranberry Island mail boat. She'd only arrived yesterday, but it had been punched seven times.

I stared at the card, thinking of the implications. Fernand might have been estranged from his family, but he'd been in contact with his sister — or at least his sister had been to the island. When? Why? I wished I had a picture to show to George McLeod, the mail boat captain. Had she come secretly the night he died, waiting for him to pass out from the scotch and then slitting his wrists when he slept?

It still didn't explain the footsteps leading to and from the water, though. Whose were they? Had two people visited Fernand the night he died — and only one killed him?

I walked through the room once more, making sure everything was in order, before heading up to the second floor and Catherine's room.

She answered as soon as I knocked, only cracking the door open.

"Hello, Natalie."

"I was just going to clean your room, if that's okay," I said.

"No, no. No need," she said, peering through the slit in the door. "I'll take care of it. I'm glad you're here, though; I was hoping you could drive me over to our old summerhouse this afternoon."

I took an involuntary step back. "I've got my knitting group, but I suppose I could take you after that," I said. "Where is it?"

"It's Cliffside, of course." She gave me a tight smile. "Didn't John tell you?"

I shook my head, surprised. I knew John had visited the island as a kid, but he'd never mentioned where he'd stayed; I'd assumed it was one of the small houses not far from the pier. Then again, with his attorney father and society mother, it made sense. "I'm not sure Torrone and her agent will want you to come in, though."

She waved my concerns aside. "Oh, I'll talk them into it. Just let me gather my things and I'll meet you downstairs. When are we leaving?"

"In about twenty minutes," I said, dreading the prospect of an afternoon with Catherine. Struggling with yarn was bad enough without my critical mother-in-law on the scene. At least I had an excuse to avoid the knitting, I thought, thinking of the bandage on my hand.

I had gathered my knitting and slipped the tin of cookies into a bag when Catherine appeared in the doorway. She had added a string of pearls to her ensemble, along with a liberal dose of a powdery scent.

"Oh, silly me. I forgot my crocheting!"

As she turned and disappeared behind the door, I jammed one of the frozen cookies into my mouth and chewed hard, then swallowed and followed it with another one. I drew the line at three and brushed the crumbs off my sweater, then stretched plastic wrap over the remaining cookies. At least there would be other people, I told myself. I wouldn't have to carry the conversation alone.

Still . . .

It was a good fifteen minutes before Catherine reappeared with a dainty cloth bag and a black wool coat. "I'm ready when you are!" she trilled. I snuck another cookie from beneath the plastic wrap and followed her out the door to the van. At the rate I was going, I'd be wearing muumuus for Christmas.

It was a quiet ride to Claudette's house — at least from my side of the van. Catherine held forth on a number of subjects, including her favorite lavender soap, the dilapidated appearance of several yards (evidently stacks of lobster traps are not recommended lawn decor), and my business at the inn. Oddly, she avoided any mention of the fake engagement ring.

"Oh, look at that front lawn. It's like a junkyard!" she said, pointing to Eleazer's boatyard. I pulled up outside the house and parked, and she looked startled.

"It's better on the inside than the outside," I told her. As she followed me up onto the porch, I debated whether I was hoping Edward Scissorhands would open the door or not.

Fortunately — or unfortunately, depending on your point of view — Claudette answered just after I knocked, her bulky form dressed in a shapeless but soft wool sweater and a black broomstick skirt, her gray hair pulled back into a thick braid. She and Catherine looked like they came from different universes. I attempted to bridge the gap.

"Hi, Claudette," I said. "This is John's mother, Catherine."

"Delighted to meet you," my future mother-in-law said, extending a claw-like hand. She still wore her whopper of an engagement ring, and I found myself wondering if it was fake, too. "I don't know if we've met, but we used to summer on the island," she said.

"Ah. I think I remember you," Claudette said, smiling. "Your son is a wonderful addition to the island — and I'm so happy for him and Natalie. You must be thrilled for him!"

There was a moment of awkward silence. Then Catherine smiled. "Of course. Thank you. And thank you so much for inviting me to your little knitting group."

Inviting her? I felt my eyebrows shoot up to my hairline, but said nothing.

"I'm glad you could come," Claudette said, opening the door wider for Catherine to step inside. "I'll take your coat for you."

"Thank you," she said. We shrugged out of our coats, and Claudette took them from us. "We're in there," I told Catherine, directing her to the next room.

I held back a moment. "How are Muffin and Pudge?" I asked quietly when she was out of earshot. Despite their reputation for

239

rampaging the gardens of the island — trailing the tire they were chained to behind them — I knew Claudette cherished the goats.

"They'll make it through," she said. The lines in her face seemed deeper than I remembered, and there were dark circles under her eyes.

"I'm sure that's the last thing you need right now. Do you have any idea who attacked them?"

She shook her head grimly. "I thought it might be Ingrid, but I just don't believe she'd do it."

"It's disturbing, isn't it?"

She nodded. "First Fernand, and now this . . ."

Not to mention the disturbed daughter-in-law and the extra children in the house, I added silently. "How's your daughter-in-law doing? She was the life of the party the other night."

Claudette's face seemed to shutter. "It's not one of her better days, I'm afraid," she said.

"If there's anything I can do . . ."

"Thanks, Natalie, but it's a family thing. My son has asked me not to say anything."

"I understand," I said. "Please know we're here to help."

She sighed. "Thanks, but we'll manage." I touched her shoulder in sympathy, and as Claudette disappeared with our coats, I followed Catherine into the living room.

Despite my knitting anxiety, I was happy to see my friends, and delighted to see that Emmeline had contributed chocolate-dipped ginger cookies. The mixture of dark chocolate and crystallized ginger was delicious — and I definitely needed the medicinal chocolate this afternoon. It was a shame Claudette refused to eat sugar; she could use some, too. Everyone but Lorraine Lockhart had turned up today.

In addition to Emmeline, who sat in yet another plaid housedress working on her jellyfish tea cozy, Charlene was next to her on the couch, the beginnings of a fuzzy purple scarf with metallic fringe in her lap. Maggie was there, too, working on a green sweater for one of her children, and looking sulky. As soon as I saw Sara, the new teacher, sitting next to Selene of Island Artists with a mostly complete red wool hat in her hands, I understood why. Charlene glanced at Catherine and shot me a quizzical look, and I realized I hadn't mentioned last night's new arrival. I responded with a look that must have been desperation, and she grinned.

"Catherine, do you want a cup of tea?" I asked, then realized I hadn't introduced her. "I'm so sorry. Has everyone met my future mother-in-law, Catherine?" I asked.

"Of course," Charlene said, giving me another pointed look. "I've heard so much about you!"

Catherine simply smiled at her. "Thank you, my dear. And Natalie, I'd love a cup of tea. Black, please."

"Have a seat," Charlene said, gesturing toward an overstuffed chair next to her as I lifted the tea cozy and poured a cup of tea. As I handed it to John's mother, I noticed the chair was a bit thread-bare on the arms; like the rest of the living room, it would never make any of the shelter magazines, but Claudette's whole house had the comfortable air of being well lived in. There were a few toys in the corner: a Nerf gun, and a stack of blocks. A small Christmas tree stood in the corner, draped in silver tinsel, and a few wrapped presents were tucked under the lower boughs. It was a cozy, homey room. I knew it probably wasn't Catherine's style, but I loved it, and despite my aversion to knitting, I was glad to be here. I pulled my tangled mass of yarn out of the bag and set it on the floor beside my chair, then headed to the coffee table to load up on goodies for myself. Everyone had been behaving so far, but it was good to be prepared.

"Such a shock about Fernand," Selene said as I set another cookie on my plate. She was a vision in red today — on me her handmade wool sweater would have resembled an afghan, but on her it was lovely. "I heard you found him."

"I did," I said, suppressing a shiver at the memory. "It was terrible."

"He killed himself, I heard," Selene said. She shook her head sadly. "You just never know about people, do you? He seemed so happy at the party."

"Do you think he was jealous of that new artist?" Marge asked.

"I heard her paintings go for millions," Emmeline said. "Hard to believe — she's so young!"

"Jealousy," Maggie said. "Maybe the party was just too much."

"And poor Nat had to find him," Charlene said. "You've got a knack for that, you know."

"I know," I said. I'd found far too many dead bodies since moving to Cranberry Island. I shot a glance at Catherine, who appeared to be concentrating on her crochet. I was sure she was taking everything in, though.

"When's the service set for?" asked Emmeline.

"I don't know yet," I said, hoping Father Timothy would be able to sort it out.

"I heard his sister and his boyfriend had it out in front of the rectory," Emmeline said.

I felt my stomach contract as I looked at my friend. "What happened?"

"She called him all kinds of names, and told him he wouldn't get a dime. Said he might as well pack up and go back to Bangor."

"Poor man," I murmured.

"That woman had murder in her eyes, I'm telling you."

"Who can blame her?" Maggie said. "She's family. This boyfriend is nothing."

I glanced at Sara, whose jaw was set, and cast about for a new subject. "Where are the children today, Claudette?"

"Eli took them to the mainland for a while," Claudette said. "Along with their dad."

I was glad to hear she was getting a break — at least from the kids. I wasn't sure about the daughter-in-law. "I hear they're settling into school beautifully," I told Sara, who was still looking upset. "I've heard wonderful things about your teaching."

Maggie huffed from the corner, but no one looked at her; in fact, the pace of gentle clacking seemed to pick up.

"Thank you," Sara said politely, and gave me a brilliant smile. "It's always nice to be appreciated. I hope to be here for a long, long time."

There was an awkward silence, except for the sound of busy needles, and I knew everyone in the room was thinking about the petition. Nice job, Nat. I'd stepped right in the middle of it again.

"How are you enjoying island life?" Claudette asked Catherine, changing the subject yet again. "A far cry from Boston, I imagine."

"Yes, but there's something to be said for the quaint island life," my future mother-in-law said.

That was news to me; from what John had told me, she'd always complained about having to spend time on the island.

"That's what Nina Torrone thinks, too. Hope we don't become the next Kennebunkport," Charlene said.

Sara looked up from her knitting. "Nina Torrone? Who is that?"

"Famous New York artist," Charlene said. "She just moved into the Katzes' old house."

"We used to spend a few months there in the summers," Catherine said. "John just loved it. Natalie is taking me to visit the house after the knitting group."

Charlene goggled at me. "The delicate flower artist's agent okayed that?" she asked, sarcasm lacing her words.

I grimaced. "They don't know we're coming yet."

"Well, good luck getting past the front door. You know, I haven't seen her since the party," Charlene said.

"Is she not coming to the store anymore?" I asked.

"The only time I ever see her is at night," Emmeline piped up. "I've noticed her a few times after dark, when I'm out with the dogs. She walks around the island, all bundled up."

"Terri saw her the other day, too," Sara said. I glanced at Maggie, who was eyeing her with disapproval. The teacher continued on, "She was trying to talk on a cell phone, but you know what the reception is like here."

"What was she saying?" I asked.

"Something about the mail. A letter she hadn't gotten. Terri told me she was practically yelling, and walked away fast when she saw her."

Yelling? "She's been pretty quiet whenever I've seen her," I said.

"Hidden depths, maybe," Charlene said. "Or bad reception. How's Gwen holding up, by the way?"

"Okay," I guess. "It looks like Zelda Chu is going to mentor her."

Charlene groaned. "Well, she's no Fernand, but she's better than that Munger character. At least she doesn't wear plaid pants."

"How's she going to have time to do that?" Selene asked.

"What do you mean?" I asked.

"Word on the street," Charlene said, "is that she and Murray have cooked up a big art school together. They want to make it a summer campus for one of the big New York art schools."

"Gwen said something about that," I said. "They made a proposal to Fernand, but I don't know what it was."

"Fernand told me about it last week," Selene said. "He told me he thought it was a bad idea. I do know that Murray bought a piece of property across the road from Fernand's place." She sighed. "I still can't believe he's gone."

"I know," I said, feeling an ache in my heart for my friend.

"Murray Selfridge is something else. He can't develop that bog he bought a few years ago, but he hasn't given up," Charlene said. "He owns the property across the street from Fernand's, but it doesn't have water access."

"Think he's planning to turn that whole area into an art school?" I asked.

"That's what I heard. And I'll bet he'll make a tidy packet if it goes through," Charlene said.

"Do you think it would be worth enough for him to kill Fernand for?" I said, thinking out loud.

Immediately, every pair of eyes in the room fastened on me.

"What do you mean?" Emmeline said, her sharp eyes fastened on me. "I thought he committed suicide."

"Nothing," I said hastily. "I don't know what I was thinking."

"Do the police think someone murdered him?" Selene asked. Her jeweled glasses sparkled as she turned her head to me.

"Not that I know of. I can't think who would have benefited from it, anyway," I said. "The police are saying it's suicide, from what I know. Still . . . well, it's just hard to understand."

"I can see what you mean," Emmeline

said. "He was a nice man."

"Do you think maybe he was in an illicit love affair?" Charlene asked. She always liked juicy stories.

"He had a boyfriend," I reminded her.

"He had a stalker, too," Selene said.

My head swiveled to look at Selene. "A stalker? Who?"

"I don't know, but it was starting to worry him. He told me he was thinking of going to the police," she said.

"What was the stalker doing?" I asked, thinking of what Frederick had told me. We definitely needed to get over there and check the caller ID.

"Lots of phone calls. Notes. Whoever it was would idle a boat just offshore sometimes at night. For hours."

I could feel my skin crawl. "Creepy."

"He also said whoever it was was trying to peek through the windows."

I ran through the women I knew on the island, trying to think who might have had an obsession with Fernand. Then I realized it might not be a woman.

"Did he have any idea who it was?"

She nodded. "He knew, but he wouldn't say anything. Said he didn't want to ruin anyone's life."

I glanced at Catherine, to see how she was

taking everything in. She was still crocheting, but she glanced up from time to time. I couldn't read the expression on her face.

"Did whoever it was ever tie up the boat and come in from the water?" I asked.

"He didn't say," Selene said. "Why?"

"Just wondering," I said, thinking of the footprints leading to and from the water. I bent down, focusing on the wad of yarn I was pulling out of my bag. The wound on my hand was throbbing.

Emmeline had just begun to say something when there was a low, moaning call from somewhere in the house.

Claudette's face paled, and she stood up quickly.

The voice continued. It was a woman's voice, but eerily childlike. "She's here, isn't she? Patricia is here. You brought her to torture me."

"Excuse me," Claudette said, and hurried to the back of the house.

"She doesn't belong here." The voice was rising into a wail. "She's got to go. Can't you see that? Someone has to stop her."

I heard Claudette's voice, and then another wail from the back of the house. I glanced at Catherine, who had stopped crocheting. Her tweezed eyebrows had risen until they were almost at her hairline.

Everyone looked at each other uneasily.

Selene broke the silence. "Is that her daughter-in-law?"

"I think so," I said quietly.

"What's wrong?" Emmeline asked. "She was so charming at the party the other night."

"I don't know," I said. "But whatever it is, it doesn't sound good."

There was another wail, and then silence, except for the sound of knitting needles.

SIXTEEN

The rest of the knitting session passed without incident, although Claudette spent most of it in the back of the house with Dawn. She was usually a fast knitter, but I noticed she'd been working on the same sweater for weeks now. She must be spending all her time with the children or with her daughter-in-law.

As the group filtered out, several of us offered Claudette help and support, but she politely refused all of it.

"When do you think Eli will be back?" I asked Charlene as we stood outside Claudette's house. Catherine had already gotten into the minivan, but I lingered a moment, despite the cold wind.

"Why?" she asked.

"I'm worried about Claudette — and what happened to their goats."

"You think whoever attacked Muffin and Pudge might go after Claudette?"

"I don't know, but it makes me worry."

"If I see him at the store, I'll tell him to hurry home," Charlene said. She glanced back at the house. A sharp wind kicked up the snow, and it whirled across the porch. "Claudette's daughter-in-law sounds like she's got some serious problems. Is she getting help?"

"I hope so, for Claudette and Eli's sake. That's got to be hard to live with."

"And not great for the kids, either."

I had to agree with her. It must be tough to have a mother who was mentally ill. It was a good thing the children had Claudette and Eli. I glanced at the house again, and a movement caught my eye. Claudette's daughter-in-law had pulled back the curtains and was staring at me, her eyes dark and haunted in her white face. There was something eerily childlike about it. Gooseflesh rose on my arms; then the curtain dropped, and she vanished. "She needs help," I said.

"Claudette? I know."

"The whole family," I said, thinking of the disturbed woman whose face still lingered in my mind like a ghost.

With a heavy heart, I said my goodbyes to Charlene and got into the van. As I turned the vehicle around to head home, Catherine said, "Well, that was interesting. I had no idea there was so much going on here." She settled into her seat, then said, "Ready to go to Cliffside?"

I turned to look at her. "Shouldn't we call first?"

"Do you have her number?"

"No," I confessed. "I don't think anyone does."

"If I remember correctly, people just dropped by all the time when we were here."

"But she's from New York," I said.

"If we can't call, then of course we have to stop by," she said. "What choice do we have?"

I thought about the rest of my afternoon, which was swiftly slipping away. I really didn't want to stop by Cliffside right now — but on the other hand, I was curious about Torrone and her relationship with Fernand. "I've got to swing by the store to pick up my order," I said, "but dinner won't take too long to put together. I think we've got time, but we can't stay long."

I turned left instead of right at the end of Egg Rock Road. The route to the store passed the road to Fernand's, and my heart tightened as we approached the familiar intersection. I had almost reached it when a beaten-up green pickup truck raced up the road, fishtailing as it pulled onto Egg Rock Road just in front of me. I slammed on the brakes and Catherine screamed as I braked and yanked the wheel to the right. The van began to skid, slewing around on the snowy road, and landed with a thud in a snowbank.

I turned to Catherine, who was gripping the armrest of the seat with whitened knuckles. "Are you okay?"

"I think so. Who was that insane driver?" she asked.

"I don't know," I said, thinking that the truck looked familiar. I'd seen it recently; but where? "Charlene will be able to tell me," I said. "She knows what everyone's car looks like."

"People like that shouldn't be allowed to drive," she said.

I opened the door and walked around the van to inspect the damage. Most of the cars here were dented, but my van was used for guests, and I needed it to look at least passably presentable.

The front right corner was embedded in a snowbank, but I didn't see any broken plastic or glass. I swiped at some of the snow; the metal looked smooth and unbuckled. I climbed back in and put the van in reverse; after pumping the gas a few times, we moved backward with a lurch. I shifted into park and got out to inspect the damage. The front bumper had a small new dimple, but other than that, the van was unscathed.

"That was lucky," Catherine said. "Still, you should pursue that driver for the damage. He didn't even stop to give you his insurance information!"

I bit back a laugh. On an island where doors and headlights were strictly optional, insurance was not exactly a priority. I nodded and put the van in drive, wondering about where that driver had been going in such a hurry — and how we were going to be received at the Torrone residence.

It had been years since I'd visited Cliffside, which was perched on a hill with a commanding view of the water and the mainland beyond. With its imposing turret and hilltop position, it had always reminded me a bit of a castle — which was a different look from the rest of the houses on the island. The last residents had experienced family tragedy, and I thought of what Emmeline said: that it was a bad luck house. Was that part of the reason it had been vacant for so long? John's family seemed to have done okay there, though. Maybe it was just because they hadn't stayed long — or maybe it was only a rumor.

The long, curving driveway hadn't been plowed, so I parked at the base of it. Someone had shoveled a path to the door, but it looked steep and slippery. "Are you sure you're up for this?" I asked Catherine.

"Of course," she said. "I'm quite fit."

And she was. By the time I was halfway up the sloping walkway, she was three-quarters of the way to the top and waiting for me.

"How do you stay in such good shape?" I asked, panting.

"Tennis," she said. "And the gym in the winter months, of course."

Not exactly an option here on the island — not that I would have joined anyway. By the time we reached the imposing front door, my face felt as red as a tomato and I was breathing like an asthmatic in a field of ragweed.

"Ready?" Catherine asked, her finger hovering over the doorbell.

"I suppose so," I wheezed, smoothing my hair back with gloved hands.

She jabbed at the doorbell and stood erect in her Burberry coat, looking like the Boston Brahmin matron that she was. I searched for traces of John in her, but other than the brilliant green eyes and the tilt of her chin, there was little to link them together. I wondered how it was that they were so different, and wished I'd had the opportunity to meet John's father. He had died of a heart attack the year before I met John.

When nobody answered, she drew herself up and rang again. We stood for a long moment, waiting in the cold. I was about to suggest we give up when there was a click, and the door opened a few inches. Nina Torrone peered out. Without her sunglasses, she looked terribly young.

My future mother-in-law's face broke into a polite smile. "I am so very sorry to disturb you," she said. "We would have called first, but your number isn't listed."

"What do you want?"

"Again, I am terribly sorry to disturb you this way. I know solitude is so important for artists, and I hate to intrude . . . but I was hoping you could do me a tiny little favor."

Nina's eyes narrowed. "What?"

Catherine sighed. "Years ago, my family and I used to spend our summers in this house . . . it's always been a favorite respite for me." I blinked at her; from what John had told me, she hated the island. "Anyway," she continued, "I am visiting my son on the island — John Quinton, he's also an artist, although not nearly as accomplished as you

— and I was hoping I might have a chance to take a look at the place. We have so many golden memories here," she said with a radiant smile. "It would kill me to go home without visiting the house again."

Nina hesitated, but opened the door an inch more.

"It's frigid out here!" Catherine said. "Hard on my old bones." I resisted the urge to roll my eyes; I'd just witnessed her "old bones" pumping up the hill at top speed. I had to hand it to her, though; she was giving a command performance. "Although being from New York, you must be used to cold weather. I promise we'll only be a minute, and we won't disturb you at all. And we won't tell anyone you let us in."

"I'm not supposed to . . . I mean, we don't have visitors." But she opened the door a few inches more.

"Oh, thank you, dear, for making an exception," Catherine said, and took a step forward. Reflexively, Nina opened the door wider, and before she could protest, we were in.

The entry hall was just as I remembered it from when the Katzes were in residence; even the furniture was the same, although the front hall table was covered with a thin film of dust. The house was cold, and had a deserted feel to it. Nina Torrone stood blinking in the middle of it, her fashionable attire of the party replaced by jeans and an NYU sweatshirt. Her hair was mussed, as if she had just woken up, and she looked incredibly young.

"Thanks so much for letting us take a look at the house," I said. "Is your agent here?"

"Uh, no . . . but he'll be back soon." She glanced around nervously, reminding me not of an accomplished artist, but of a teenager whose parents would be returning at any moment. "I guess you can look around, but you'll have to go fast. You should probably not be here when he gets back."

"This room looks almost identical to the way it was when we stayed here!" Catherine said, moving past us into the living room. "I like this rug better, though. The blues bring out the color of the walls. Wonderful view, don't you think?" she asked as she looked out over the panoramic view of the dock and the island beyond. "Not as nice as from the back porches, though. Natalie, my dear, I'm surprised you didn't snap this place up for your inn."

"It wasn't for sale," I said. In truth, I much preferred the Gray Whale Inn's classic cape lines to the faux majesty of Cliffside. The views were lovely, though. Not that that was what interested me.

Although the decor of the room was formal, with a rich Oriental rug and stylish chairs, the coffee table was littered with tabloid magazines and empty coffee cups. A manila envelope similar to the one I'd seen Gladstone and Torrone pick up at the store was open on the couch, beside a stack of what looked to be bills and letters. Nina spotted them at the same time I did, and hurried over to scoop them up.

"So hard to get good help, isn't it?" Catherine said with an understanding tone of voice. "I understand you're here to focus on your work. Which room are you using for your studio?"

She froze, hugging the pile of correspondence to her chest. "It's upstairs," she said.

"Can I see?"

"No!" she blurted. "No, no, no. You shouldn't be here at all. I have to ask you to leave now."

"But we've only just arrived," Catherine said. "I'll only be a minute." And with that regal way of hers, she swept past Nina into the kitchen. The young artist and I trailed after her

"Sorry about that," I murmured to the distressed artist. "She's kind of a force of nature."

"As long as she stays downstairs," Nina said. I stole a glance at the papers as she stuffed them into a drawer. One of them appeared to be a utility bill; New York Power and Light was emblazoned at the top of the page. Why did she feel the need to hide that? I wondered.

"I understand you and Fernand knew each other," I said as we watched Catherine admire the view from the kitchen window. Like the living room, this room was full of dirty dishes and stacks of newspapers — only in this room, it was the *New York Times.* Apparently Nina and her agent had widely differing reading tastes — or they had designated different rooms for different periodicals.

"Not really," she said.

"But you studied under the same artist," I said.

A hand darted up to her face. The nails were polished a bright pink, and there was no stray paint on her hands. Either she was an unusually neat painter, or the art retreat wasn't going as well as expected. Had she come here because she was undergoing an artistic crisis?

"Fernand and I hardly knew each other," she said.

"Still, it must have been upsetting to learn that he had died."

That was enough to make her find her resolve. "You really must be going now," she said. "I never should have let you in."

"All right," Catherine sighed. "It has been a nice trip down memory lane. Very different in winter, though. More stark, somehow." She surveyed the living room, then turned her critical eye on Nina. "You really should make your agent take better care of you. He should earn his 15 percent, don't you think?"

Nina Torrone's eyes widened in fear. I wondered again what their relationship was.

"I'm sure Natalie could help you find some good household help, if you need it. She's at the Gray Whale Inn — I'm sure she wouldn't mind if you stopped by sometime."

"You have to leave now," she said, all but running to the front door. A cold blast of wind came through as she threw it open. "Goodbye."

"I'm sorry to have disturbed you," Catherine said as she breezed through the door, her leather-soled boots clicking on the parquet floor. "Thank you again."

The door slammed behind us, and John's mother looked at me. "She's terrified of him," she said, and began to head down the path.

"Why?" I asked, hurrying after her.

"I don't know," she said. "But she certainly didn't want to invite us up to her studio, did she?"

"No, she didn't,"

She said nothing else until we had reached the minivan. I turned the van around and headed back down the road, passing Gladstone, who was huffing with a *New York Times* under one arm and a bag of groceries in the other.

"Do you think they're having an affair?" I asked.

"No," she said. "I'd know the signs of that." There was a bitterness in her voice that I'd never heard before.

"Why did you want to visit the house?" I asked.

She stared straight ahead. "Because the last summer we stayed there was the last time John's father and I were happy together."

SEVENTEEN

It was a quiet ride back to the inn. I stopped briefly at the store to pick up my food order — Charlene wasn't there, but her niece Tania helped me load up the van — before turning the van toward home. I wanted to ask more about what had happened after that last summer at Cliffside, but could sense her closing up as quickly as she'd revealed herself. She excused herself as soon as we got back into the inn, leaving me with several crates of groceries and as many unanswered questions.

As I put away a box of mushrooms, I glanced at the clock. I was dying to go over to Fernand's house with Frederick and see if we could find out who had been making harassing phone calls, but I needed to get dinner started. I also wanted to check in with John.

Once I got the groceries stowed, I ran up to check on Gwen, who was painting in the

Crow's Nest. She looked miserable, and the canvas she was struggling with didn't look much better, but I said a few encouraging words before closing the door behind me. I grabbed a coat and headed down to John's workshop, but he wasn't there — or in the carriage house, either. As I headed back up the path, I found myself wondering what to do with the little house. We could rent it out as a summer place . . . or John could keep it for himself. Would it be better if we both moved in there? I sighed and pushed the thoughts from my head. We had enough to deal with without adding more complications to the equation.

I jogged back up the path to the inn, did a last check to make sure I had the dinner prep taken care of, and checked my messages; John told me he'd be in late and would hitch a ride from the dock, and the new attorney had called to confirm an appointment tomorrow. Feeling more hopeful that at least some progress was being made on the mortgage front, I pushed through the swinging door to the public portion of the inn.

As it turned out, I didn't need to knock on Frederick's door; he was sitting on the sofa in the parlor, gazing moodily at the fire.

"How did it go with Father Timothy?" I

asked, sitting down across from him.

He barely glanced at me. "That witch showed up," he said. "She wants everything. The memorial service, the house . . . the whole shebang."

"Was he able to calm her down?" I asked.

He snorted. "He kept suggesting we work together, but she rejected it out of hand. She told him she'd have the service back in Bangor if he kept giving her a hard time."

"I'm so sorry," I said.

He shrugged. "What can you do?" Despite the light words, I could hear the despair in his voice. "At least I have the key to his house."

I blinked in surprise. "She doesn't?"

"Why would she? She hasn't seen him in years."

I thought of the mail boat card I'd seen in her room. "Did Fernand tell you that?" I asked.

"He told me she hadn't been in touch with him since he moved to the island."

I didn't contradict him, but filed that bit of information away. Why had she been on the island recently? And why hadn't Fernand mentioned it to Frederick?

"So," he said, standing up and giving himself a shake, as if trying to discard Fernand's sister's words. "Shall we go and see if we can find out who Fernand's secret admirer was?"

"If you're up for it," I said.

"I am," he said grimly. "As long as that woman isn't in the car with us. He drove us both back to the inn, you know."

"That can't have been pleasant."

"It wasn't," he said, and left it at that.

Evening had begun to fall as we pulled up outside of Fernand's house. The Christmas lights still dangled from the trees outside the gallery, and the wreath still hung on the front door, its red ribbon flapping in the wind. My heart ached, knowing my friend would never celebrate Christmas again.

Frederick, too, was feeling the wash of emotion, and swiped at his eyes as I put the van in park and turned the ignition off. "Ready?" I asked.

He nodded, and together we marched up to the front door, Frederick fumbling with his keys.

The house was almost as cold inside as out, and a breeze pushed through the front hallway, almost tearing the doorknob from Frederick's hand. "It's not locked," he said, pushing the door open.

"Did you turn the heat off?" I asked as he switched on a light.

"No," he said. A breeze gusted, and the door slammed itself shut behind us, making us both jump. "Why is it so cold in here?"

My feet crunched on something as I took a step back. Frederick and I both looked down: broken glass.

"Somebody broke the window," he said.

"Somebody broke into the house," I corrected. "That's why the front door was open." The glass had been knocked clean out of the sidelight, which is why I hadn't noticed it initially. I felt a shiver course through me. If Fernand had killed himself, why would someone feel the need to break in?

Frederick evidently had the same thought. "What would someone be looking for that they needed to break in?" he asked. "Unless it was that sister of his."

I turned toward the living room and gasped. The couches had been pulled apart, the floor was littered with pillows, and the books had been pulled from the bookshelf and lay scattered across the rug.

"No," Frederick said, his hand to his mouth. "No, no, no." Tears welled in his eyes. "Fernand would have hated this."

"We'll put it back in order after we call the police," I said, putting a hand on his shoulder. "Whoever it was was looking for

269

something. Can you go with me and tell me if you notice anything missing?" I asked.

"I . . . I'll do my best," he said.

"Thank you, Frederick. I know how hard this must be for you."

He nodded and followed me into the living room. Automatically, he bent to pick up a book; I touched his shoulder again.

"Try not to touch anything. The detectives may want to dust for fingerprints."

He straightened, but his shoulders were slumped. The chaos was bothering both of us; it felt like a desecration of Fernand's space. When Frederick ascertained that he couldn't tell if anything was missing, we moved on, both feeling jumpy. We walked into Fernand's study; the neat stack of papers had been shuffled through and left in a messy pile on the floor.

"There's a phone," Frederick said in a hoarse voice, pointing to the handset on the desk. "Can we touch that at least? To check the calls?"

"I have gloves," I said, pulling my wool gloves out of my pockets and slipping them on to turn the phone over gingerly. I pushed the button for recent calls; the first number that popped up had a 202 area code.

"Do you have a piece of paper?" I asked.

"No, but there's a blank one here," he

said, stooping down to pick up a sheet that had drifted free, but he froze before he touched it. "Do you think it's okay to pick it up and use it?"

"If whoever did this left prints, there will be enough on other things, probably," I said, looking around at the messy room. I plucked a pen from the mug on the back of Fernand's desk — I couldn't imagine the intruder had fingered the Bic pens — and jotted down times, dates, and numbers as I scrolled through the calls. There was only one 202 area code, which I recognized as New York, and it had come the day of the party. Torrone's agent? I wondered. The others were all from Maine. A few were from the island — I recognized the phone numbers — but many were from elsewhere. His sister in Bangor, perhaps?

And then there was the most frequent caller: Blocked. Blocked, blocked, blocked, blocked. Whoever it was had called repeatedly, though; up to fifteen times in a row. I marked down the times and dates until the phone history ran out. Whoever it was had called 65 times over a three-day period. The last call was the evening of the party; there were none after it. Was it because the caller was the killer, and knew Fernand was dead? A chill ran up my spine.

"Looks like we found Fernand's secret admirer," Frederick said.

"Too bad he knows star 69," I said. I wrote down the last number and looked up from the phone. "Do you have any idea where Fernand might have kept the letters the mystery person sent?"

"If he kept them at all," Frederick said. "Fernand might well have burned them. He didn't appreciate the attention."

I surveyed the room. "Whoever broke in was looking for something."

"The letters?"

"Maybe. I wish I knew," I said, pocketing the paper with the numbers.

We searched the rest of the house, but found nothing incriminating. Whoever had broken in had been very thorough; every room had been torn apart. As we entered the bedroom, Frederick blanched. "It's a desecration," he said, looking at the dresser. The drawers had been pulled out and dumped, and Fernand's cashmere sweaters were scattered like used towels on the floor. I glanced at Frederick; his face was white, and he looked as if he might be sick. He picked up one of the sweaters and brought it to his nose. "I bought this for him for his birthday," he said, touching the soft wool as if it were Fernand himself.

"I'm so sorry," I said.

"Can I keep it?"

"I can't think why not," I said. "Do you see anything missing?" I asked gently.

"Just Fernand," he said miserably.

The smell of sautéing bacon and garlic filled the inn when Frederick and I got back a while later. Frederick returned to his room, still holding Fernand's sweater, and I walked into the kitchen to find John at the stove.

"Smells great in here," I said as he added butter to the pan.

"Where were you?" he asked, worry creasing his forehead.

"Frederick and I went over to Fernand's house. Someone had turned the place upside-down." I hung my coat on the hook by the door and pulled up a chair at the table. Biscuit abandoned her post on the radiator and crossed the floor to leap up onto my lap.

"A break-in?" John put down the spatula and turned to face me.

I nodded, stroking the purring cat. "Whoever it was broke the window next to the door."

"When did you arrive?" he asked.

"Just a few minutes ago."

"Was there anything missing?"

"Not that Frederick or I could tell." I rubbed behind Biscuit's ears, and she purred louder. "Frederick told me Fernand had a secret admirer; we were wondering if he might have something to do with what happened to Fernand. I checked the phone and wrote down all the callers for the last several days," I said, pulling the piece of paper from my back pocket.

John took it from me and scanned it, frowning. "Until we get this sorted out, I don't want you to go anywhere alone with Frederick," he said. "Or with Fernand's sister." Then, before I could ask more, he continued. "What's all this about a secret admirer? Gwen didn't say anything about it."

"Frederick mentioned it." The pan on the stove sizzled loudly. "You'd better check on the food," I said, and he put down the paper and picked up the spatula.

"Any other evidence of this admirer?" he asked as he stirred garlic into the pan.

I scratched Biscuit under her chin. "Somebody called a lot — but blocked his number."

"How do you know it's a man?"

"According to Frederick, Fernand told him it was a man."

John made a skeptical noise. "We don't

274

even know if Fernand and Frederick were still together. It could be that Frederick was the caller."

I thought of Frederick, cradling Fernand's sweater as if it were the most precious thing in the world. Had Fernand broken up with him? Was Frederick desperate to get him back — and had he perhaps killed Fernand when he wouldn't continue to see him? Biscuit gave a rumbling purr, then meowed to remind me to continue petting her.

"Did Fernand say anything to anyone else about this admirer?" John asked.

"Selene of Island Artists mentioned something about a stalker today at Winter Knitters. She said Fernand was thinking about talking to the police about it."

"I'll have to pass that on to Detective Penney," he said, giving the onions he'd just added a stir.

"You never told me how it went on the mainland," I said.

"I dropped off the doll and the blood sample," he said. "I talked with Detective Penney, too. The toxicology reports came back."

I paused with my cookie halfway to my mouth. "And?"

"Ativan and alcohol in his system," he said.

"Did he have a prescription for Ativan?"

"No." John added mushrooms to the pan, making the kitchen smell heavenly. "They have a copy of the will, now, too."

"Who inherits?"

"Fernand changed it six months ago. The old version left everything to his sister, but the new one changed everything."

"Who did he leave the house to, then?" I asked, leaning forward as Biscuit, tired of being petted, leaped off my lap.

"Frederick."

"So they were still together?"

"They were last summer, at least," John said. "A lot can happen in a few months." He added a handful of sliced carrots to the pan. "Frederick wasn't the only one in the will, though."

"No?"

"He left the studio and gallery to Gwen," John said.

I sat back and let out a low whistle. "Does she know?"

"I hope not," John said. "Because if she does, she might be a murer suspect."

EIGHTEEN

"Are you saying they're reopening the investigation?" I asked, stunned.

"It looks like he was unconscious at the time he slit his wrists." John grimaced. "His death is now considered a homicide."

"Gwen was right, then," I said.

"Seems that way. They're sealing the house this afternoon and will be questioning people again tomorrow.

I sat up straight. "My fingerprints are on the door."

"Did you touch anything else?"

"Once I figured out the house had been broken into, no," I said, thinking back to our visit to the house. I had put my gloves on before touching the phone, and hadn't taken them off.

"Good."

"What you said about Gwen being a suspect. Do you really think she is one?"

"They'll consider everyone," he said.

"She's told everyone she thought it was murder from the beginning. Shouldn't that count for something?"

"One would hope so," he said. "I don't know much about this detective."

"Have you told Gwen yet?"

"I wanted to talk to you first," he said. "And get this chicken in the oven."

"Anything I can do to help?"

"You got bread, right?"

"Came over from Little Notch Bakery on the mail boat."

"We'll make a salad right before dinner and cook up a pot of noodles, and I think we're set."

"Dessert?"

"I defrosted a cheesecake." He pointed to the creamy round cake on the counter.

"You're amazing," I told him, breaking off a piece of cookie and nibbling at it.

"Of course, my mother won't touch it."

Catherine. I'd almost forgotten about her. "Would you believe your mother got us into Cliffside today?"

"Why?"

"For old time's sake. You never told me that was where you stayed!"

He shrugged. "I guess it didn't seem important. Mother always complained about the house — I'm surprised she

278

wanted to go back to see it."

I sucked in my breath. "She told me it was the last place she and your father were happy," I said.

John ran a hand through his sandy hair and leaned against the counter. "What the heck does that mean?"

"I don't know. She clammed up after that," I said.

"They never were particularly happy, from what I can remember." John shook his head. "My father wasn't home much, and my mother was always off at society luncheons or benefits."

"Where was your father?" I asked, inhaling the scent of garlic as the pan sizzled.

"Working. The only time we really spent together as a family was when we were in Maine."

"Maybe that's what she meant," I said.

Before we could take the conversation further, Gwen pushed through the door, her shoulders slumped. "It's useless," she said.

"What is?" I asked.

"This whole art thing. I'm meeting with Mr. Munger tomorrow, and I know he's going to hate all of my paintings. And with Fernand gone . . ." She slumped into the chair next to mine. "Maybe my mother's right, and I should go back to California."

"I think you're being too hard on yourself," I said, reaching out to rub her back. "I think the change in medium is the problem."

"I just don't know anymore, Aunt Nat. With Fernand gone . . ."

"I believe in you," John said. "And Fernand did, too." He lifted the last pieces of chicken out of the pan and turned to face Gwen. "In fact, he believed in you enough that he left you his studio."

Gwen sat up straight. "He *what*?"

"It's in his will," I said. "He left the studio to you. He wouldn't have done that if he didn't believe in you."

As she sat looking stunned, John added, "The police finally believe you, too."

She was quiet for a moment, then comprehension dawned. "You mean . . ."

"They believe Fernand was murdered," John said.

"I knew it," she said. "I knew he didn't kill himself." Then she put her head down on the table and burst into tears.

Detective Penney arrived the next morning, just after I finished serving breakfast to Frederick and Irene. Catherine stayed in the kitchen, eating a thimbleful of plain oatmeal and looking fidgety. I didn't know if it was because of what she'd told me yesterday or because of the jeweler's appraisal of the ring; we hadn't discussed it since. She had been surprised by the appraisal, but not shocked, or even guilty, I decided. What was going on with her?

Irene and Frederick had sat on opposite ends of the dining room. While Irene had made quite a dent in the French toast casserole, Frederick, as usual, hadn't touched much. Was it guilt over murdering Fernand? I wondered. Or grief? Despite John's warning, I was tempted to believe the latter. Although it could, as he suggested, be both.

Irene was a puzzle, too. If she had loved her brother, she was hiding it well; she seemed tense, but not grief-stricken, although Father Timothy had told me once that different people expressed grief in different ways. Had she heard about the will yet? I wondered as I filled her coffee cup with dark French Roast coffee. If not, I wished I could be a fly on the wall when she learned about the change her brother had made. I thought again about the mail boat ticket in her room. When had she been on the island? Again, I wished I had a photo of her to show to George McLeod; he remembered faces pretty well, and would likely be able to tell me if and when he'd seen her.

I had just returned to the kitchen and asked Catherine if she'd like a little more oatmeal when the front doorbell rang. I passed through the dining room and hurried to the front door of the inn.

"Good morning," Detective Penney said when I opened the door, her thin mouth in a polite smile. Her face was all sharp angles and planes, but her brown eyes were kind. Next to her stood a young man in police blues.

"Are you here about Fernand?" I asked.

"Yes," she said. "We'd like to ask you and your guests a few more questions."

"John mentioned there'd been a change in the status of the case," I said. A gust of wind blew a flurry of ice crystals at us, and I invited them in. "Any word back yet on the doll or the fake blood?" I asked as I closed the door behind them.

"The lab is working on that," Penney said. "We'll let you know as soon as we hear anything."

"Thank you," I said.

"Now. I understand Frederick Johnson and Irene LaChaise are both staying at the inn." When I nodded, she asked, "Are they here this morning?"

"Right this way," I said, leading them to

the dining room.

As we walked into the room, Frederick looked up first. There was a flash of surprise, then relief. Either he was a very good actor, I thought, or he was innocent. I looked at Irene, who was facing away from the door. She turned and looked; like Frederick, the first expression was surprise, but there was another emotion that flickered across her face so fast I almost missed it.

It was fear.

"Good morning, everyone," Detective Penney said. "I'm sorry to disturb your breakfast, but there's been a change in status in the case of Fernand LaChaise's death, and we'd like to ask you a few questions."

"What do you mean?" Irene voice was shrill.

"We are considering it a homicide," the detective said.

Both Frederick and Irene looked shocked.

"I'll be talking to you one at a time. Do you have a room we can use?" the policewoman asked me.

"Of course," I said. "You can take one of the guest rooms."

"We'll also be needing fingerprints," she said, nodding toward her partner, who was eyeing the buffet table.

"No problem. Can I get you a cup of coffee?" I offered, and they both accepted. "You're welcome to help yourselves to breakfast, as well," I added.

"Thank you," Detective Penney said, "I think we may take you up on that; we didn't get a chance to stop for breakfast." She hesitated before continuing. "I'll also have to talk to you and your niece. We'll need fingerprints, too."

My heart contracted, but I smiled. "I'll let her know," I said.

"Actually I'd prefer if you didn't," she said.

"I understand," I said, feeling sick, and retreated to the front desk to get the key to one of the guest rooms. I gave it to her a minute later, telling her where the Beach Rose was located. "I have to leave by 9:30," I told her. "I have an appointment on the mainland."

"I'm sure it won't take that long," she told me with a sympathetic smile that did nothing to ease my nervousness. I retreated to the kitchen, where John was pouring himself a cup of coffee.

"Good morning," he said, a smile making his eyes crinkle in the way that made my heart melt.

"Detective Penney is here," I told him in

284

a low voice. "She wants fingerprints — and she wants to talk with Gwen."

He read my concern in my face. "It'll be fine, Natalie," he said, coming over to give me a hug. As I let him wrap his arms around me, I looked over his shoulder and saw my future mother-in-law watching us with a look of sadness in her eyes.

"I hope you're right," I said, averting my eyes from the look on Catherine's face. "I hope you're right."

Detective Penney had just begun questioning Gwen when John and I fired up the van and headed for the pier. Despite multiple scrubbings, my fingertips were still black with ink. I'd told them about Frederick's and my visit to Fernand's house; I only hoped they'd believe me. I was thankful Gwen hadn't gone upstairs; they might suspect her, but they would find no trace of her beyond the downstairs of Fernand's house. When I told Detective Penney that it was Gwen who insisted he was murdered, she simply wrote it down and asked me another question — which was not encouraging, despite John's assurances that my niece would be okay.

"So, who do you think killed him?" I asked John as we crested the hill behind the inn.

"Frederick stood to benefit from his death," he said.

"As did Gwen."

"True, but we know it wasn't her. His sister may have believed she was in the will, too," he said.

"She's been on the island in the past few months," I told him.

"How do you know?"

"I found a mail boat ticket in her room."

He shot me a sideways glance. "Natalie . . ."

"It was on the dresser," I said. "I didn't open any drawers or anything."

He didn't look convinced, but let it drop as he parked the van near the pier and opened the door. I zipped up my coat and followed him down to the pier, grabbing the hand he held out to me. In my other hand, I clutched the envelope with all of my mortgage paperwork in it. I said a small prayer that we'd find a solution to the problem today — or at least something to give me peace of mind.

The mail boat arrived just as we reached the dock, and George McLeod smiled as he hustled us aboard. "A bit of chop this morning; hope you don't get seasick too easy!" he said. I lurched to the side as the boat shifted under me; George, on the other hand, looked as if he were standing on dry land.

"Not too many people this morning!" I said; we were the only ones on the boat.

"Slows down a lot in the winter," he said as he handed off the mail bag to Tania, who had followed us down the pier.

"My aunt wants you to call her," she told me when she spotted me, giving me a big, lip-glossed smile. Like her aunt, she was a magnet for the island's men.

"Tell her I'll stop by later," I said. "Lots to catch up on."

"That's why she wants you to call her!" Tania said, retreating up the wheelhouse with the bag.

George cast off the ropes, and John and I hurried to the seats closest to the front, which were the most sheltered from the wind. The mail boat captain took his place behind the wheel of the boat a moment later, propelling the boat forward over the waves.

Even with the cold, the exhilaration of being on the water filled my heart. I reached for John's hand and squeezed it, breathing in the heady aroma of salt and fish and snow and fuel.

"How's your niece holding up?" George asked as the boat bobbed up and down, cutting a frothy wake behind it.

"As well as can be expected," I said.

"Heard they're saying it's murder now," he said. "Saw the police launch at the dock."

"Looks like it," I said. I thought again of Irene and the ticket on her dresser. "George, do you know what Fernand's sister looks like?"

"Don't know," he said.

"She was on the boat a couple of days ago," I said. "About my height, slender, blue eyes like Fernand."

"Short red hair?" he asked.

"That's the one," I said. "Have you seen her before?"

"Not in a few weeks," he said.

I glanced at John, who raised his eyebrows. "When was she here last?"

"Just before Thanksgiving," he said. "Didn't talk much. I tried to engage her in conversation, you know, but she seemed like the quiet type."

"How long was she here?"

"I dropped her off on the ten o'clock, and picked her up in time for lunch."

"I don't imagine she mentioned why she was here."

"Nope," he said, steering the boat slightly to the left.

"Had she been here before?"

"Might have been, in the summer, but we get lots of folks then, so I wouldn't necessarily remember."

"She wasn't here the night of the party, was she?"

"You mean the night Fernand died?" he asked.

"Exactly." I shivered, remembering Fernand, and John put his arm around me. I leaned into him as George answered.

"I don't remember seeing her, but there were a lot of folks over from the mainland that night. Do you think she might be mixed up in her brother's murder?"

"I wish I knew," I said gloomily.

"Did Fernand ever find out who was sending him all those notes?" George asked.

"You know about that?"

"Ayuh." He nodded. "Fernand told me to keep an eye out as I made my rounds."

"For what?" I asked.

"Said someone in a skiff kept idling out near his house."

I thought of the footprints John and I had seen in the snow, leading to and from the water.

"Did you ever see anyone?" John asked, leaning forward.

"I spotted the skiff a time or two," he said, "but only after dark."

"So you don't know who it was," I said.

"No, but I can see why Fernand didn't like it. Apparently whoever it was came ashore a couple of times at night, was peeking through the windows."

"Did Fernand say who he thought it might be?"

George rearranged his cap and shook his head. "Never breathed a word. I asked him once, but he wouldn't tell me."

"I wonder why not," John mused, and we both looked back toward the island — and Fernand's house, which was rapidly disappearing into the distance.

"I'm afraid you're not the only one he defrauded, Ms. Barnes," Marina Zapp said as she pushed a stack of paperwork toward me. The tall attorney wore jeans and a casual blazer, but I knew she had been one of Boston's top legal minds before she decided to move to Maine. "He made off with millions."

"And he's disappeared completely," I said.

"Skipped town," she said, shaking her head. "Probably in the Cayman Islands by now."

So much for Colorado. I slumped in my chair, feeling as if she had just punched me.

"What can we do about it?" John asked,

his voice calm and composed. Just hearing his voice steadied me.

"I called the mortgage company; the bad news is, they've accelerated the loan payments so that the entire balance is due."

My stomach dropped to the vicinity of my ankles. "I thought it was only $15,000."

"No longer," Marina said, with a grimace. "The good news is, I can probably talk them down, given the circumstances."

"What about the funds the new company sent?"

"They'll have to go after Forester to get them," she said.

"So I'm not responsible for that?"

"The funds were never in your account."

That was some consolation. "What's our next step?" John asked, leaning forward.

"We'll probably have to pay the fees," she said, "and we may not get back the money you've paid over the last several months. I can't make any promises, but I think if you can handle the $15,000, you'll probably be okay."

Relief flooded me, followed by a second wave of panic. Where was I going to come up with that kind of money?

John didn't hesitate. "I've got it covered," he said.

I turned to look at him. "Are you sure?" I

asked, warmth flooding my heart.

"Absolutely," he said, and reached over to squeeze my hand. He turned to the attorney. "When will you know what the mortgage company says?"

"I'll call this afternoon," she said. "It's a good thing you got in touch with me when you did; you're not the only one going through this — and not everyone will be as fortunate."

"You mean they'll be foreclosed on?"

She grimaced. "I'm doing what I can, but it's a mess."

We stepped out of her office feeling as if a weight had been lifted from our shoulders — not completely, but at least in part. Zelda Chu was in the waiting room, looking pale and drawn. "Hi, Zelda," I said. "I heard about your offer to Gwen. Thank you so much for supporting her."

She gave a quick nod, but said nothing. What was she doing here? I wondered.

"We didn't see you on the mail boat this morning," John said.

"I came over earlier," she said. "I had to visit with a gallery owner."

"Ms. Chu?" Marina said from the doorway behind us.

We said our goodbyes, and Zelda entered the room we had just left, looking as if she was going to the executioner.

"Do you think she got caught by Forester, too?" I asked as we stepped out of the small converted house into the crisp December air. I'd barely noticed the Christmas lights and slender icicles festooning the shop fronts when we arrived; now that I knew Marina thought we would keep the inn, I felt like the world was sparkling.

"I don't know, but I'm sure Charlene will find out," John said.

"What if she did, and she can't be Gwen's mentor?" I asked.

"We'll deal with that if and when it comes," he said.

I snuggled into him as we walked down the street, thankful for his warm presence. A small tree glowed in an upstairs window, and I thought of the inn. "We still haven't gotten a Christmas tree," I said.

"Or lunch," he pointed out. "My treat."

"I don't think so," I said. "You just agreed to pony up 15K to bail me out."

"In a few months, it'll all be coming from the same account," he said, leaning down to kiss the top of my head. "What would you say to some pizza?"

"I'd say that sounds terrific," I said. As much as I loved to cook, I'd never mastered the kind of chewy crust I loved — and Rosalie's did a great job of it. Together we started toward the pizza place, which was one of the few restaurants open in Bar Harbor during December.

"What are we going to do about the carriage house?" I asked as we turned onto Cottage Street.

"I hadn't thought about it," he said. "I've enjoyed living there, but it might make more sense to rent it out. And it might be more comfortable for you to stay in the inn."

"We've got room in the inn for the books," I said. "But do you want to keep your own space?"

"I have my workshop," he said. "If we rent it out, we can pay down the mortgage faster."

"It's worth thinking about," I said as we arrived at Rosalie's. He opened the door for me, and my stomach rumbled as I entered the garlic-scented restaurant.

"Would you rent it out for the whole summer, or by the week?"

"We should talk to a real estate agent," he said. We ordered a large sausage and mushroom pizza and sat in a booth by the window, enjoying the bustle. "We still need to pick out a ring for you, too," he said.

"I have a ring," I said.

"It's not real, though." John reached for

my hands. "I'm so sorry about that."

"It's not your fault," I said.

"Still." He grimaced. "I've asked my mother about it twice, and she refuses to discuss it."

"Why?" I asked, taking a sip of my Diet Coke.

"There's something she's not telling me," he said, a furrow forming between his sandy brows. "And it's about something more than the ring."

"Do you think she's ill?"

"She looks healthy enough," he said. "But it's hard to tell." He sighed. "I'll ask her about it again tonight. Too bad she doesn't drink . . . it might help loosen her up a bit."

The pizza arrived at that moment, steaming and fragrant, and we forgot about our cares and dug in. It was the best meal I'd had in weeks.

I was still feeling a warm glow when we stepped off the mail boat almost two hours later. The glow dissipated immediately when Charlene rushed up to us, her face pale.

"What's wrong?" I asked.

"It's Gwen," she said. "Somebody attacked her."

NINETEEN

"Where is she?" John asked.

"They flew her to the hospital on the mainland," Charlene said. "She was unconscious."

"Is she going to be okay? Who was it?" The words tumbled out of my mouth. Gwen. Attacked. My heart squeezed in my chest. "Where was she?"

"Munger found her in the studio," Charlene said, the wind whipping her words away. "I don't know what happened, but it was a head injury of some sort." She almost had to yell to be heard. "Adam went with her to the mainland."

"We have to go back," I said, feeling my knees turn to water. I turned to wave down George McLeod, but he had already pulled away from the dock. "What now? The next boat isn't for three hours!"

"I'll take you in the skiff," John said, his voice firm.

"But the waves . . ." I looked at the white caps. John's skiff was no match for some of the waves we'd just crossed.

"We'll be fine," he said. "I've been sailing for twenty years; I know what I'm doing. Let's move out of the wind for a moment," he said, shepherding us off the dock to the side of the building where it was still windy, but not strong enough to blow us over. He turned to Charlene. "Were the police notified?"

"They were still at the inn," my friend told him. "They came over immediately."

"When we get back, I'll see what I can find out from the detective."

"I have to call my sister and tell her," I said, feeling racked with guilt. If only I'd kept a better eye on Gwen . . .

"Do you know the phone number?" Charlene asked.

I nodded.

"Let's go to the store. It's closer than the inn."

"You go with Charlene. I'll get the skiff and meet you back here," John said. He squeezed my gloved hand and headed to the van, while I went with Charlene to her pickup truck.

It was only a few minutes from the dock to the store. The snowy landscape that had looked so enchanting just a few minutes earlier now looked bleak. I dreaded the phone call; Bridget had been against Gwen staying on the island, and I'd talked her into it. Had that been a terrible mistake?

Charlene walked beside me as I headed to the back of the shop; a hush fell over the conversation as we passed the lobstermen at the counter. News traveled fast, I knew.

My friend shut the door of the back room tight and handed me the phone. "Are you going to be okay?" she asked.

"It depends on Gwen."

"I mean calling your sister."

"It's got to be done," I said. I picked up the phone and dialed my sister's cell number. There was no answer, so I left a message for her to call me at the inn and hung up. I felt both guilt and relief; because I had no cell phone, she couldn't reach me.

"Let's get back to the dock," I said. "John will be there soon."

I could feel eyes on me as we walked through the store, but I ignored them. When we stepped outside, I noticed a familiar green truck parked in one of the six spots. "Whose is that?" I asked, jabbing a finger at it.

"Belongs to Rob Perkins, one of the lobstermen. He's a single guy, originally from

Ellsworth. Helps out on Ernie's boat."

I remembered the truck peeling out of the road to Fernand's house — and the mess Frederick and I had found when we got there. "Does he have a skiff?" I asked, thinking of what George had told me about a skiff hanging out behind Fernand's house at night — and the footprints leading to Fernand's back door.

"Who doesn't?" Charlene asked.

I sighed. Unfortunately, she had a point.

It took just over an hour to make it to the hospital; although the trip across the water was rough, John handled the skiff expertly. It wasn't a long drive in the truck, but it felt like hours. How was my niece? Had it been the murderer who attacked her? Why was she at the studio on her own? The questions whirled through my head as I waited impatiently to arrive at the hospital.

Adam was standing by Gwen's bed when we got there. His handsome face looked haggard; after greeting me, he ran a hand through his tousled hair, obviously very upset. I looked at my niece; her dark ringlets tumbled over the bandage that wrapped her head, and her eye was swollen. Her cheeks were hollow, and her hand was almost skeletal on the pillow; she looked terribly fragile. "How is she?" I asked, breathless with fear.

"They think she's going to be okay," he said.

I let out my breath — but not all of it. Thinking she was going to be okay wasn't nearly as good as knowing it. "What happened?"

"There was a fallen ladder near her, and a broken light bulb, but the police think someone hit her with a blunt object and tried to make it look like an accident."

"Has she woken up at all?"

"Briefly," he said. "The doctors said she's got a bit of a concussion, but she should be fine."

Relief flooded me as I looked at my niece's young, pale face. "Thank God," I said. "When she was awake, did she say anything about what happened?"

"I didn't get a chance to ask," he said, grimacing. He reached over and smoothed a stray curl from her forehead, looking at her with a tenderness that made my heart swell.

I sat down on the side of Gwen's bed and reached for her hand. "Poor, poor, girl. Why did she go to the studio alone?"

"We should get a police guard on her," John said. "Whoever it was might try again."

"The detective already took care of that; she told me an officer would be here within the hour," Adam said.

"We'll stay until then," I said.

"Can we? What about dinner at the inn?" John asked.

"There'll be time," I said. "If it's late, the guests will have to deal." I looked back to Adam. "Munger found her?"

"He got a ride from the dock from one of the locals," Adam said. "He said he knocked twice; when she didn't answer, he let himself in."

"Sounds about right," I said.

"Are we sure Munger didn't do it himself?" John asked.

"Why would he?"

"You mentioned that you don't trust him," John said, lifting an eyebrow in my direction.

"I don't," I said, "but I can't think why he'd whack Gwen over the head." If anything, I was more worried that he might try to take advantage of her. "Her clothes weren't . . . mussed, or anything, were they?"

Adam shook his head. "I don't trust Munger either," he said, "but if he did hit her on the head, it appears as if that's all he did."

I looked at my niece's ashen face and felt

guilt rush through me. "If only I'd been there with her . . ."

"You can't be with her every moment," John said, stepping up to touch my hair. "And you and I both told her not to go to the studio alone."

"Still . . ." I shivered, thinking of what might have happened. "She's going to be okay," John said.

"I certainly hope so," I said, squeezing my niece's cool hand and feeling tears well in my eyes.

I couldn't imagine the alternative.

We got back to the inn at twilight, and I was surprised to see all the windows of the inn blazing in the semidarkness. John tied up the skiff, and we hurried up the walkway. We were greeted by Detective Penney at the kitchen door.

"What's going on?" I asked breathlessly, my face numb from the chill wind. John closed the kitchen door behind us; the toasty warmth of the room and the scent of cloves and cinnamon did nothing to alleviate the coldness that gripped my heart. "Has there been another incident?"

"No. Everyone's fine," she said. "We were just about to head out. The police launch will pick us up at your dock, if that's okay."

"That's fine," I said, "but it's windy out there." My face still felt numb from the cold; I knew I needed to make dinner for my guests, but first I was making John and me a cup of hot chocolate, I decided. "Thanks for being there to help Gwen," I said. "Did you find anything out?"

"I'm sorry about your niece, but I'm afraid I have nothing to tell you. We're still investigating that incident," she said, and my heart sank. "We'll keep you apprised."

John's mother stood up; I had been so focused on the detective I hadn't noticed she was sitting at the kitchen table. She wore a dark sweater and a tailored pair of jeans, and her face was lined with worry. "How's your niece?" she asked.

"It looks like she should be okay," I said.

"Does she have any recollection of what happened?" the detective asked.

I shook my head. "Not so far, but Adam told me she was only awake for a little bit."

"Her mother called," Catherine said. "I didn't want to say anything until you got back."

"Thank you," I said, relieved. "I'll call her in just a minute."

Detective Penney, who had been waiting patiently, looked at me with compassion in her brown eyes. "I'm sorry you're having to go through this. I'll pray for her," the detective said, and I found myself warming to her. She was a lovely change from Detective Grimes, who had been as nasty and condescending a man as I'd ever met.

"Thank you, Detective," John said.

"I need to call my sister again," I said. "Is Frederick doing okay?"

"It's a bit of a shock, of course, but he seems to be holding up. He's in the parlor," Catherine told me.

"Want me to start dinner?" John asked.

"That would be great," I said. "I think we have enough for the detectives, too."

"You don't need to cook for us," Detective Penney said.

"You're welcome to stay," I said.

She smiled politely. "Thanks for the invitation, but the launch will be here at any minute."

After saying our goodbyes, John and I headed to the kitchen. I poured milk into a saucepan before picking up the phone to call my sister Bridget. It had started to snow; fat flakes whipped by outside the window as I told my sister what had happened and reassured her that her daughter would be fine.

"I had no idea how dangerous living on

the island would be," Bridget said. "I don't like it."

"I don't either," I said, "but she's going to be all right."

"Maybe I should fly out. I've got a meeting tomorrow, but . . ."

"Bridget, she's going to be in California in just a couple of days — no need for the extra trip. Adam's with her, and she's doing okay." I loved my sister, but I knew the last thing Gwen needed right now was her mother in the hospital room with her. With Fernand's death and the upcoming show, not to mention her injury, she had enough on her plate already.

"I just keep thinking she'll get over this," my sister said, "and come back to her normal life. I hate to see her throw her future away."

"She's doing what she loves," I told my sister. A high-powered attorney in California, she'd never understood my decision to leave my career and open a bed-and-breakfast on a small island in Maine — or her daughter's love for something as impractical as art. Like me, Gwen was doing what she loved; or at least she had been, before she met Munger. I looked around my warm yellow kitchen, with the white curtains and the ancient pine farm table, and then at

John, who was chopping tomatoes near the sink, his shoulders broad under his flannel shirt. I said a brief prayer of thanks that the inn wouldn't be stolen from me, and I would soon be married to a man I loved. Gwen was on that road, too; as soon as she was able to recognize that she, not a former vacuum salesman, was the master of her destiny. I had mixed feelings about the upcoming art show; if the oils didn't do well, Gwen would be distraught, but if they did sell well, she'd feel compelled to paint more. I fervently hoped we could convince Munger to include some of her watercolors, and that the response would be what I suspected it would.

"She may *think* she loves it," my sister said, pulling me back from my woolgathering, "but is it the practical thing for her future?"

"Practicality is only part of the equation," I said.

"She told me her mentor died." My sister's voice was high and anxious. "What's she going to do without a mentor?"

"There's another artist who volunteered to take that role over," I said, not having the energy for this conversation but knowing it was necessary. I stirred the milk and added in cocoa and sugar, inhaling the comforting aroma. "She's a talented artist. And her former mentor left her the studio."

"Really? How much is it worth?"

How much was it worth? "That's not the point," I said. "She's got a place to work — and to display and sell her paintings."

Bridget sighed. "I know you think I'm being bossy and controlling, Natalie." I was startled to hear her say it, but stayed silent and let her talk. "But this is my daughter we're talking about. Her future is important to me."

"I know," I said. "It's important to me, too."

"Is she really going to be okay?" My sister's voice cracked on the phone, and I suddenly understood that her harangue had been about fear — and about missing her daughter. She loved Gwen. So did I.

"The doctors say she'll be fine," I said. "She'll be in California in a few days, and you can see for yourself."

"What about whatever lunatic attacked her?"

"She has a police officer watching over her," I said, "and they're investigating the incident. John's a deputy; we won't let her out of our sight." I took a deep breath. "Bridget, I love her as if she were my own daughter. I'll make sure she's safe," I said, feeling a twist of guilt that I hadn't been with her when she was attacked.

Bridget was quiet for a moment. "Do you promise?"

"I promise," I said, still stirring the rich cocoa on the stove.

"She's coming home for Christmas," my sister said.

I paused in my stirring. "Will you send her back in January?"

She was quiet for a moment. "If that's what she wants," she said, "then yes."

I hung up a moment later feeling a new uneasiness in my stomach despite the aroma of hot chocolate.

"You okay?" John asked. He'd left the kitchen a few minutes ago, and returned with a slip of paper in his hand.

"I think so," I said, grabbing two mugs and ladling hot chocolate into them.

"Is she coming?"

I shook my head and handed him a mug. "Not at the moment. But she wants Gwen home for Christmas . . . and I'm guessing beyond that."

"She's an adult now," John said. "She'll make her own decision."

"I know," I sighed, then took a sip of the warm, cocoa-laced drink. There was not enough chocolate in the world to soothe me, unfortunately. Biscuit, seeming to sense my upset, wound between my legs. I picked her up and snuggled her in my lap, but even a purring cat did nothing to dispel my worries.

"I have some interesting news on a completely different topic, if you're interested," John said.

"What?"

He took another sip of his hot chocolate and held up a paper in his hand. "I ran Irene's credit card number; the service was down the day she checked in."

I petted Biscuit's silky head. "And?"

"It was declined," he said.

I groaned. "Did you talk to her?"

He shook his head. "No: but I'll be telling Detective Penney."

"Why?"

"She may be in over her head financially; I'm guessing that's why she came back to visit her brother. To ask for help."

"She found out about the will this morning, when the detectives told her. That might have prompted the attack on Gwen."

"How do you know?" I asked.

"Her attorney called. I was around the corner."

I thought of my niece in her hospital bed and gave Biscuit a little hug. "You think she

309

may have attacked Gwen out of anger that Fernand changed his will?"

"Perhaps. It may be that she killed him thinking she'd inherit," John said. "The previous will favored her, and she didn't know about the new one, so there's motivation there. We don't have confirmation that she's been on the island. They're doing a search on her prescription history right now to see if she's had access to Ativan," he said. "I'm not going to say anything about the card, if that's all right with you."

"We're already out 15K," I said, trying not to sound bitter. "What's another couple hundred dollars?"

"In the meantime, be careful," he said. "If Irene is the murderer, I'm glad Gwen's safe on the mainland."

"She is. But we're not," I said, shivering.

Breakfast was quiet the next morning. I served coffeecake and omelets to my guests, who sat in their accustomed corners of the dining room and refused to look at each other. Despite the seductive aroma of my favorite sour cream coffeecake, my appetite was low; I was too worried about Gwen and the fact that I might be harboring a murderer under my roof. We'd slept with the kitchen and bedroom doors locked, and I'd woken up almost every time the wind blew the night before.

John had gone out to work carving more of the toy boats he sold in the summers at Island Artists. With the continuing education and all the hullabaloo of the last several days, he was behind schedule and needed to catch up. Catherine, dressed in a dove-colored sweater and dark blue jeans, ate her oatmeal slowly, saying little.

When I opened the dishwasher to clean up, she stood up. "Let me take care of that this morning," she said. "I know I can't cook, but I can clean."

I blushed a little bit, remembering the cabbage, and stammered, "Oh, no . . . please. You're our guest."

"I'm *family,*" she said, stressing the word. "I want to help. Besides, I know you want to call the hospital. Go ahead; it's nine o'clock."

I was surprised by the offer but grateful for the help, and stepped away from the sink. "Thanks," I said, drying my hands on a dishtowel. "It's been on my mind all morning."

As she busied herself putting plates into the dishwasher, I picked up the phone and dialed the hospital. Gwen answered on the third ring.

"You're awake!" I said, feeling my whole body relax.

"I've got a heck of a headache, but I'm up," I said.

"Do you remember what happened? You got a nasty knock on the head."

"I don't know," she said. "Last thing I remember was painting. Then I woke up here."

"You didn't fall off a ladder?"

"Ladder? Why would I need a ladder?"

"They found one next to you," I said, watching Catherine as she rinsed a mug. "With a broken light bulb. I think somebody attacked you, then tried to rig it to make it look like you fell."

"I'm just glad they didn't finish the job," she said.

"Me too," I said. "The only thing is, how did they get in without alerting you?"

"I was wearing my iPod," Gwen said, a bit sheepishly.

"And you were there alone," I reminded her. "Until we get this cleared up, no more of that. Okay?"

"I know, Aunt Nat. I was only there because I was supposed to meet Mr. Munger."

"We were lucky this time," I said. I stared out the window at the mainland, its pink-gray granite shrouded in snow. If it was the murderer who attacked Gwen, why not finish the job? Had Munger interrupted him or her? And why attack Gwen at all? Was it rage because she inherited some of Fernand's estate? If that was the case, both Gwen and Frederick were in danger.

"Is there an officer guarding you?" I asked, thinking of my niece, unprotected in her hospital bed.

"Yes," she said. "Adam went down to get him a bagel just now."

That's right; Adam was there, too. "He's a good man," I said. "Well, you just focus on getting better; everything's fine around here."

"Have you talked with Mr. Munger yet?" I could hear the tension in her voice.

"No . . . but I understand he's the one who found you."

"That's what Adam said. I'm worried; we never got a chance to talk about the paintings."

"It'll keep," I said, gazing out the window toward the mainland, which was dusted with white after last night's snow. "I'll give him a call. What's his number?"

"I don't know it by heart, but it's in the phone book. Cottage Street Gallery."

"Got it," I said, flipping through the

313

phone book. "I'm so glad you're okay, Gwen."

"Me too," she said. "But I'll be even gladder when this show is over."

I hung up with Gwen and checked my watch; too early to call Bridget on the West Coast, but not too early to call Munger. I wanted to hear what he'd found when he discovered Gwen, anyway. I grabbed a sliver of coffeecake and took a bite of the moist, cinnamon-pecan studded cake and dialed again.

Munger answered on the fifth ring, sounding irritated.

"Herb, this is Natalie Barnes — Gwen's aunt."

"How is she?" he asked. "Will she be able to attend the show?"

I swallowed down my irritation. "She's going to be fine," I said, "and I assume she'll be in good shape for the show, but that'll be up to her doctors."

"I've already paid for advertising," he said in a peeved voice.

"I know," I replied. "I wanted to ask you a few questions about how you found her. What time was it?" I asked.

"It must have been at around 1:20," he said. "I came over on the 12:30 mail boat and walked over to the studio. She was supposed to meet me at the dock, but when she didn't show up, I figured she'd forgotten. Typical artist."

I bristled, but said, "How did you find her?"

"I knocked twice, but no one answered. I thought I heard someone inside, though, so I tried the door — it was unlocked — and let myself in."

"Where was Gwen?"

"In the studio," he said. "Near her easel."

"I heard there was a ladder?"

"It was right next to her."

"Anything strange or out of place?"

"No," he said, sounding irritated by the question. "Wait — there might have been one thing."

"What?"

"There was snow on the floor. Right next to her."

"It can't have been there long," I said. "The studio was heated."

"You think someone else was there?"

"I think it's likely," I said. "And I think you interrupted whoever it was." A chill went down my spine as I thought of what might have happened if Munger hadn't showed up. As much as I disliked him, I was thankful — he might have saved my niece's life.

315

"I just hope she gets those oils done," he said. "When did they say she'll be out of the hospital?"

"I don't know," I said. "But even if she doesn't get the oils done, she's got tons of gorgeous watercolors. In fact, I think they're better than the oils."

"I'll show them if I have to, but oils are what's selling. If Gwen wants to make a name for herself, that's where it's at."

"I think her watercolors are beautiful."

"Yes, but watercolors aren't hot right now. To be a successful artist, you need to learn what the market likes."

I swallowed back what I wanted to say, and made a choked sound that he evidently took as assent.

"Well, let me know when your niece is back in the saddle. The show's only a few days away; she'd better heal fast."

"I'll keep you posted. I would hate for your advertising to go to waste," I said, sarcasm lacing my voice. Maybe Gwen did need a mentor, but Herb Munger was nowhere near the top of my list. Or even on it.

When I'd hung up, I turned to survey the kitchen; Catherine had put away all the dishes and was wiping down the counters. I had rarely seen her in jeans, but they suited her; she almost looked as if she belonged on the island. Except for the cashmere. "Someone attacked her, then," she said, shaking her platinum-dyed head.

"Looks like it."

"I can't think who would want to hurt that lovely young woman."

"Me neither," I said.

She hung up the dishtowel and sat down at the table. "There's always darkness under the surface, it seems. This seems like such a peaceful place, and yet . . ." She hesitated, then turned to me, the dishtowel twisted between her hands. "Natalie, I'm sorry about the ring."

I looked at her, surprised by the non sequitur. "What do you mean?"

She gave a deep sigh and twisted the dishtowel again. "I never wanted to tell John, but his father . . . had some problems." She looked out the window; I sensed she was having difficulty meeting my gaze. "I tried to hide it from John — he worshiped his father — but it was difficult."

"I'm sorry," I said. "Family relationships are hard."

"Yes, they are," she said. She looked older this morning, the lines in her face deeper.

I stood quietly, waiting for her to continue and wondering how this related to the ring.

"When we went to Cliffside," she said, "I told you it was the last place John's father and I had been happy."

"I know."

"John was fifteen at the time," she said. "Paul and I had a stable marriage — happy, even. We'd been together almost twenty years by then." Her eyes seemed to be focused on a different scene than the cozy kitchen around us. "It was a lovely summer — I hated to be away from my friends in Boston, but the weather was fine, and the house was lovely, and John — well, he loved it here." She took a deep breath, then continued.

Her voice hardened. "The gambling started when we got back to Boston." She looked out the window, into the distance. "And the womanizing."

I stood, silent. I'd never heard about gambling from John. Or affairs.

"He started with small things," she said. "A few hundred dollars here and there. But then it got bigger." She took a ragged breath. "It took years. And I didn't know it was happening."

"I'm so sorry," I said.

She gave a bitter laugh. "I figured out the womanizing after a few years, but didn't want to ruin the family for John. That's why

I stayed with him."

"What about the gambling?" I asked.

"I knew about the savings — some of it, anyway. I didn't know how bad it was until after he died. There was a small life insurance policy, enough to keep me going for a few years. But I didn't know about my mother's ring."

"He sold the original and used it to cover his debts?"

Her face was pale, devoid of color. "I wouldn't have thought it possible that he would stoop so low, but that's the only explanation I can come up with. And now, I'm faced with a situation I swore I'd never find myself in."

"What's that?" I asked. Paul had died years ago. What had happened?

"They're foreclosing on my home," she said. I could see the pain in her face; she had lived in her grand Boston townhome for almost forty years. "I refinanced when . . . when I found out all that Paul had done to our savings. But the insurance policy money ran out in the summer. I haven't been able to make payments in months."

"Oh, Catherine . . ." I said, feeling like all the wind had been knocked out of me. "Why didn't you say something earlier? Is it too late to talk with the mortgage company?"

Tears welled in her eyes. "I didn't want to burden you," she said. "I didn't want John to know what his father had really done. And I . . . I was embarrassed."

She looked away, flushed with shame. All the facade had cracked, and her pain was plain to see. I crossed the kitchen and opened my arms, holding her thin body as she sobbed. As I held her, John walked into the kitchen, then froze just inside the door.

"What's wrong?" he asked. "Is it Gwen?"

"No," I said. "Gwen's fine." Catherine pulled away from me, wiping at her eyes.

"I was just explaining to Natalie what happened with the ring," she said. "I suppose it's time you knew, as well."

"What's wrong?" he asked, eyes dark with worry.

"It's like this," she said, taking a deep breath and then telling John what she'd told me. I sat quietly as she explained what had happened with his father. "He wasn't a bad man, John. It's . . . it's an addiction. Like alcohol, or drugs."

"Mom, I'm so sorry you had to suffer this by yourself," he said, sitting down at the table and shaking his head. "You should have told me."

"I knew how much you loved him," she said. "I didn't want to ruin your image of him — taint the relationship."

John ran a hand through his sandy hair; his voice was calm, but I could tell he was upset. "If he drained your savings, how are you making it financially?" he asked.

"That's the thing," she said. "The insurance money ran out a few months ago, and . . . I didn't know what to do." She took a deep breath. "The reason I came here . . . is that they're foreclosing on the house." Her face was bleak. "I have nowhere to go."

John leaned back in his chair, looking stunned. "You lost the house?"

She nodded, looking at a spot on the floor.

"But Thanksgiving . . . you must have known then. Why didn't you say something?"

"I was ashamed," she said in a low, quavering voice. Then she straightened her shoulders and raised her chin, looking her son in the eye. "It galls me to ask this, but I have no choice. If you can give me a place to stay for a while, until I can get things figured out, I would appreciate it."

John glanced at me, and I nodded slightly. "Of course," he said. "But let's see if we can talk to an attorney first, see if we can rescue the house."

"It's no use," she said. "It's in the beginning of January. I have just enough time to clear my things out — the problem is, I don't have anywhere to move them."

"We'll take care of it," John said, running his hand through his hair again. I could hear the take-charge tone of voice. Catherine could, too — I could sense her relaxing.

"Thank you," she said, her voice low and sincere.

John walked over and gave her a huge hug. "We'll get through this," he said. "That's what family is for."

Not for the first time, I was grateful to be engaged to such a wonderful man.

"Is Gwen okay?" Charlene asked when I stopped by the store with the extra muffins from this morning's breakfast. The green pickup truck was in front of the store again; I spotted its driver sitting at the end of the bar, staring into his cup of coffee. I found my eyes drawn to him — and was tempted to ask him where he'd been going in such a hurry the other day.

"Natalie?"

"Sorry," I said, turning my attention back to Charlene. "She seems to be recovering fine, but she has no idea what happened. She was wearing earbuds when she was attacked. She must have left the door unlocked." The police had found no sign of forced entry. Again — what had she been thinking?

"I'm just glad she's going to be okay."

"She'll be fine, but I may not."

"Why?" Charlene's eyes widened in alarm.

"Looks like our mortgage troubles may be in hand," I said, "but my future mother-in-law will most likely be moving in with us for a while."

"You're kidding me," my friend said.

I glanced around at the other people in the store; Charlene, understanding, moved us toward one of the side aisles so we could talk more comfortably. "Financial troubles," I said in a low voice.

Charlene's eyebrows rose almost to her hairline. "Really? I know the economy hasn't been terrific, but I thought they were loaded. Isn't she a Boston Brahmin type?"

"She is, but things have changed," I said. "Her husband was a gambling man, evidently. Gambled their life savings away."

My friend winced. "Ouch."

"I'm actually starting to like her, now that I get to know her. She's devoted to John. And she's got a lot of chutzpah, for sure," I said, remembering how she'd talked her way into the Torrone compound. "She's actually been volunteering to help out around the inn — and as long as it's not cooking, she does a great job."

"No more cabbage?" Charlene asked. I'd told her about the steaming incident.

"Nope — and I think I've got the smell out at last."

"Well, that's something," Charlene said, not sounding convinced. "Any more weird dolls or blood?" she asked.

"None," I said. "Haven't heard back from the lab yet, but John will let me know."

"Speaking of interesting things, I've got something to show you," she said, her eyes glinting with excitement.

"What is it?" I asked, stealing a glance at the man at the end of the bar. I thought about how he'd pulled out in front of me the other day, fishtailing into the road. What was he doing on Fernand's road — and why the agitated driving? There were only three houses down there; did he live in one of them?

"You'll see," she said. I followed her into the back room, where she pulled out an open manila envelope addressed to Nina Torrone.

"Did you open it?" I asked. "That's a federal offense!" Not that I should be talking — I'd done my share of snooping in the past — but still. She was the postmistress.

"Chill, Nat. It was open when it got here," she said. "And these fell out while I was putting it into her mailbox." She flipped open the flap and dumped out a short stack of envelopes.

"What about them?" I asked.

"They're addressed to somebody other than Nina Torrone," Charlene said.

I picked up one of the envelopes. It was from Sprint, and was addressed to a Jennifer Salinas, at a New York City address.

"Why is she getting somebody else's phone bills?"

"Not just phone bills," Charlene said. "There's a postcard here, too."

"Weird," I said, picking up the card. It was addressed to a Jennifer Salinas, and featured a picture of a beach with palm trees and crashing surf. Despite my love of Maine, with the cold weather we'd been having, it looked pretty darned appealing. There was a brief note on the back.

Miss having you in Padre this year, girlfriend! Call when you're back in town! XXX OOO Nikki

"Who's Jennifer Salinas?"

"Good question," Charlene said. "Let's go see if she's on Facebook."

She headed toward the front of the store,

but I grabbed her arm. "That man out there at the end of the bar. Does he live on Seal Point Road?"

"No," she said. "He lives in a garage apartment down by the pier. Why?"

I told her what Frederick had said about Fernand's secret admirer. "I saw him tearing out of Fernand's street the other day — just before we found out the house had been broken into."

Charlene pursed her frosted lips. "Do you really think he broke into Fernand's house? Why would he have? Fernand was dead."

"Yes, but Frederick told me whoever was stalking Fernand wrote letters."

"And he didn't say who it was?"

"Not to Frederick," I said. "And not to anyone else, either — or at least not that I know. I was thinking whoever broke into his house might have been after the letters. If whoever it was was married, I could see how they could be pretty incriminating."

"I'll see what I can find out," Charlene said, and I followed her to the front of the store, where her desktop computer sat. Both of us shot furtive glances at Rob Perkins. He was a thirtyish man with scraggly hair and rubber boots that came up to his knees. Could he really have been Fernand's admirer? I wondered. "Is he married?" I whispered.

"Not that I know of," Charlene said, reaching for one of the ricotta muffins I'd brought. "These are to die for," she said as she bit into one of the plump little cakes and settled herself at the stool in front of her computer. A few crumbs dropped onto her ample chest, and she brushed them off. She wore leggings and a sparkly green tunic today, and as usual, was garnering appreciative glances from the two men nearest the register.

"You look just like Christmas," one of them told her.

"Thanks, Al," she said, smiling. "Let me know when you need a refill."

"Will do," he said. "Although I could use something a bit stronger than coffee," he said.

"Sorry to disappoint," she said, eyes twinkling. "You'll have to bring a flask." While Al and his friend seemed to light up at the sight of Charlene — a not uncommon occurrence on the island — I noticed that Rob barely looked up. I filed that away and turned my attention to the computer screen.

"Let's see here," Charlene said, pulling up Facebook and typing in "Jennifer Salinas."

There was quite a list of results, unfortunately.

"Can't you refine the search geographically?" I asked.

She hit the button marked "Advanced Search" and typed in "New York."

Only one entry popped up.

"Bingo," Charlene said.

"Is her profile locked?" I asked, peering at the entry. I could tell the profile picture was of a young woman, but it was too small to tell anything by.

"Her public 'wall' is," Charlene said.

"What's a 'wall'?"

"That's where she updates her status and people can comment," Charlene said. "Really, Natalie — you should think about doing a page for the inn."

"I know, I know," I said. I was hopelessly behind on the electronic frontier, and hated the reminder. "Can you find anything out?"

"I can't get into her wall, but it looks like I might be able to see her photos."

She clicked on photos, and an album turned up. "Bingo," Charlene said. The first three were a blurry series of group shots, but the fourth was a picture of a young woman with long, dark hair and a NY Jets sweatshirt.

"Is that who I think that is?" I asked in a

low voice, stealing a glance at the lobster-men at the counter. They were busy talking about another line-cutting episode, and didn't seem to be paying attention.

Charlene looked at me. "If you cut the hair and add a pillbox hat, I think so. See the little mole by her mouth?"

"You're right," I said, focusing on the small beauty spot just above her lip. I hadn't noticed it when I met her, but it was definitely there. I stared at the photo, trying to compute what I was seeing. Nina Torrone and Jennifer Salinas were the same person.

TWENTY

How could that be?

"It doesn't make sense," I said.

"It explains why Mr. Agent is so protective of her," Charlene said in a low voice.

"And why he never lets her speak — and high-tailed it up to Maine from New York." I thought about it. "She never has paint on her hands."

"She's probably not painting," Charlene said, casting a glance at the lobstermen and speaking barely above a whisper, "because she's not Nina Torrone."

It took a moment for that to sink in, and an unsettling thought presented itself. "If she's *not* Nina Torrone," I hissed, "then where is Nina Torrone?"

Charlene's face was grim. "I think that's an excellent question."

"Does Nina Torrone have a page?" I asked.

Charlene typed the name into Facebook, and one entry came up. She grimaced. "It's a fan page — not run by the artist."

I leaned forward. "The photo looks remarkably similar," I said. "Do you see a mole?"

"Nope. The resemblance is eerie, though," Charlene agreed. "Do you think she has two identities? Maybe she covered up the mole for the publicity shots."

"Why would she want a fake name?" I asked. I glanced at the men at the counter; they were discussing the best places to put lobster pots in December and seemed unaware of our conversation.

"Privacy?"

"If she wanted privacy, wouldn't she come up here incognito — as Jennifer Salinas?" I thought about it. "When Catherine barged into Cliffside, she was very nervous — probably worried about being discovered. And there were all kinds of magazines, but nothing about art."

"You're right — if she's real but wanted privacy, she'd use the Jennifer Salinas name, wouldn't she?"

"You'd think. But if she's not — if she's an imposter — why go through the charade?" I asked.

Charlene cocked a penciled eyebrow. "Maybe something bad happened to the real Nina Torrone."

I thought about that for a moment. "But wouldn't that be in the news?"

"Not if her agent covered it up," she said. "If everyone knew something had happened to her, there'd be no need for a fake Nina Torrone."

"What would be his motivation?" I asked.

"Money," she said, with a glint in her eye. "What else? I know: let's Google him, and see what we find out. Maybe he's got a history." She typed in the name Mortimer Gladstone, and a whole slew of pages came up. She clicked on the Wikipedia entry and let out a low whistle. "He's cleaning up on Torrone's work," she said. "Her paintings are going for a million each."

"And commission is what — 15 percent?" I asked.

"Not bad work if you can get it," Charlene said, scrolling through the page. "Wait a moment," she said. "Torrone's not his only high-stakes client."

"Who else?" I asked, leaning forward.

"This sculptor named Anne Stokes." Charlene clicked on a link and scanned the page. "Oh, my," she said.

"What?"

Charlene gave me a meaningful look. "Evidently her sailboat went down about seven years ago, and she was lost at sea."

"How awful," I breathed, thinking of the accidents that occasionally occurred off the coast here.

"Wait — there's more."

"What?" I asked.

"They apparently had such a close relationship that she left her entire estate to him." Charlene leaned back. "He must have made millions from her death."

"She didn't have family?" I asked.

"According to this," she said, scrolling through the entry, "she was estranged from her parents."

"Like Fernand," I said, gloomily. Then something occurred to me. "Look up Torrone on Wikipedia."

Charlene dutifully typed in her name.

"Does it say anything about her family?"

"Daughter of a moderately known painter who died about ten years ago. Grew up without her mother, who left the family when Nina was young." Charlene looked at me. "Creepy."

"Yes."

Charlene hugged herself. "Are you thinking what I'm thinking?"

Goosebumps prickled my arms, and a sick feeling settled in my stomach. "Let's discuss this in the back," I said. I didn't think the lobstermen were listening, but I didn't want

333

to take chances. "We should talk to her," I said when the door closed behind us.

"If it's what we think it is, I think she already knows. She's clearly in on the scam."

"But she may not know this happened before. And that the artist was 'lost at sea'."

"No body to identify," Charlene mused. "Although if there was someone acting as the artist, maybe she just picked up her old life."

"She's still a liability if she does that," I said, not liking the direction my mind was heading.

Charlene shivered. "You think he's going to kill her?"

"We're on an island, right?" I asked. "And as long as she's alive, she can blackmail him."

We sat in silence for a moment, listening as the wind moaned around the corners of the store. I could hear the voices of the lobstermen through the door, but only faintly. "If we're right and it was a scam, what do you think happened to the real Nina Torrone?" Charlene asked, her eyes big.

I shivered. "Wherever she is, she sure isn't here. Do you really think he might have killed her? And that other artist?"

"I can't come up with another explanation," Charlene said. "Maybe she died suddenly, and he realized the gravy train was about to dry up."

"So he came up with an impostor and then drowned her so there would be no body to find?"

"Or just sent her away," Charlene said.

"It doesn't explain why two of his clients died unexpectedly."

"Assuming Torrone is dead," Charlene said.

I leaned against a stack of ramen noodle boxes. "If Jennifer Salinas is taking her place, then I can't come up with another explanation."

"Fernand was giving her a funny look at the party," Charlene said. "And her reaction when he handed her that drink was strange."

"I know he had several articles about her at his house. I saw them the day I took Frederick over there."

"Think he suspected she wasn't who she said she was?" Charlene asked.

"If she was a fake, he'd know — they studied under the same mentor. There's a problem, though," I said.

"What?"

"The thing is, if the same person who killed Fernand went after Gwen, what was the motive?"

Charlene shrugged an emerald-clad shoulder. "Maybe Fernand was killed because he knew Torrone was a fake — and Gwen saw something she shouldn't have."

"If this has anything to do with Torrone, Catherine and I saw more than we should have. We barged into the place."

"But Gladstone doesn't know you were there, does he?"

"That's true," I said. "Jennifer wouldn't have told him; she seemed afraid he'd find out we were there." I thought about it for a moment. "If Gwen knew something, though, she never said anything to me."

"Maybe she doesn't realize what she saw," Charlene said.

I had a bad feeling about this. "This is all speculation," I said, trying to make myself feel better.

"Tell you what. Have John check and see if Gladstone's got a record," Charlene said. "Violent criminals often have a history."

"Good idea," I said. "But what do we do about Torrone — I mean, Jennifer Salinas — in the interim?"

"Warn her?" Charlene asked.

"We're still not sure of what really happened — it's all speculation."

"Better safe than sorry," Charlene said.

"I can see that. But if we warn her, she'll know we're onto her — and if she breathes a word of it to Gladstone, that might spur him to get rid of her sooner than later."

"We've got to try," Charlene said. "Don't you think?"

As much as I hated to face it, she was right.

But how were we supposed to do it?

I walked out of the store ten minutes later, deep in thought. I was dying to go and talk with Nina/Jennifer immediately, but Charlene had made me promise not to. "Let's find out what we know about Gladstone first," she said. "If we're right, it's too dangerous to just knock on the door and tell her."

"How do we warn her, then?"

"I'm sure one more day won't hurt," Charlene said. I wasn't so sure, but told her I'd wait at least until I'd had a chance to talk with John.

I turned the key in the ignition and fastened my seatbelt, shivering despite my winter coat. As I was about to back out of the parking place, I heard another engine roar to life: it was the green pickup truck.

Curiosity flared in me, and I waited until he'd pulled out and turned out of the lot before putting the van in reverse and following him.

As I pulled out onto road, hanging back from the pickup truck, I wondered what I was doing — and what I hoped to accomplish by following Rob. When he turned right onto Seal Point Road, I felt my heart contract, and turned in after him. The road curved, and I lost sight of him for a while behind the stands of trees that were thick along the narrow strip of roadway, but I wasn't surprised when I rounded the last bend and found the truck idling outside Fernand's house.

There was no way I could turn around without attracting attention, and since Fernand's house was at the end of the road, it was the only likely destination, so I went ahead and parked next to the truck. I expected it to pull out and go tearing down the road, but it didn't.

I got out of the van and slowly walked around the front of it. Rob was bent over the steering wheel, his body shaking with sobs.

Not knowing what to do, I stood at the front of the van and waited until he looked up. When his eyes met mine, there was a flash of fear, then a heartrending mix of resignation and grief.

Instinctively, I closed the distance between us and knocked gently on the window. I held my breath and waited, half-expecting him to put the truck in reverse and peel out, but after a moment, he opened the door and stepped out of the truck, looking at the ground as he shut the door, then jamming his hands in his pockets. We stood there for a moment, the wind stealing our breath away.

"I miss him, too," I finally said quietly, when the wind died down for a moment.

He looked up at me, a darting glance filled with misery. He was skin and bones, his hair unkempt, his jeans smudged with dirt. I found myself wondering if this was normal for him, or if this was a grief response. "Don't say anything to anyone," he said, a desperate tone in his voice.

"I won't," I assured him.

"I can't believe he's gone," he said, kicking the tire of the truck.

I stood quietly, feeling as if I were near a spooked animal. I didn't want to say anything to scare him off.

"Why would he kill himself?" he asked. "I could have been there for him. He knew I would have been. Why wouldn't he let me in?" His face was a mask of misery. "I was here that last night, you know. After the party. I went home and had a drink, then finally screwed up my courage to talk to him. I tied up out there," he said, waving a hand toward the back of the house, "and walked up to the back door." His eyes were focused on something far away, as if he were reliving the scene. "He was already with someone, though, so I left."

"Who?" I asked, feeling my heartbeat pick up. That explained the footprints — but had he seen who was with Fernand the night he died?

"I couldn't tell who — the windows were too foggy, and his back was to me," he said. "But they were sitting at the kitchen table, drinking something. Laughing. I could tell it was another man. He was big, with dark hair." He sounded miserable.

Big, with dark hair, and laughing. That could describe Gladstone. But it could also describe about half of the island's male population. And Frederick, too, come to think of it. "Did it look like it might have been Scotch?" I asked, thinking of the doctored drink.

"I don't know," he said. "I lost my nerve and went back to the boat. I wish I hadn't, though. I didn't know it would be my last chance." He looked up at me again. "Don't tell anyone. The guys wouldn't understand. Please."

"I won't," I said again, and took a deep

breath. "You were his secret admirer, weren't you?" The wind kicked up again, carrying my words away.

He snorted, making puffs of dragonlike smoke that the wind whirled away. "Sounds like something out of junior high school. Yes, I was." He glanced up at me, and again I saw that fear in his eyes. "I shouldn't have told you all of this. You can't tell anyone. If they knew . . ."

"I promised I wouldn't say anything," I said, wondering why he was so worried about people knowing he was attracted to Fernand. Sara and Terri were "out," after all, and it didn't seem to be a problem, except for a few islanders. On the other hand, Fernand's family had disowned him. And I knew that men for some reason had a harder time accepting gay men than lesbians.

I turned the conversation back to the house, which felt empty even from where we were standing. I glanced at it, my heart contracting at the sight of the wreath on the door — a decoration for a holiday that Fernand would never have a chance to celebrate. "Were you the one who broke in the other day?" I asked.

He dropped his head and his shoulders slumped. "Yes. I was looking for some letters I wrote to him."

"I saw you when you left," I said. "You were in a pretty big hurry."

"That was your van I almost hit?" he asked.

"Yeah," I said.

"Sorry."

"No harm done," I said gently. "Did you find what you were looking for?"

"No," he shook his head abruptly. "I have no idea where they are. I knew I never should have sent them."

"You know the police are thinking he might have been murdered," I told him, watching his reaction.

His head jerked up. "Murdered?"

I nodded.

He shook his head, looking mystified. "I don't understand. Who would have killed Fernand?"

"I was hoping you might be able to tell me that," I said. "Had he argued with anyone that you knew of?"

"Not that I saw," he said, "but again, it's not like we talked or anything. I just sat on the sidelines, wishing . . ." Again, a forlorn look passed over his face.

"I think we've all been there," I said gently.

He folded his arms as if closing himself off again, then turned toward the truck. "I gotta go," he said. "I shouldn't have come here."

"If you ever need to talk . . ."

He shrugged his shoulders and got into his truck. Pity stirred in my heart as I watched as he drove up Seal Point Road. It must be awful to feel you had to hide who you were — and I knew the pain of losing someone you cared about must be even harder when you felt you couldn't share your grief. I hoped he would someday feel safe enough to come out.

At least I'd solved the mystery of the footprints and the break-in, I reflected as I climbed back into the van and closed the door behind me. I just wished he'd gotten a better glimpse of whoever was having drinks with Fernand the night he died.

I stared at the lonely house, wishing there were some way to make it speak to me — to tell me what had happened that cold winter night. Who had killed Fernand? It didn't appear to be his sister — after all, Rob had told me it was a man who was with him the night he died. Had Torrone's agent come back the night he died?

If only walls could talk.

Twenty-One

I hurried home to look for John, but he wasn't in his workshop or the carriage house; he'd left me a note telling me that he was headed to the mainland. Catherine wasn't there, either — evidently she'd joined him on the mail boat. Detective Penney's card was on the top of the desk; I called her number and left a message, asking her to tell John to call me — and requesting that she do a criminal background check on Mortimer Gladstone.

I hung up feeling uneasy. Gwen had been attacked yesterday, and the police were starting to investigate Fernand's death as a murder. Were both issues linked to the fake artist?

If only I had some proof.

Then I remembered the slip of paper I'd found in Fernand's parka pocket the other day. I hurried to the coat hook in the kitchen and fished in the pocket for it. The address was familiar, of course — because it was the New York address on the utility bills Torrone had been receiving. I hurried to the computer and typed in the web site; it was an account of the death of Gladstone's first client. The one who had drowned offshore and never been recovered.

Despite the warm radiator and the cat weaving around my ankles, I felt suddenly cold. Fernand had known — or suspected — what Gladstone was up to.

I stared at the screen and reached down to pet Biscuit, trying to figure out how everything was connected. If Gladstone had attacked Gwen, there must have been a reason. But what was it? She hadn't remembered anything . . . but maybe she didn't realize what she'd heard.

I called the hospital, praying that Gwen would be awake. Adam answered, and handed the phone off to my niece.

"Aunt Nat?" Her voice sounded bright; my heart swelled with gratitude that she was okay.

"How are you doing?" I asked.

"Better — I'm hoping they'll release me today," she said. "I still have to work on that show."

I was actually much happier with her in the hospital, but said, "Great. Is the police guard still with you?"

"Hasn't left the door," she said.

"Good."

"Do you really think it's necessary?" she asked. "I still don't know why anyone would hit me over the head," she said.

"I wanted to talk to you about that, actually. Do you remember having any contact with Nina Torrone or her agent over the last few days?"

"Not really," she said, and I felt my theory evaporate. Maybe Fernand's sister had been the one to kill him after all. But if so, who had been the man in Fernand's kitchen? Then my niece said, "Wait. I did see them."

I gripped the phone tight. "When?"

"Remember when I ran to the store to get milk a few days ago? I ran into Nina Torrone and her agent."

"What did you say?"

"I didn't say anything," she said. "I was walking behind them; they didn't know I was there. He said something about getting a boat, and that everything would be taken care of in a couple of days."

"What did she say?" I asked, feeling dread curdle in my veins.

"That it was harder than she thought it would be. That she was convinced someone would find out she was faking it."

Bingo, I thought.

"It made me feel better, really, knowing that another artist was struggling, too. I mean, if Nina Torrone thinks her paintings aren't very good, then what are the rest of us supposed to think of our own work?"

"What did he say then?" I asked.

"He told her she was doing fine. And that's when Gladstone turned around and noticed me." She paused. "Not very incriminating, I'm afraid. I don't think either of them would attack me for knowing Nina was insecure about her work, do you?"

"I think Nina Torrone wasn't talking about artistic insecurity when she told Gladstone she was worried someone would find out she was faking it," I said.

"What are you saying?" She sounded puzzled.

"I think she isn't Nina Torrone. She's an imposter."

Gwen was silent for a moment. "You're kidding me."

"I'm not. But don't say anything to anyone," I told her. "I think something happened to the real Nina Torrone, and the woman we met is really named Jennifer Salinas."

"What does that have to do with the boat?"

"He had a well-known client who ended up lost at sea a few years back," I said. "She was estranged from her family, and he was the sole beneficiary of her estate."

"Oh, my God. What about the real Nina?" she breathed. "Do you think he killed her?" she asked.

"I don't know," I said, "but I'm afraid whoever is posing as her is in grave danger."

"Is there some way to find out what her will says?" Gwen asked.

"I don't think so," I said. "I'll ask John when I see him."

"You have to warn her," Gwen said, her voice urgent. "He knows I'm still alive — and I heard what she said."

"I'm waiting until John gets back," I said. "I called and asked the detective to do a search on his criminal background."

"Does he have the boat?"

"I don't know," I said.

"Call Eli," she said. "Find out. If he already has the boat, you've got to go and talk with her."

My blood froze in my veins as I realized she was right.

"I'll call her right now," I said.

"Be careful, Aunt Nat. I already lost Fernand. I couldn't bear to lose you, too."

■ ■ ■ ■

Claudette answered the phone just before I was about to hang up.

"I'm sorry to bother you," I said. "I know you're busy with your family, but I've got an urgent question."

"Natalie," she said. "I'm so glad you called. I've got something I've got to tell you."

Whatever it was could wait until later. "Claudette," I interrupted. "Did Eli deliver a boat to Mortimer Gladstone?"

"He did this morning," she said. My heart sank. "I really need to talk to you . . ."

"I've got an emergency. I promise I'll call you later," I said.

"But . . ."

I put the phone down with shaking hands and reached for my jacket. What if I was too late? What if she was already dead?

Don't think about that, I told myself as I scrawled a note for John telling him where I was going — and why — and hurried out the kitchen door to the van. At the last second, I doubled back and dug in the freezer for a bag of sugar cookies, which I hastily dumped into one of the Christmas tins I'd bought on the mainland and was planning to fill with goodies for my island neighbors. It wasn't a great excuse, but it was better than nothing.

Even though the drive to Cliffside was only about five minutes, it seemed to take an hour. I parked at the bottom of the hill and slammed the van door shut, looking up at the imposing building as I clutched the tin in my gloved hands. If Jennifer Salinas was there by herself, I'd tell her. If Gladstone was there, I'd hand off the tin and watch for a sign of Torrone — Salinas, I corrected myself.

If only John were with me. If only I'd thought to tell him what I was doing. If Gladstone didn't kill me, there was every likelihood my future husband would when I had to tell him I'd gone off half-cocked again.

Although the drive had seemed slow, I made it up the steps all too quickly, and was staring at the heavy wood front door. Like a drawbridge door, I thought. I knocked, wishing I had Catherine's bravado, and straightened my shoulders as I waited for someone to answer the door.

After a long minute, I heard the snick of a dead bolt sliding back. The sound reminded me of a gun being cocked, but I pasted a smile on my face and waited for the door to open.

Which it did, about two inches.

Nina — or Jennifer, I reminded myself — peered out of the crack. "What do you want?"

Relief poured through me. "Nina," I said. "We need to talk."

"You want to pry into my house again?"

"No," I said. "I'm afraid for your life."

She hesitated; I could see the door swing slightly open, then back. "I don't know what you're talking about."

A cold gust of wind blew, slicing through my coat and pushing against the door. "Is your agent here?"

"Yes, but he's in the shower."

"Can I come in for a moment?"

"Why?"

"Because I need to talk to you about something important, and I'm freezing to death on your front stoop."

She glanced behind her, hesitating. "How important?"

"Life and death important," I said.

She opened the door an inch or two more, wavering. I channeled my future mother-in-law and said, "Thanks," taking a step forward as I spoke. Reflexively, she opened the door more — and I was in.

"You can only stay a minute," she said, her eyes darting to the staircase. She wore sweatpants with JUICY emblazoned on the butt and a hot pink sweatshirt studded with rhinestones. I listened; I could hear the sound of water running in the pipes in the walls.

Relieved that Gladstone was out of commission, I plunged ahead. "You're Jennifer Salinas, aren't you?"

Her eyes widened in terror. "How do you know that?"

"It doesn't matter. What happened to Nina Torrone?"

"She's on an artist retreat down in the Virgin Islands," she said, looking startled. "Mort told me she needed some time off; I'm the decoy."

"How did he find you?"

"Through a modeling agency in New York. He told me I'd be perfect for the role."

"And what happens when you're done playing the part?"

"I get twenty thousand dollars," she said. "Enough to pay down my credit cards. He told me the whole thing will be done this week, and I'll get my check."

I shivered and glanced at the staircase myself. "Do you know why he asked you to pretend to be Nina?"

"It's business. I didn't ask," she said. "And he didn't tell me."

"Fernand figured out that you were a fake, didn't he?"

She nodded.

"He's dead now."

"So? He killed himself!" she said.

"The police have ruled it a homicide now," I said. Her face drained of color as I continued. "This isn't the first time Gladstone has done this. Another artist he represented disappeared. Her name was Anne Stokes. She was lost at sea seven years ago, and he inherited her estate."

"What are you saying?" she asked

"My niece overheard you telling him you were afraid someone would find out you were a fake. She was attacked yesterday, and is in the hospital now."

"It couldn't be Mort. He'd never do that . . ."

"Two artists he has represented have disappeared. Don't you think that's a bit of a coincidence?"

"But what does that have to do with me?"

"If he can make the artists disappear," I said, "he can do the same to you. That's why you have to leave with me. I'll take you back to the inn where you'll be safe." I listened; the water was no longer running in the pipes. "Come on," I said, feeling dread coalesce in the pit of my stomach.

A bewildered look crossed her round face, and she looked terribly young all of a sudden. "Why would he hurt me?" she asked. "I haven't done anything."

"Because you'll know," I said, feeling adrenaline pulse through me. Why could she not see? "When Nina Torrone is pronounced lost at sea in Maine next week, you'll know she was supposed to be in the Virgin Islands."

Her eyes got wide. "He just got a skiff this morning."

"I did." The voice came from the staircase. "And I thought I told you not to let anyone in."

TWENTY-TWO

Dread washed through me, but I masked it as well as I could. I turned to look at Gladstone. He was wearing a bathrobe, and held a gun in his hand. His hair — or what was left of it — was wet.

"I'm so sorry to interrupt you," I said, ignoring the gun. How much had he heard? More than enough, I was sure — but I was going to pretend I knew nothing. "I was just dropping off some cookies."

"I thought I heard the doorbell. And it sounds like you've brought more than cookies, from what I heard," he said. He waved the gun toward the living room and walked to the bottom of the stairs. "Why don't you go and sit down?"

"I really have to go," I said. "My fiancé is expecting me. I told him I was just going to drop off these cookies for you and Nina." I forced a brittle smile. "He's the island deputy, you know."

"Sit down." His voice was like iron, and his eyes were flat. Predatory. Like a shark's.

I was an idiot for coming here.

He waved the gun, directing us both toward the living room. My eyes strayed to Jennifer's; they were wide in her young face. I could see she believed me now — only five minutes too late.

Holding the cookies in front of me as if they could block a bullet, I shuffled through to the next room, turning over my options in my mind. Which didn't take long, as I couldn't come up with many.

I glanced around the room, searching for a weapon. There was a tall brass lamp on the corner table; I sat down on the sofa next to it. If I could distract him long enough, maybe I could whack him on the head. Jennifer sat down gingerly on the other side of the couch from me.

"I really need to be going," I said.

"You're not going anywhere," he told me. "Except maybe a boat ride."

"They'll figure it out," I blurted. "And there are eyes everywhere on this island. You'll never get away with it."

"No?" he asked. "It's worked out pretty well so far."

"John will come looking for me."

"And I'll tell him I haven't seen you," he

said mildly.

"My van is at the base of the hill."

"Thanks for reminding me. I'll take care of that in a little bit." He sat down across from us, in an easy chair, and leaned forward.

"What happened to the real Nina Torrone?" I asked.

"She was thinking of switching agents," he said. "I couldn't have that."

"So you killed her," I said.

"We argued. She slipped and hit her head. Fortunately," he nodded at Jennifer, "there was an adequate replacement available."

"What did you do with the body?"

"It's long gone, I'm afraid," he said.

"Like Anne Stokes," I said. "Did Nina change her will, just like Anne did?"

"You've been doing your research, Ms. Barnes," he said, adjusting the belt of his smoking-jacket-style robe. He looked like an actor in a bad movie. Too bad the gun was real. "Unfortunately not," he said. "But I negotiated with a major museum to sell a group of paintings worth a few million dollars. The sale should be finalized this afternoon, with the funds wired to an account in Switzerland. I will 'follow the money', so they say, and all of this unpleasantness will be behind us."

"Don't you think they'll be suspicious if you disappear?"

"They may suspect, but with no evidence . . . what can they do?" He gave me a smile that didn't reach his eyes. "I will leak the rumor that Nina and I ran off together. We're very close, you know," he said with a lecherous grin at Jennifer, who was now chalk white.

"Why did you kill Fernand?" I blurted.

"Ms. Barnes, surely you've deduced the reason by now. He figured out that Nina wasn't Nina, of course," Gladstone said. "He knew her personally, and could tell the difference." He sighed. "I didn't realize how much time they'd spent together, or I never would have moved to this island. The party was a mistake, but there was no avoiding it. I suspected he knew when he handed her that awful crème de menthe drink — I never could understand why she liked that cocktail. When I came to visit later that night, he confirmed it."

"So you drugged him."

"Yes," he said. "A pill in his scotch. And I'm sure you can figure out the rest."

I eyed the lamp, trying to track the cord. If I was going to grab it and start swinging, I didn't want to be hampered by a plug refusing to come out of the wall. Why hadn't

I waited until John came home to come and talk to Jennifer? Why hadn't I dragged her to the van immediately and told her what I knew in the safety of the inn? I took a deep breath and kept talking, stalling for time. Maybe John would come home and see the note. Maybe he'd show up at the front door with the entire police force. "Did you plan it all the first time it happened? With Anne Stokes?"

"It was a happy accident," he said. "But I really can't discuss that right now. I need you both to head downstairs."

"To the cellar? Why?" Jennifer asked in a breathy voice.

"I just do," he said, standing up and leveling the gun at me. "Now. Ladies first!"

Jennifer stood up quickly and obediently. "You're not going to hurt us, are you?"

"Of course not, my dear," he said, trying to sound avuncular. Which he did, but only in a creepy old uncle kind of way. "You've been wonderful. The gun is because I don't trust your friend, here. I know you wouldn't betray me."

She smiled faintly. Could she really believe him? He had just confessed to murder in front of her. Did she really believe she'd be able to walk away from this? For a moment I regretted prompting him to be honest in front of Jennifer, fearing that I had made her situation worse. But he was always going to kill her anyway, I realized, feeling my stomach turn over at the thought.

"But why do I have to go to the cellar?" she asked, sounding like a five-year-old girl.

Gladstone's voice was soothing. "It's only for a little bit, my dear. I promise, you'll be back in New York by the end of the week. I just have a few preparations to do — and I want you to keep an eye on her for me."

"Promise?"

"I promise," he said. "Why don't you take a few magazines with you? Keep you busy." He scooped up a handful from the coffee table and handed them to her; she took them peacefully. "Now," he said, "if you'll lead our friend to the cellar?"

She swallowed, but did as she was bidden, leading me to a narrow door at the end of the kitchen. It stuck as she opened it, and my heart sank when I noticed there was a dead bolt on the kitchen side of the door.

I went first down the rickety stairs, already shivering as the cold, dank air rushed up to greet me. The light from the kitchen illuminated only the top few stairs; I clutched at the railing and stepped gingerly forward, shuddering as the ancient steps creaked underfoot. When I got to the bottom, I peered into the gloom, looking for something I might use as a weapon, but could see nothing in the darkness. Only once Jennifer had descended did he turn on the light — a feeble 60-watt bulb suspended from a wire — and follow us down.

He was carrying a roll of duct tape.

"What's that for?"

"It's to keep our friend from getting any ideas," he said. "Where are your keys?" he asked me.

"In my jacket pocket."

"Toss them to me," he said. I pulled them out and did as he asked. Seeing my keys in his hand made me suddenly realize how vulnerable I was. "Thank you," he said, then turned back to Jennifer and held out the duct tape. "I'll need you to do the honors, my dear."

"What do you mean?"

His eyes flicked to me. "Ms. Barnes, if you would just put your hands behind your back."

"No," I said.

I heard the safety snick back. Even in the dim cellar, I could see that the flat look was back in his eyes, and his voice sent a shaft of ice through me. "I can end this now, you know."

"Okay, okay," I said, and thrust my hands

behind my back.

"My dear," Gladstone said, turning to Jennifer. "If you'll just tape them together for me?"

Eyes wide, she took the tape he handed her. A moment later, I heard a ripping sound as she pulled the tape from the roll. I moved my hands so they were a couple of inches apart, hoping that would allow me to wriggle out of it.

The doorbell rang upstairs. Hope flared in me. Was it John? My van was still at the base of the hill; he'd have to know I was there.

"Quickly," he said, and I felt the tape pulling at the skin of my wrists as she wrapped my hands three times.

"Is that enough?" she asked.

"It will do for now," Gladstone said. "And put a piece over her mouth."

"Her mouth?" To her credit, she sounded horrified.

"So she doesn't make noise. I don't want her alerting our guest."

Another rip, and a claustrophobic feeling as the tape covered my mouth. The doorbell rang again, and he hurried up the steps. The light bulb blinked off, the door slammed shut, and the dead bolt made a sick thud as he slammed it home.

■ ■ ■ ■

"Why did he turn off the light?" Jennifer's voice quavered. "I can't read if he turned off the light."

I would have responded, but she'd taped my mouth shut.

"I'm sorry about the tape, by the way," she said.

I made something of a soothing sound — or at least I tried to — and prayed she would shut up so I could listen. As I craned my head to listen, I worked at the tape around my wrists. There were definitely voices upstairs. I could hear Gladstone's stentorious baritone, and then a lighter, familiar, female voice. But whose was it?

"I had no idea he was such a terrible man," Jennifer rambled on, "or I never would have agreed to play the part. I can't believe he murdered that artist. I can't wait until I'm out of here and back to New York."

As if she'd ever leave this house alive, I thought. As if I'd ever leave this house alive. I strained again, trying to hear who was upstairs. Whoever it was had made it into the house; the voices were getting louder.

"I simply must speak to her," I heard from somewhere above, and recognized the voice instantly. *Catherine.* "Her niece has taken a turn for the worse."

Gwen. I felt a sharp pang of fear for my niece. Was she going to be okay?

"I'm afraid I don't know where she is," Gladstone lied.

"But her van is here," Catherine said. "Where else would she be?"

"I do not know, Madam. Now, I'm afraid I have a conference call coming up, so I'm going to have to ask you to leave."

"Where's Ms. Torrone?"

"She is unavailable at the moment. And not taking visitors."

"I was here just the other day," Catherine said. "She never leaves this house without you."

"She is indisposed," Gladstone repeated, a hint of steel in his voice. "I will thank you to depart, or I will have to call the police."

"My son *is* the police, thank you very much," she retorted. "And I will take my leave." There was a pause, and then she said, "Natalie was here. She left her cookies."

I felt my entire body tense. Would he shove her down in the cellar with us? Would my rash action result in yet another death?

"Perhaps she left them with Ms. Torrone."

"Why don't we ask her, then?" Catherine

364

said. *Leave!* I thought. *Go tell John I was here!*

Catherine might not have picked up on my thoughts, but it sounded like Gladstone did. "I wish you a very good afternoon, Madam."

"But . . ."

"Good bye."

I let out my breath as I heard the front door shut. The good news was, Catherine knew I had at least been here, and knew my van was here — but had left without being added to our little menagerie in the cellar. The bad news was, the pressure was now on Gladstone to get rid of us before the police came knocking at his door.

It was no surprise at all when Gladstone's footsteps grew louder, sounding as if they were stopped at the cellar door. I sucked in my breath — as best I could, with duct tape covering my mouth — and braced for the sound of the dead bolt sliding back, but it didn't come.

"Mort!" Jennifer's voice was high and scared. "Can you turn on the light?"

"Turn it on yourself," he barked, and then tramped away again. I heard the front door close a moment later; he must be going down to deal with the van. Which meant if I was lucky, I had at least a few minutes to figure out what to do.

I began working at the tape on my hands. If nothing else, Catherine's arrival had come at a good time; it had distracted Gladstone from checking Jennifer's tape job. As she fumbled up the stairs and flipped the switch, lighting the naked bulb, I twisted my hands, sucking in my breath as it ripped the hair off the backs of my wrists. By the time she made it to the bottom of the stairs, I was missing a good bit of skin, but one of my hands was free.

I reached up and ripped the tape from my mouth, sucking in a big breath of cold, musty air.

"What are you doing?"

"Getting out of your tape job," I said.

"But you're not supposed to be free," she said. I could see the whites all around her irises; she was terrified.

As was I, but I didn't let myself think about it. "He's planning on killing both of us anyway," I said, in the same tone of voice I usually used to tell John what I'd planned for dinner. "If both of us are free, we have a fighting chance of getting out of here alive."

She hugged herself. "Do you really think he's going to kill us?"

After hearing what her employer had told me just fifteen minutes ago, it boggled the mind that she had to ask — I didn't bother answering. As Jennifer wrung her hands, I headed up the stairs and tested the door, even though I was sure I'd heard the dead bolt. Sure enough, it was locked, and the solid wood didn't budge when I gave it an experimental thrust with my shoulder. I hurried back down the stairs. "Are there any windows in here?" I hadn't seen any daylight when the light was off, but it was always possible.

"I don't know," she said. "I've never been down here before."

I searched the tops of the walls, but the rock went all the way up, except for one slit the approximate size of a mail slot. So much for the window exit. If we were going to get out, it would have to be through the door. I peered into the gloomy corners of the basement. If only there were a sledgehammer, or a pick axe, somewhere buried in the clutter. "We have to break through the door," I told Jennifer. "Help me look for something big and heavy — an axe would be good, but even a two-by-four might help us ram through the door."

"Okay," she said, and dutifully began picking through the piles of debris scattered around the basement.

There was a pile of old plywood in one

corner, along with the remains of an old wood stove and an ancient mop that looked like it had had a major hair loss problem. I picked it up, wondering if I could use it as a battering ram — or at least a weapon — and set it near the steps as I continued to search.

I glanced over at Jennifer, who was peering into the corner farthest from the stairs. "See anything useful?" I asked, trying to be encouraging.

"A bunch of old *Reader's Digest* magazines — they're kind of moldy, though." She poked at the stack with a sneakered foot.

"Keep looking," I ordered.

We spent the next ten minutes — precious minutes, I knew, as I listened for the sound of Gladstone returning — searching the basement, but finished with nothing more than an over-the-hill mop and a small box of mason jars containing a black substance. I took a couple of cracks at the door with the mop, but it barely dented the wood.

"Looks like it's time to come up with Plan B," I said, sinking down on the step.

"Okay," she said. "What would that look like?"

"Putting him out of commission," I said.

"But he's got a gun!"

"That's the hitch." I picked up one of the

dusty jars and held it up to the light. "What do you think is in here?" I wondered. Out of curiosity, I unscrewed the lid — which was a bit of a challenge, as it had corroded over the years — and took a sniff. "Blueberries," I said. "In a liquid. Still smells surprisingly berrylike. I wonder how long it's been here?"

"Not much help against a gun, is it?" she asked.

"No," I said. It was not looking encouraging; although at least it sounded now as if she was on board with the plan. "I wish we could take out one of the steps, so he would stumble or something on the way down." Unfortunately, unless a saw magically appeared or I figured out how to gnaw through it with my teeth, that wasn't going to happen.

"We could always blow out the light bulb," she said. "Then attack him."

"Good idea," I said, surprised.

"The problem is, how would we know where he was to attack him? There would only be light at the top of the stairs; by the time he got down, we couldn't be sure to hit him in the right spot."

My spirits sank as fast as they'd risen. "You're right. If we whack him, we'd better get him the first time.

"Wait," I said, looking at the jar in my hand. I swirled the contents around. "I have an idea."

TWENTY-THREE

It was a long, tense wait as we crouched at the bottom of the stairs, waiting for Gladstone to arrive. Finally, after what seemed a small eternity, I heard the front door open and close. Jennifer and I exchanged glances, and I stood up and took my position near the bottom of the steps. The tape was affixed over my mouth, and my hands were behind my back — but clenched in my fists was the mop.

The footsteps moved around for a few minutes before drawing close to the door upstairs. I heard the chunk of the lock being pulled back. The door swung open, and I said a small prayer and glanced at Jennifer with what I hoped was a look of encouragement.

He stood, framed in the doorway, surveying us in the cellar. "You did well," he said, acknowledging the tape that appeared to be still plastered over my mouth. I stared at her, hoping her resolve wouldn't falter, and was relieved to see her give me a quick nod. He descended the stairs, the ancient wood creaking under his bulk. He had changed out of his smoking jacket and was now dressed in slacks and a winter coat, I noticed, but the gun was still in his hand. Did the coat mean he was planning on taking us outside? It didn't matter, I reminded myself. If all went well, he wouldn't be taking us anywhere.

He got to the bottom step and looked at me, gun trained on me. I stared at him, waiting for him to drop the gun for a moment; it was too risky to do anything with it pointed directly at me. I choked up on the mop behind my back, trying to figure out a way to distract him. Unfortunately, with my mouth taped shut, there wasn't a whole lot I could do. He turned to Jennifer. "I'm surprised you didn't . . ."

Before he could finish his sentence, Jennifer was in motion, slinging a jar full of berries in his face. No! I thought as an explosion went off in his hand. I lurched instinctively to one side. There was a stinging sensation on my leg, but I barely registered it as I swung the mop around, connecting with Gladstone's chest.

His face was coated in a dark purple fluid,

the blueberries sticking to him like dark blemishes. He was swiping at his eyes with his free hand as I hit him, and he let out a grunt. I pulled back to hit him again, and realized my mistake. I should have gone for the gun.

"Stop," he ordered me. And since his finger was on the trigger, I did.

He took a wheezy breath — the mop had made a bit of an impact, evidently — and ordered me to drop the mop. I did.

"I'm disappointed in you, Jennifer," he said, waving her over to stand next to me. "I'm afraid I'll have to consider our agreement void."

"But . . ."

I ripped the duct tape off my mouth. "He was going to kill you anyway," I reminded her.

"That's true," he admitted. Jennifer blanched.

"Did you do the same thing last time?" I asked. "With your first artist? Did you get a decoy and finish her off?"

"It really doesn't matter at this point, does it?" he asked. Despite the assured tone of voice, his eyes darted around nervously. "Now, let's go, before your fiancé's mother decides to come back."

"Where are we going?" I asked.

"For a ride," he said. "Get going." I took a step toward the stairs, but he stopped me. "Jennifer first, then you."

We filed upstairs, my stomach clenched tight with dread. Could I shut the door behind me and lock him in the cellar? As if reading my thoughts, he pushed the gun muzzle into my back, ending all speculation in that direction. I caught a whiff of blueberries, and thought how incongruous it was that the air smelled like a grandmother's kitchen, but I was facing an open grave.

As was Jennifer, who couldn't have been more than twenty-five. Poor girl. What would her family think? They wouldn't ever know what had happened to their daughter, I realized. She would just disappear.

I couldn't let that happen.

He herded us toward the side door off the kitchen. I scanned the countertops and table for anything I could grab, but there was nothing — and I wouldn't have had a chance to grab something if there was.

"Open it," he ordered Jennifer, who turned the knob with a shaking hand.

"Where are we going?" I asked.

"Down to the dock," he said.

I searched the water for a boat to flag as I picked my way down the shoveled walkway to the small dock off the back. With a sinking heart, I saw that the skiff Eleazer had brought over was moored there. It was the second time someone had tried to drown me from a dinghy, I thought as my foot slid on a patch of ice. If history insisted on repeating itself, I wished it would rerun the more pleasant aspects of life, instead of the parts where people were trying to tie bricks to me and toss me overboard.

I glanced over my shoulder, wondering if my van was still at the base of the driveway, but Gladstone jammed the gun harder into me and pushed me forward. A blast of cold air made me shiver, and I stumbled slightly as I made my way down to the water's edge, making the wound in my leg sting. The gun wavered, but only for a moment. Ahead of me, Jennifer was hugging herself as she picked her way down to the water. I could hear her sobbing, and resolved to do anything I could to save her. And me.

But what?

All too soon, we were at the dock.

"Get in," Gladstone said gruffly. Jennifer went first, letting out a small scream as she almost capsized the dinghy. I hesitated, trying to come up with a plan B. "You too," he said, giving me a shove that sent me reeling forward. I fell hard onto the bench seat, and a sharp pain bloomed in my hip. I reached down to steady myself, and my hand closed on an oar.

I didn't let it go.

Gladstone managed to train the gun on me as he clambered onto the bench seat at the back of the boat. We were still tied up, though. How was he going to manage that?

"Untie the ropes," he barked at me as he sat with one hand on the rudder. Well, that explained that. I let go of the oar and un-looped the rope from the cleats on the dock. The motor roared to life as I released the second knot, and I felt my stomach drop as he gunned the motor and we pushed away from the dock.

I sat back down and let my hand fall back to the oar. It was my only weapon. Would I find an opportunity to use it?

Not likely, I thought. Jennifer and I were positioned in front of Gladstone in the boat, with him in the back, one hand on the rudder and the other on the gun — which was still pointed directly at me. I knew Eleazer had just repaired the motor, so it should work like a charm.

The wind sliced through my coat and the storm-whipped waves made the small boat slam down on the water again and again as I scanned the horizon, hoping to see someone I could flag down. It was late in the day, though; all the lobstermen were miles off shore, checking their traps, and there weren't a lot of pleasure boats out in December. As I watched the little strip of land that was Cranberry Island recede into the distance, my hopes began to sputter. Was it really going to end here, on the cold water of the Gulf of Maine? My inn, my future with John, my life . . . was this the final chapter? For me — and for the young woman on the bench seat behind me, who was sobbing quietly, her cries stolen by the wind?

As I stared at the black barrel of the gun and came to terms with my fate, there was a sputtering sound. Gladstone swore, and my heart leapt as the engine gave one last guttural sound and died.

He pulled the starter cord, yanking at it again and again. It almost took on the third pull, but died into nothingness. We were adrift.

He narrowed his eyes at me. "Do you know anything about boat engines?"

I shook my head, still staring at the gun, my hand resting on the oar. Surely he'd have to put it down to check the engine — or at least turn it away from me.

"Go to the end of the boat," he barked. "Next to Jennifer." He trained the gun on me as I followed his instructions, sitting next to Jennifer's slender, shaking body. The oar was still in reach, and my hand sought it as he turned to look at the motor, pulling back the casing and peering at it. The gun was still pointed in my direction, but instead of aiming at my head, it was directed at my left arm. I spread my jacket over my hand as I lifted the oar, praying he wouldn't turn around, and slid it up over the bench seat. He glanced back at me, then swore again and turned to the motor. He tried to pull it out of the water with one hand, but was forced to use both. He still held the gun in his hand as he yanked at the engine cord, but it wasn't pointed at me — it was aimed at the bottom of the boat.

Adrenaline pulsed through me. I gripped the oar and pulled it up, leaping toward the front of the boat at the same time. Gladstone's head swiveled around as I brought the heavy wood around toward his head. As the oar made contact with his temple, the gun came up and went off with a deafening explosion.

His body went limp, sagging like a rag doll, and he slumped toward the side of the boat. I reached for the gun as it clattered from his hand, but it hit the edge of the boat and went over, vanishing into the leaden water.

I glanced down at myself, looking for blood. I hadn't felt a bullet, but I'd heard you don't always. Then I whirled around to check Jennifer; had the bullet hit her?

She was huddled in the back of the boat and crying, but appeared to be intact.

"You okay?" I asked.

"Yes," she said. "But there's a hole in the boat." I followed her pointing finger to where the water was rushing in, filling the bottom of the boat. We were no longer being held hostage by a lunatic with a gun — but we were in a boat with no engine in the middle of nowhere, with water gushing into our skiff and the murderer still in the boat with us.

"We need to stop up the hole," I said, digging in my pocket for a glove and jamming it into the hole. It didn't stop the water, but at least it slowed it. I looked around for a bailing bucket; thankfully, Eli had left a cut-open bleach bottle in the bottom of the boat. I handed it to Jennifer. "Bail with this," I said. "I'll tie up Gladstone."

"I wish we could just push him overboard," she said.

"Me too," I said, "but we can't. Throw me that rope, will you?"

She tossed me the rope I'd untied just minutes ago — although by now, it felt like hours — and I shoved Gladstone onto his side and reached for his arms, pulling them behind his back. Try as I might, I couldn't keep them from flopping onto the bench.

"Need a hand with that?" Jennifer asked as she scooped some water overboard. Getting rid of Gladstone — and having a task — seemed to have revived her. As a cold gust slammed into us, I hoped it would be enough. How would anyone find us out here?

I pushed that thought away. If I didn't get Gladstone incapacitated, it wouldn't matter.

Jennifer held his hands together as I wrapped the rope around them a half dozen times, then pulled it tight and tied it using one of the knots John had taught me.

"We should do the feet, too, don't you think?" I asked.

"I've got another rope here," Jennifer said, reaching for the second one. Together we bound his ankles together; then we pushed him sideways, so that he was wedged between the back bench of the boat and the motor.

The water had crept up as we worked; I readjusted the glove in the hole and Jennifer started bailing again. With no motor, no food and water, a hole in the bottom of the boat, and not much to keep us warm — I had a coat, but Jennifer was shaking with cold — we wouldn't last long. I picked up the oar I'd used to whack Gladstone and then reached for its sister, thankful that there were oarlocks.

"You're going to row us back in?" Jennifer asked as she scooped another bucket of water out of the boat.

"What choice do we have?" I asked. I fitted the oars in and slipped my coat off, shivering violently at the cold.

"What are you doing?" she asked as I handed it to her.

"I'll work up a sweat rowing," I said. "We'll take turns."

"Are you sure?" she asked, teeth chattering.

"Take it," I said.

I sat on the bench and began to turn the boat around, sending salt water spraying into both of our faces. Jennifer bailed from the front of the boat, Gladstone lay on the floor of the back of the boat, and I fought with the waves, trying to pilot the boat back toward land.

I rowed hard for what must have been twenty minutes, then looked back over my shoulder. My heart sank at what I saw. The little strip of land I knew was Cranberry Island appeared no bigger, and the sky was already darkening. The temperature was dropping, too; even with the rowing, the wind whipped away any shred of body heat I was able to generate. Gladstone hadn't come to, but he had groaned a few times.

"We don't seem to be getting any closer, do we?" Jennifer asked.

"No," I said. Hearing it from her made it more real.

"What are we going to do?"

"I don't know what we can do," I said. If only I had a cell phone that worked. "You don't have your cell phone with you, do you?" I asked, wondering why it hadn't occurred to me earlier.

"No," she said, shaking her head. "But he might."

We both looked at Gladstone, wedged into the back of the boat, with something like dread. "I'll look," I volunteered.

I checked his jacket pockets first. The top one was easy, but only filled with Kleenex. It occurred to me that we should have taken his coat off before tying him up. He groaned as I shifted him; I didn't dare do it now. I dug in the bottom pocket, but only found my van keys.

"Where did he keep his phone?" I asked.

"In the back pocket of his pants," she said.

To my relief, it was in the pocket closest to me. I felt a surge of triumph as I pulled the rectangular phone from his pocket and jabbed at the button at the bottom. I gave a little whoop as the screen came to life, then turned on the screen and dialed 911. I couldn't tell them where we were, but if they knew we were out here, at least they could look for us.

I held it to my ear and sent up a little prayer, but nothing happened. I looked at the screen: out of service area.

I dropped the phone to my lap and closed my eyes. "No signal?" she asked.

"No signal," I said, my last shreds of hope dissipating on the icy wind.

"Guess we'd better keep rowing then," Jennifer said. I could hear despair in her voice.

"Guess so," I said, and even though both of us knew it was fruitless — the wind was more powerful than we were — I picked up the oars again.

After another thirty minutes, we traded spots; I took the coat and the bailing bucket and Jennifer began rowing. Jennifer was not in good shape, though, and began huffing after the first few minutes. I tried not to look at the small strip of land, which seemed to be getting smaller by the moment. And darker. Already I could see the first lights twinkling as night began to fall.

"Maybe we should try the motor again," I said, shivering even under the coat.

"Worth a try," she said.

I pulled the starter cord, but nothing happened. I tried again, but nothing happened. I pulled again and again, praying that the motor would roar to life, but it remained cold and silent.

"What are we going to do?" Jennifer asked after I'd pulled the cord for the twentieth time. Why didn't I know about boat motors? I wished Eli were here. Or John. What had Gladstone done with my van? Surely Catherine had told the police my van was at Gladstone's house. John must be back by now, and looking for me. But how would he know to look for me a mile out to sea?

I readjusted the glove, wedging it farther into the hole, and looked at Jennifer. The oars barely skimmed the surface of the water as she rowed; the spray kept blowing back into her face. She looked absolutely miserable.

"I'll take over," I said, shrugging out of the coat again. "Take this and stay warm." I took the oars and began rowing again, wishing I still had both gloves. I was going to get frostbite on my right hand; already I could feel the numbness creeping up to my knuckles.

Then again, unless there was a miracle, frostbite would be the least of my troubles.

TWENTY-FOUR

Evening faded into night, and still we drifted. Gladstone was murmuring now, showing signs of waking. My fingers had grown numb, and my body cried out with every fruitless stroke.

"Take a break," Jennifer finally said. "Let's share the coat." As the moon rose and the wind howled, we huddled together in the middle of the boat, our feet damp from the leak, our fingers icy as we took turns bailing.

"I'm so sorry it's turned out this way," I said to her as we watched the distant lights of Cranberry Island. They were as far away as the stars. "Does your family know where you are?"

"They just know I got an acting job, and that I was going to be out of town," she said. "My last conversation was with my mother; she wanted me to get an office job, and I told her I didn't want to." She gave a muffled sob. "I wish I'd listened to her."

"You didn't know," I said. "And just because this job didn't work out, it doesn't mean you can't get another, better one." I realized as I spoke that the likelihood of her getting any job — or getting out of this boat alive — were extremely remote. Still . . .

"Do you think?" she asked.

"Absolutely," I said.

She voiced the fear that had been growing in my mind as night fell on the empty water. "It's a little late, isn't it?"

"You never know," I said. "My fiancé should be home soon, and looking for me. And Catherine — my future mother-in-law — knows we were at Cliffside. Besides, the lobstermen should be coming back soon." As I had constantly since we began drifting, I scanned the horizon, looking for a boat. Twice we had heard the thrum of an engine and tried to wave the captain down, but both times the sound had drifted away.

"Why would they look for us on a boat? We don't even have a light!" Her teeth chattered as she talked, and I huddled closer to her thin, cold body.

"Eli knows he delivered a boat to Gladstone. When it's not there, they'll start looking for it." At least I hoped so.

We lapsed into silence, listening to the

wind as it lashed the boat — and the incoherent mutterings of Gladstone, who thankfully hadn't woken up yet. How frustrating to have gotten rid of our attacker only to be stranded in a leaky boat in the middle of the Gulf of Maine . . .

Night fell, cloaking us in darkness. The wind picked up, and it began to sleet, soaking our one jacket and tossing the little boat like a child's toy. Jennifer's quaking became stronger, and Gladstone began to stir, his murmuring turning to yelling. He thrashed around as I bailed furiously. My hands and feet were now soaked and half-frozen, the stinging pain of cold replaced by a numbness that worried me. Jennifer had retreated into quiet sobbing; she had given up. I was tempted to, but as the water reached my ankles, I found myself reaching for the bailing bucket. Again and again I filled it, dumping the water over the sides with unfeeling fingers. But the cold took its toll on me; I was dumping a scoop of water over the side when a rogue wind knocked the bucket from my fingers.

"No!" I cried as the bleach bottle skittered over the waves, out of reach, and vanished into the darkness. Panic welled in my throat as I looked down at the hole in the boat; already the water level was rising. I jammed my fingers into the icy water, pushing at the glove, trying to keep the seal. The sleet rained down on me, the cold water seeping up my legs. I had never been so cold in my life.

I was tempted to pull the plug and let the water claim us quickly, but a glance at Jennifer stayed my hand. She was no older than my niece. How could I make that decision when there was any hope left? I gritted my teeth and cupped my hands, scooping the icy water up and dumping it over the side. I kept moving even though I knew it was no use. The water still rose.

I knelt, my hands in the icy water, my existence reduced to the water and the cold, fighting off the feeling of faintness and fatigue that threatened to swallow me, when Jennifer cried out. "A motor!"

I looked up, barely able to focus.

"And a light. Over there!" she said. She stood up in the boat just as a wave knocked the little skiff sideways. I watched in horror as she lost her balance, then toppled into the water.

"Jennifer!" A burst of energy from reserves I didn't know I had shot through me, and I lurched toward her. I thrust my arm into the inky water, searching for her hand. Her head popped up above the water, and I heard her gasp. "Here!" I yelled. "Take my hand!"

I felt something close around my numb fingers and squeeze them. I tried to pull, but my strength had left me. The boat was already filling with water; I could feel it on my shins now as I leaned over the boat, grasping Jennifer's hand.

"Help!" I called, my voice hoarse. The motor was close, and I could make out a light in the darkness. "Help! Over here!"

"Natalie!" The voice was one I'd thought I'd never hear again.

"John," I whispered.

He'd come.

I didn't speak again until I was swathed in three blankets and encased in the wheelhouse. Terri and John had pulled Jennifer onto Terri's lobster boat, then me, managing to extricate Gladstone just before the boat went under. John threw a blanket on the agent's prone body while Sara swathed Jennifer and me in blankets and coats.

"Take me home," I said in a voice so dry and small it was hard even for me to hear.

"Soon, my love," John said, coming over to press my icy hands between his own. "We have to go to the mainland first, and get you checked out. You've got hypothermia, and Jennifer's in even worse shape."

"And Gladstone . . ."

"We have to deal with him, too." He peeled off my wet socks and tossed them aside. The tingling as he warmed my feet made me gasp with pain.

"Tell me what happened," John said. "It will distract you."

"How did you find me?" I whispered.

"It was Catherine," he said, nodding to my future mother-in-law, who was tucking a second blanket around Jennifer. "She saw your note and headed over to find you. When she saw the van but Gladstone said you weren't there, she got suspicious and called me."

I gave Catherine a grateful look, and she smiled.

"But by the time we got to the house," John continued, "the van was gone. We found it near Fernand's house, but you weren't in it. I had no idea where to find you until Eli mentioned that he'd dropped off a skiff. We've been searching for you ever since." He pushed a strand of wet hair from my face. "I was afraid we were too late. I thought I'd lost you," he added in a low voice that made my heart ache with love. How could I have wondered if this was the right man for me?

"You almost did," I said. "If you'd been five minutes later . . ."

"Don't think about it," he said.

"He confessed to killing Fernand," I said, looking at Gladstone's prone form. "Jennifer isn't Nina. I mean, Nina isn't Nina."

His eyebrows rose. "She's an imposter?"

I nodded. "Fernand knew the night of the party. That's why he died. I think Gladstone killed the real Nina, too. And he did it once before."

"I ran a criminal background check on him," John said. "There was one assault case, but no murder."

"He wasn't caught," I said, suddenly feeling dizzy. "He tried to kill me, and Jennifer. He attacked Gwen, too . . ." My voice trailed off.

"Sshh," he said. "Take it easy. We can get the details later."

"Is the van okay?"

"It's fine," he said. "The van's okay, and I got a call from the attorney today."

"Oh, no." My stomach tightened. "Is everything okay?"

"Better than okay. They located your mortgage attorney."

"Where?"

"He'd fled to the Yucatan peninsula and was in the process of buying an estate with your money. They're charging him with fraud and have frozen his accounts. It looks like there should be enough to reimburse the mortgage company — they're filing suit against him."

"So we're off the hook?"

"We might have to pay a few extra months of mortgage — the attorney is negotiating that right now — but there's a good chance that even if we're out of pocket now, we'll be reimbursed later. Best of all, they've reversed the foreclosure proceedings; the inn is safe."

The inn is safe. Despite the cold in my body, those words sent a wave of warmth through me.

"I love you," I said.

He kissed me lightly on the forehead, and I felt my body relax for the first time in weeks. John sat down beside me, wrapping me in his arms to warm me, and I drifted off to sleep with my head on his shoulder.

Sara and Catherine stayed with us as the hospital checked us out; Terri had gone out in search of a coffee shop and returned with two steaming cups of good coffee. "Better than hospital fare," she said, her blue eyes twinkling as she handed me a cup. Gladstone had been taken to a different room, and was under police guard. Evidently the crack on the head was enough to knock him out, but not enough to do permanent damage. He'd be able to stand trial. The police were taking Jennifer's statement in a nearby room; Catherine had gone with her for support.

I took a grateful sip of the dark roast coffee and smiled at Terri's friendly, open face. "Thanks," I said. "And I wanted to let you know how glad I am you two are on the island — tell Sara I'm sorry Maggie started that stupid petition."

"Maggie won't be here for long," Sara said from her chair in the corner. Like Terri, she had blue eyes, but while Terri wore her hair close cropped, Sara's hair was long and pulled back in a low ponytail. Her cheeks were still pink from the wind; evidently they'd been on the water searching for us for hours, along with the rest of Cranberry Island's lobster boat fleet. "She's moving back to Illinois."

I almost spilled my coffee. "What?"

"She got caught up in the mortgage fiasco, too," John said. "But to be honest, I'm not sure island life suited her."

"It's a shame, really," Sara said, pursing her chapped lips. "I loved her kids. The school will miss them."

"Really?" I asked, surprised at her response. "Even though she started that nasty petition?"

"Everyone pretty much ignored it," Terri said, leaning back in her chair and crossing her jean-clad legs. She'd traded her waders in for duck boots, I noticed. "Except Ingrid, and she was backing away from it because it wasn't too popular and she didn't want to lose the next election."

"I don't understand what the big deal is," I said, thinking of Rob, and how he was terrified to let anyone know how he felt about Fernand. And how Fernand was nervous about going public with his own relationship. "Maybe you two will be the vanguard."

"We're just living our lives," Terri said, her eyes meeting Sara's. A tender look passed between them, and I instinctively turned to John. His green eyes crinkled at the corners as he smiled at me.

"I'm glad you're okay," he said, reaching over to squeeze my hand.

"Me too," I said, squeezing back. "I'm worried about the real Nina Torrone, though," I said, feeling a pit in my stomach. "I hope the police are able to get Gladstone to tell them what happened."

"We can't change what happened to Nina,

but at least you and Jennifer are okay," he said.

"It was awfully close. If you hadn't gotten there when you did . . ."

"But we did," Sara said. "And you did a great job dealing with Gladstone. We had to cut the rope off of him — those knots were tight."

I shuddered, remembering the long hours in the boat. "I was sure we were dead," I said. "I can't figure out what happened to the motor, though. Eli had just fixed it."

"He told me he didn't fill up the tank before he delivered it to Gladstone," Terri said.

"So we ran out of gas?" I asked.

"Most likely," Terri said. "He wasn't much of a seaman, I'm afraid."

"Good thing, too," I said. "If he hadn't turned to check out the motor, I never would have had a chance to bean him." I shivered, thinking of where I would be now.

"Aunt Nat?"

I looked up to see Gwen, who was standing in the doorway, Adam at her side, in a hospital gown.

"I hope you don't mind; I thought she'd want to see you," Catherine said, smiling.

My niece came over and hugged me. "Catherine told me what happened. How terrifying!"

"Yes, but it's over," I said.

"And you saved Jennifer."

"I almost got us both killed," I said. "Maybe our plan wasn't the best, after all."

"I've been so worried about you. I tried to call the inn, but nobody answered."

"That's because they were all out looking for your aunt," Terri said, and Gwen hugged me again. She was still skinny as a rail; the hospital food didn't appear to be helping.

"I'm sorry I didn't think to tell you as soon as we got here," I said. "With all the hullabaloo . . ."

"It's okay," Gwen said. "You're okay. And as long as we're all together, that's the most important thing."

I looked around the room at John, and Gwen and Adam, and Cathcrine, who stood by the doorway with a half smile on her face. Even Terri and Sara, who had spent hours in the cold and the dark searching for a stranded boat.

Gwen was right. I loved the inn . . . but I loved the people in my life even more.

"I'm so nervous," Gwen said as I pulled three pans of Eggnog Bread from the oven a few days later. She was dressed in a simple black sheath, with a dangly pair of crystal earrings that sparkled in the afternoon light.

"All the art is out and displayed, right?"

"Mostly. John is going to head over with me to put the finishing touches on it."

"So really, all you have to do is show up," I said as I set the last pan on a cooling rack. The entire kitchen was wreathed in its spicy vanilla scent; it was all I could do not to slice off a hunk and eat it warm from the oven. I resisted the urge, though; it was for the show. "You put your watercolors in, too, right?"

"Yes," she said. "Of course. But what if nobody likes them?"

"They will," I reassured her, but I could tell the words were lost on her.

"I'm going to go try on the other dress," she said, and disappeared back upstairs.

I sighed, wishing there were some way to tell her the show was bound to be a success. Or at least a partial success; I wasn't sure her oils would sell, but I knew her watercolors would shine. Ever since she'd gotten back from the hospital, Gwen had been working night and day at the studio — and with the murderer safe behind bars, I'd given up trying to stop her. It would be over soon enough.

I slid a knife around the edges of the golden brown loaves and thought about the changes the last week had wrought in my life. Gladstone had been charged with Fernand's murder and the assault on Gwen, and the police were looking into Nina Torrone's disappearance — and the disappearance of Anne Stokes years earlier. Both Jennifer and I had been discharged from the hospital after recovering from hypothermia. As soon as she'd given the police her statement, Jennifer had high-tailed it home to her family . . . and, I hoped, a less dangerous future in the acting business.

The phone rang as I turned off the oven; it was Charlene.

"How are you feeling?"

"Positively chipper," I said. "And I'll be even better when this art show is over."

"Even though your future mother-in-law is moving in next door?"

"How did you hear that?"

"She's down at the store drinking black coffee and munching on celery sticks. She's told everyone how wonderful you are."

"I think it'll be okay, actually," I said, and was surprised to realize that I meant it. I was glad to help her out. Not only was she John's mother, but without her quick thinking, I wouldn't be alive.

"Really?"

"Really," I said. "I'm actually starting to

like her. She seems stiff at first, but there's a good person in there." It was funny; at first she'd seemed standoffish, but now that I got to know her, I found myself warming to her gutsy personality. John and I had agreed to let her stay in the carriage house until she got her feet under her; in exchange, she would help with some of the hotel chores (with the exception of cooking). I was nervous about the arrangement, but felt it was the right thing to do; after all, what was family for but to help each other out? Besides, now that her shameful secret was out, she had really relaxed. I didn't know how things would turn out, but we'd give it a shot.

"I heard you got stiffed."

"Yeah, by Fernand's sister. As soon as she found out she wasn't in the will, she skipped town. Her credit card was declined, so she stayed for free."

"Ouch."

"Actually, it's fine. Now that the mortgage fiasco is worked out, it's a loss we can absorb. And she is Fernand's sister, after all."

"So Frederick's getting to plan the service himself?"

"No more conflicts of interest," I said. Frederick had stayed on, thankfully — we'd taken to inviting him to dinner in the kitchen with us, where we reminisced about our evenings with Fernand. With Irene out of the way, Frederick had thrown himself into planning Fernand's memorial service. He'd taken me up on my offer to host the reception at the inn: a sad event, but one I felt compelled to hold. He was still grieving, but I had come to enjoy his company.

"Do you think he'll stay on the island?"

"I don't know. I hope he doesn't sell Fernand's house — I'd love it if he at least came to visit from time to time — but I think it's too soon to think about that."

Rob, too, seemed to be recovering from the loss of Fernand. Sara had come to visit me the day after she rescued Jennifer and me from the sinking dinghy, and she'd told me confidentially that Rob had approached her about what it was like being "out" on Cranberry Island. He wasn't ready to spill the beans yet, and was still grieving Fernand's loss, but Sara had told him to come talk to her whenever he needed to and had put him in touch with a group in Bar Harbor. It wouldn't heal his pain, but maybe he would feel less alone.

"Well, I'd better figure out what to wear," Charlene said. "I ordered a cocktail dress the other day, and I'm thinking this might be just the event to take it for a test drive."

"Can't wait to see it," I said, hoping I remembered where I'd put my 'all-purpose' dress.

"Have you called Claudette, by the way? She's been bugging me about it. She told me she swung by to see you yesterday, but you weren't there."

"Shoot. With everything going on, I forgot to call her back."

"It's been a crazy week, hasn't it?"

"You can say that again," I told her as I poured myself a cup of coffee. I cradled the warm mug in my hands and looked out the window toward the cold water, thinking of those long hours in the leaky skiff. The skin of my fingers and toes still stung with frostbite; the doctor had told me it would take a while to heal, but that I was lucky I hadn't lost a finger or toe. Another thing to be grateful for. "At least we figured out what happened to Fernand," I said.

"And you get to keep the inn. Which is better than what happened to Zelda."

"Poor Zelda," I said. Zelda Chu, as it turned out, had used the same mortgage at-torney I had — but either the company she'd worked with had been less forgiving, or she'd let the problem go on too long before dealing with it. Word was her new future retreat center had been foreclosed on, and she was heading back to New York. Which was not good news for Zelda — or for Gwen, who had been counting on her as a mentor. "I'm surprised Murray isn't helping her out," I said.

"Apparently he got burned, too, on some speculation property farther down the coast. The attorney had all the paperwork forwarded to his office, so they didn't know it was in foreclosure until it was too late."

"That's awful!" I said.

"It is. You got really lucky, Natalie."

"In more ways than one," I said, thinking of all the blessings in my life. John, the inn, my near-miraculous rescue by Terri and Sara . . .

But there was still something bothering me — some piece of business that seemed unfinished. I just couldn't put my finger on what it was.

TWENTY-FIVE

"Shoot — customers," Charlene said. "We're short on baked goods, by the way."

"I'll whip something up this afternoon," I told her.

"Great," she said. "See you tonight!"

"Looking forward to it!" I hung up and took a sip of coffee, then turned on my computer and checked my gift orders. John's new set of woodworking tools were scheduled to be delivered tomorrow, as was the silk scarf I'd ordered for my mother-in-law and the books on creativity I'd ordered for Gwen. Biscuit wove between my legs, meowing. "Don't worry, your Christmas catnip is coming," I told her, reaching down to stroke her head. Her rumbling purr vibrated against my hand.

I wiped my hands on a dishtowel and walked into the parlor, mentally ticking off the things I needed to do. The balsam fir John had cut down for us twinkled from the corner of the parlor, filling the room with its green, festive scent. John and I had gotten the lights up, but Charlene, Gwen, Frederick, John, Adam and I would decorate it that evening, after the show; I was planning on putting the cider in the crockpot with cloves and cinnamon before we left for the gallery, and reserving one loaf of Eggnog Bread for home consumption.

I had finished my coffee and was headed down to bring the boxes of ornaments up from the cellar when there was a heavy "thunk" at the kitchen door. I turned to look; a figure moved behind the glass of the kitchen door.

"Hello!"

No answer.

I hurried over to the door, feeling uneasy, and opened it. A headless Barbie doll lay on the porch, spattered with red paint, and a woman was running toward the woods. "Hey!" I called. The woman tripped and went sprawling into the snow. I leaped over the porch steps and into the snow, determined to find out who had been leaving those awful dolls at my doorstep.

As the woman — she had dark hair, and was wrapped in a shapeless coat — struggled to her feet, Claudette's ancient Pinto crested the hill. I barely spared it a glance, though;

I was focused on catching my stalker. The snow filled my sneakers as I ran toward her. I was ten feet away when she turned, a look of hatred and fear on her face that made me stop in my tracks.

"I knew you'd follow me here! You're always after me."

"Dawn?" I said, confused.

"Dawn!" Claudette called. She had gotten out of the car and was hurrying over to us. "Natalie, I'm so sorry . . . I've been trying to tell you."

"Stop calling me that!" Claudette's daughter-in-law said. Gone was the coiffed woman I'd seen at Fernand's party; her face was pale and drawn, and the look in her eyes sent a shiver of fear through me.

"Dawn," she said. "This is Natalie. It's not Patricia."

"You're lying," she hissed, her pale face contorted with fear and hatred. "She's just pretending."

"Natalie isn't here to get you. She just reminds you of the woman you're afraid of."

"No," she said, shaking her head vehemently. "You're wrong."

"Come home with me, Frances," Claudette said. Frances? I wondered. I thought her name was Dawn! "It's cold out here. I'll make you hot chocolate."

The woman's face softened slightly. "With marshmallows?"

"With marshmallows," Claudette said. "And whipped cream, just like you like it."

"Are there any cookies?" Her voice was that of an eight-year-old's. It was eerie to watch.

"We can make some," my friend said. "Why don't you get into the car where it's warm?"

"She's not coming with us, is she?" Dawn/Frances said, narrowing her eyes at me.

"No, it's just us," Claudette said, coming up and putting an arm around her daughter-in-law. "Come on, sweetheart." Suddenly docile, the woman followed Claudette to the little Pinto, allowing the older woman to buckle her in as if she was a child. When Claudette had closed the door behind the woman, she turned to me. "I'm so sorry, Natalie. I tried to tell you, but I couldn't reach you."

"What's going on?" I asked.

Claudette gave a deep sigh. "She's suffering from dissociative personality disorder. Apparently she was abused as a child. It used to be manageable — it only happened once in a while — but lately . . ."

"No wonder you're looking so exhausted all the time," I said. "Is the disorder why she has two names?"

Claudette nodded. "This personality is called Frances; her psychiatrist thinks it's a throwback to her younger self. She had some bad experiences as a child . . . and unfortunately, she seems to think you're a woman who abused her."

"Her abuser was named Patricia?"

Claudette nodded.

"No wonder she's been leaving the dolls," I said. "But why dolls?"

"I don't know. She cut the goats, too," she said. "I think she was using the blood for something, but I don't know what."

I did, but I wasn't going to tell Claudette right now. Dawn was evidently very disturbed.

"We're taking her to the hospital on the mainland tomorrow," Claudette said in almost a whisper. "They're going to keep her for observation."

"I hope they're able to figure out what's going on and fix it," I said.

"Me too," she said.

"If you need anything . . . Help with the kids, anything at all . . ."

"I know who to call," Claudette said. I gave her a big hug and watched as she climbed into the Pinto and drove back up the hill.

I walked back to the inn, hugging myself for warmth, and stooped to pick up the doll from the steps. Poor woman: trapped between adulthood and a traumatized childhood. I walked into the warm kitchen to find John leaning against the kitchen table with a cup of coffee in his hand. "Hey there, pretty lady," he said with a rakish grin, but the smile on his face evaporated as he saw the doll in my hand. "Another one?"

"Yes, but I know who it was now."

"How?"

I told him what had just happened, and he shook his head. "Poor Claudette."

"Every family has its secrets, I suppose," I said, dumping the doll into the trash can and pouring myself a cup of coffee.

"Including mine," John said, with a grimace. "Are you sure you're okay with my mother moving into the carriage house?"

I walked to John and gave him a kiss on the cheek. "We're family now — or will be, soon. That's what we do for each other."

"Are you sure?" he asked. "It'll be a big change. And I know you two don't get along too well."

"We're getting better," I said. "Besides, she saved my life, remember?"

"I don't want you to do this just because you feel indebted."

"I'm not. I'm glad to be able to help," I said. "Just like you helped me out — and Claudette's helping her son and daughter-in-law out."

John ran a hand through his hair. "I wish she hadn't tried so hard to protect me from the truth," John said. "We might have been able to save the house."

"We can't go back and change it," I said. "She's here now, and needs a place to stay; and it just so happens we have one." I smiled at him. "Besides, that solves our question of where to live. If your mother takes over the carriage house, you'll just have to join me here at the inn."

There was still a crease between his eyebrows. "Are you sure you're okay with that?"

I thought of the retreat I had made for myself, up above the kitchen. Was I willing to share my room with the views of the water, and the blue and white quilt I'd bought at the antique fair last year? With the wooden bookshelves overflowing with my favorite mysteries? Yes, I realized, looking at this man with his shock of sandy hair and his caring green eyes. "Absolutely," I said, feeling my heart overflow with warmth as he took me into his arms. I closed my eyes, relishing his warm, woody smell. I'd never felt this way about anyone before. To think I'd be able to spend the rest of my life with this man . . . I tilted my chin up, and he kissed me.

At that moment, Gwen appeared on the stairs. "Sorry to interrupt, but the boat leaves in twenty minutes."

I sighed as we broke our embrace, but told myself that there would be plenty of time later.

The rest of our lives, in fact.

Charlene, Catherine, and I arrived at the gallery twenty minutes before it was scheduled to open. One of Gwen's oils was highlighted in the front window. It wasn't my favorite, but I tried to tell myself that taste was completely subjective.

Herb Munger met us at the doorway, resplendent in plaid Sansabelt pants and a virulently orange sweater. I handed him the tray of Eggnog Bread, which I had had to defend from Charlene on the entire trip over from Cranberry Island, then put my coat on a hook and smoothed my black, tea-length dress. It was actually a little looser than it had been last time I put it on; all the stress of the last week must have gotten to me. "Looks great, don't you think?" he beamed.

Charlene's eyebrows rose at the sight of his ensemble, but she smiled politely. She was decked out in a form-fitting purple dress spangled with sequins that made my simple black dress look positively plain. "Sure does," I said, looking around the room, which was filled with enormous oil paintings, none of which were to my taste. On the back wall, however, were a half dozen watercolors that were beyond anything I'd ever seen Gwen paint before.

"Wow," Charlene said, as we gravitated to the back of the gallery, both entranced by a watercolor of a small pond ringed by verdant green trees. A lone boat floated in the pond's center, and the light was so pure I felt as if I could walk into the painting. "This is just gorgeous," I breathed. "She really has improved."

"And how," Charlene said, adding a low whistle. "The girl's got talent."

"She did an oil of the same scene," Munger said, pointing to a large, square canvas that vaguely mirrored the delicate watercolor, but lacked its ethereal beauty. "So much more impact. It's more of a representational piece — not so exacting. A statement piece."

"I still like this one better," I said.

"Me too," Charlene said.

"Hey, you," John said, materializing at my right arm with two glasses of white wine. He looked good enough to eat in a dark green sweater that brought out the color of his eyes and a pair of khaki pants. He bent down to give me a kiss. "You look lovely," he said.

"Thanks — but not as lovely as these new watercolors. Where's Gwen?"

"She's freaking out in the back room," he said, handing Charlene and me each a glass. "Here. Drink this."

I thanked him and took a sip of the slightly sweet wine. "I'll leave you two lovebirds alone," Charlene said, and headed toward the snack table.

"It's really just an excuse for a snack," I said, leaning against John. "I wish Fernand could be here," I said.

"He's here in spirit."

"Maybe." I sighed. "I'm worried Gwen won't come back. Zelda was going to be her mentor, but with her going back to New York . . ."

"Something will turn up," John said. "She's got too much here to abandon it. You, the inn, Adam, the studio . . . and her art has grown so much recently."

"Her watercolors, anyway," I said, eyeing a lurid blue canvas.

"That's her art," John said. "This is a business proposition. A misguided one, in my opinion, despite Fernand's encouragement. I hate what happened to him, but Gwen probably needed to find a mentor who would help her be true to her instinct."

"I hope she finds one," I said, and took another sip of wine.

"I can't believe they sold in ten minutes," Gwen said, eyes shining, as we trundled in through the front door of the Gray Whale Inn three hours later. The snow had started outside, falling in fat flakes that would almost certainly blanket the island by morning, and for the first time since Fernand died, I was feeling the Christmas spirit. Charlene and Adam had joined Gwen, Catherine, John, and me, and were planning to stay as we trimmed the tree; if it snowed too heavily, I'd just put them up in the inn. The air was scented with cinnamon and cloves from the apple cider I'd put in the crockpot before leaving the island, and our spirits were high as we peeled off our coats and filled the mugs I'd set out on the counter.

"I told you watercolor was the way to go!" I said, grinning at my niece as she wrapped her hands around a mug.

"Munger was kicking himself for not charging more for them," she said.

"Mimi Kuhn seemed interested in your work," John said as I unwrapped the last plate of Eggnog Bread and opened a tin of fudge. Biscuit had perked up at our arrival, meowing hopefully; as I arranged a plate of goodies for the humans, John took pity on her and gave her a can of her favorite food.

"She did," Gwen said. "I'm so honored; she does the most beautiful work."

"Another mentor possibility?" I asked.

"She wanted to have lunch in January, after I get back from California."

"So you will be back?"

"Absolutely," she said, grinning at Adam.

"I certainly hope so," he said. "Not too many lobsters in California."

She looked at him with shining eyes, and I found myself smiling. We had our old Gwen back — and she wasn't planning on leaving.

"Let's go into the parlor," I said, nibbling at a piece of Eggnog Bread and deciding I needed to make it again — soon. I pushed through the swinging kitchen door, my mug in one hand and the plate of bread in the other, and felt another surge of Christmas spirit at the scent of the fir tree in the corner. When I went to set the tray down

415

on the table, I was surprised to see a small box with a red ribbon.

"Why isn't this under the tree?" I asked, setting down the tray and picking up the small package.

"I want you to open it now," John said, his eyes crinkling as he smiled.

I carefully removed the silver paper; it was a jewelry box. I looked up at John. "But the mortgage back payment . . ."

"Shh," he said. "Just open it."

What was inside took my breath away. A beautiful sapphire, the color of the water out behind the inn, nestled between two starry diamonds on a slender gold band.

"It's beautiful," I breathed.

"So are you," John said, taking my hand and slipping the ring onto my finger. I held it up to the light; it caught the twinkle of the lights on the tree and sparkled.

"It's just perfect," Catherine said.

"You don't mind?" I said, looking at her.

"Why would I? It's absolutely beautiful," she said. "I'm just so sorry about what happened to the original ring." Her cheeks turned pink.

"Not to worry," I said, looking at Catherine, and Gwen, and John, and feeling a deep contentment surge through me. My family.

I squeezed John's hand, relishing the feel

of the band on my finger, and gave him a quick kiss. "Now, then," I said, turning to the tree. "Who wants to put up the first ornament?"

RECIPES

WINTER KNITTERS CANDY CANE CHOCOLATE SANDWICH COOKIES

Cookies:
3 1/2 cups all-purpose flour
1 cup cocoa powder
1/2 teaspoon salt
2 cups sugar
1 1/2 cups butter, room temperature
2 large eggs

Filling:
2 cups plus 4 tablespoons powdered sugar
1 1/2 cups unsalted butter, room temperature
1 1/2 teaspoons peppermint extract
4 drops red food coloring
1 cup crushed red-and-white-striped candy canes

Cookies:

Blend flour, cocoa, and salt in medium bowl. Beat sugar and butter in large bowl until well blended, then beat in eggs. Add dry ingredients; beat until blended. Refrigerate dough 1–2 hours.

Preheat oven to 350 degrees F. Line 2 baking sheets with parchment paper. Scoop out dough by level tablespoonfuls, then roll into smooth balls. Place balls on prepared baking sheets, spacing about 2 inches apart. Using bottom of glass or hands, flatten each ball to 2-inch round (edges will crack). Bake until cookies no longer look wet and small indentation appears when tops of cookies are lightly touched with fingers, about 11 minutes (do not overbake or cookies will become too crisp). Cool on sheet 5 minutes. Transfer cookies to racks and cool completely, then repeat process with remaining batter.

Filling:

Beat powdered sugar and butter in medium bowl until well blended. Add peppermint extract and food coloring. Beat until light pink and well blended, adding more food coloring by dropfuls if darker pink color is desired. Spread 2 generous teaspoons filling evenly over flat side of 1 cookie to edges;

top with another cookie, flat side down, pressing gently to adhere. Repeat with remaining cookies and peppermint filling.

Place crushed candy canes on plate. Roll edges of cookie sandwiches in crushed candies. Store in single layer in airtight container at room temperature for up to 3 days or freeze for up to 2 weeks.

CHILLY NIGHT HATCH CHILE STEW

2 tablespoons olive oil
3 cloves garlic, crushed
1 onion, chopped
3 large carrots, finely chopped
1 large Yukon Gold potato, peel on, finely chopped
2 cups chicken broth (more if needed)
2 pounds shredded cooked pork
1 teaspoon dried oregano
1 teaspoon ground cumin
1/2 teaspoon salt
Ground black pepper
2 bay leaves
2 4-ounce cans fire-roasted diced mild Hatch green chiles
1 teaspoon salt
1 teaspoon chili powder
Fresh cilantro for garnishing

Sauté garlic and onion in olive oil; add carrots and potato, then add remaining ingredients. Bring to a boil, then simmer until vegetables are tender, 1–2 hours. Remove bay leaves before serving.

Garnish with sour cream, grated jack cheese (if desired), and fresh cilantro. Serve with corn muffins or tortillas.

CRUSTED GARLIC AND ROSEMARY PORK TENDERLOIN

Two pork tenderloins

1/4–1/2 cup fresh rosemary (or more), chopped roughly

7–8 garlic cloves, crushed

1 tablespoon fresh thyme leaves (if you have them)

1–2 tablespoons sea salt

1/4–1/2 cup olive oil

Remove tenderloins from the refrigerator and let them rest for 30–60 minutes. Combine rosemary, garlic, thyme, sea salt, and oil, and rub on pork tenderloins until they are well coated. Brown both sides of tenderloins in oven-safe pan, then transfer to 325 degree F oven (still in pan) and roast until internal temperature is at 140 degrees. Terrific with roasted rosemary potatoes and/or crusty bread and a salad!

RUSTIC SAUSAGE AND CHEESE LASAGNA

1/2 pound lasagna noodles, boiled for five minutes, tossed with olive oil, and set aside

3 tablespoons olive oil

1/2 pound Italian sausage (sweet or hot, to taste)

1 cup water

5 large garlic cloves, thinly sliced

One 28-ounce can chopped tomatoes, juices reserved

Salt and freshly ground pepper

Freshly grated Parmigiano-Reggiano cheese

1/2 pound fresh mozzarella, cut into 8 pieces

6 ounces Provolone cheese, cut into 8 pieces

2 tablespoons unsalted butter, softened

1/4 cup thinly sliced basil leaves

Preheat the oven to 425 degrees F. In a medium skillet, heat 1 tablespoon olive oil. Add the Italian sausage, cover and cook over moderate heat, turning once, until browned all over. Add the water, cover and simmer until the sausage is just cooked through, about 4 minutes.

In a large skillet, heat the remaining 2 tablespoons of olive oil. Add the garlic and cook over low heat until golden, about 3 minutes. Add the tomatoes with their juices and cook over moderate heat for 10 minutes, stirring occasionally. Add the sausage and its poaching liquid and simmer for 4 minutes. Transfer the sausage to a plate. Simmer the sauce over moderate heat until thickened, about 12 minutes. Coarsely break up the sausage and season the sauce with salt and pepper.

In a greased, 9-by-13-inch ceramic baking dish, arrange 3 lasagna noodles in different directions in the dish, leaving about 2 inches of overhang. Spoon a scant 1/4 cup of the tomato sauce over each lasagna noodle and sprinkle with a little grated Parmigiano-Reggiano cheese. Set a piece of mozzarella and Provolone on each lasagna noodle and add a few chunks of sausage. Fold the overhanging lasagna noodles on top of the cheese and sausage. Repeat the process with the remaining lasagna noodles, tomato sauce, mozzarella, Provolone, and sausage, sprinkling with a little more Parmigiano-Reggiano cheese. Brush the softened butter on any bare pasta and curly edges and sprinkle with Parmigiano-Reggiano.

Bake the lasagna on the top rack of the oven for 20 minutes, until the sauce starts to bubble. Raise the oven temperature to 450 degrees F and bake for about 7 minutes longer, until the top is nicely browned. Let the lasagna rest for about 10 minutes, then scatter the sliced basil on top, cut into squares, and serve.

EGGNOG BREAD

Loaf:

2 1/4 cups all-purpose flour

2 teaspoons baking powder

1/2 teaspoon salt

1/4 teaspoon nutmeg

2 eggs

1 cup sugar

1 cup eggnog

1/2 cup salted butter, melted

1 teaspoon vanilla or eggnog extract

1/2 teaspoon rum extract (optional)

Preheat the oven to 350 degrees F., then butter the bottom and 1/2 inch up the sides of a 9×5×3-inch loaf pan. In a large bowl, whisk together flour, baking powder, salt, and nutmeg. Make a well in the center of the flour mixture and set aside. In a medium bowl, combine the eggs, sugar, eggnog, melted butter, vanilla, and rum extract (if using). Add egg mixture to the flour mixture and stir just until moistened (batter will be lumpy). Spoon batter into the prepared pan and bake for 45 to 50 minutes. Loaf is done if top springs back when touched. Cool in the pan on a wire rack for 10 minutes, then remove from pan and cool completely on a rack. Cool before icing!

Eggnog Icing:
1/2 cup powdered sugar
1/4 teaspoon vanilla extract
Dash of nutmeg
2 to 3 teaspoons eggnog

Combine sugar, vanilla, and nutmeg. Stir in enough eggnog to reach drizzling consistency. Drizzle cooled loaf with icing. Grate a little bit of fresh nutmeg over the icing, then let icing set completely before wrapping loaf.

GWEN'S FAVORITE
LEMON BLUEBERRY RICOTTA
BERRY MUFFINS

2 cups flour
1/2 cup sugar
2 1/2 teaspoons baking powder
1/2 teaspoon salt
1 cup ricotta cheese
1/2 cup milk
4 tablespoons butter, room temperature
2 eggs
Zest of 2 lemons
1 cup blueberries

Preheat oven to 400 degrees F.

In a medium-sized bowl, whisk together flour, sugar, baking powder, and salt. In a large bowl, use an electric mixer to blend together the ricotta, milk, and butter until completely blended. Beat in eggs one at a time. Add the lemon zest and mix well.

Slowly add the dry ingredients into the wet ingredients and mix together just until incorporated. Add the blueberries and stir together with a rubber spatula. Your batter should be relatively firm, but if it's on the dry side you can add just a splash of milk.

Divide batter evenly into 12 pre-greased or lined baking cups. Bake for 26–30 minutes, or until the tops are a light golden brown color. Remove from the oven and let cool on a wire rack for around 15 minutes. Remove from the pan and let cool completely.

Makes 12 muffins.

CHRISTMAS SIMMERING POTPOURRI

Two cinnamon sticks, broken up
One tablespoon star anise
One tablespoon cardamom pods
One tablespoon cloves
One tablespoon dried orange peel (optional)

Add to potpourri warmer with a bit of water, light, and enjoy!

ACKNOWLEDGMENTS

Thank yous, as always, go first to my family — Eric, Abby, and Ian — for all their love and support; also to Dave and Carol Swartz and Ed and Dorothy MacInerney. I am so lucky to have my extended family so close! Thanks also to Bethann and Beau Eccles, my adopted family; my wonderful nieces and nephews on both sides; to my sister, Lisa, and her family; and to my fabulous grandmother, Marian Quinton (and Nora Bestwick). Thanks as always to Clovis and Maryann Heimsath, who introduced me to this beautiful corner of the world and inspired Cranberry Island.

Many thanks go to my agent Jessica Faust, who is there for me at every plot turn. I cannot say enough good things about the fabulous Midnight Ink team — particularly Terri Bischoff, whose support and patience as I finished the manuscript has been amazing. Thanks also to Connie Hill, editor extraordinaire, for finding my mistakes and making me look good, and Ellen Dahl, whose cover concepts for the original publisher's editions rock.

And a big thank you to all those supportive friends out there — particularly my wonderful Facebook community, who offer recipes and encouragement, along with all my friends at the Westbank Library and my local coffee haunts. Thanks also to all of the kind readers who take the time to tell me you enjoyed the books; I couldn't do it without you!

ABOUT THE AUTHOR

Although she currently lives in Texas with her husband and two children, Agatha-nominated author **Karen MacInerney** was born and bred in the Northeast, and she escapes there as often as possible. When she isn't in Maine eating lobster, she spends her time in Austin with her cookbooks, her family, her computer, and the local walking trail (not necessarily in that order).

In addition to writing the Gray Whale Inn mysteries, Karen is the author of the Tales of an Urban Werewolf series. You can visit her online at www.karenmacinerney.com.

CPSIA information can be obtained
at www.ICGtesting.com
Printed in the USA
FFOW02n2137040913
1727FF